Heaven Ride

Book 2:
BLOOD RED

by

John Eccleston

and

Kerry Gleason

For Theodore, Kristen, Megan, Isabella and Tucker
Dedication

To the memories of my parents, especially my mom whose untimely death made me wonder about the afterlife and how one's soul and consciousness finds it way there. This was the nugget of an idea that led to the Heaven Ride trilogy. One day I will see her again and share this book with her.

- John J. Eccleston

For Al Milazzo, Paul Graham and Tom Eckert
Dedication

True friends who have believed in me and lent their encouragement to my crazy schemes and stories through the decades. Through laughter, tears and all the wild years, our camaraderie has been a constant.

- Kerry T. Gleason

"Who was the fool, who the wise man, beggar or king?
Whether poor or rich, all's the same in death."

- Inscription at Yale University

Chapter 1: Danger Level High

Turbulence created a rocky landing as David Brownington's flight touched down in Salt Lake City.

David's entire world had been rocked, as though an earthquake destroyed the very foundation on which he built everything. Only one pillar of truth remained, one bastion of sanity, one rock that had not crumbled: his friendship with James William Gomez.

Marty Martin and Thomas Steinman – and others – tried mightily to drive a wedge between that friendship, and nearly succeeded, but JW was beyond betraying his longtime friend, grad school buddy, one-time house mate and business partner in Heaven Ride, the world's most significant socio-political phenomenon since the splitting of the atom.

It was just a few hours earlier at Reagan National Airport in D.C. that David ditched a would-be assassin. He spent the flight contemplating who might have set him up. Was it Steinman? Could it have been Martin, whose penchant for violence had already reared itself? Or some other party trying to stop David from shutting down the Heaven Ride enterprise? During the length of his flight, whomever plotted his demise might have arranged for someone to pursue him at the airport.

He texted JW before the flight left Reagan National Airport. During the flight, he monitored the charge left on the Tracfone he was using. As it hit single digits, he turned it off, praying that it wouldn't crap out on him once he left the sanctuary of the plane. He stared straight ahead, his brain working overtime to solve the whodunit.

On the SLC runway, he activated his burner phone. Just 7% left on the charge. He texted JW: *"On the ground at SLC now. Delta flight 643 from DC. Meet me at Terminal 2."* Then, he texted again. *"Like I told you earlier, use caution. Danger level high. Karl level high. Tell you later."*

When passengers were allowed to stand, David got up, an envelope fell to the floor. The elderly woman sitting in the same row called to him.

"Sir! You dropped this."

She picked it up, and her expression changed. She could tell that the contents were a fat stack of bills, and she became curious about David. Their eyes met, and when she didn't readily offer the envelope to David, he snatched it from her hand. In it was a bank-processed bundle of $100 bills, the $10,000 "escape money" that Alison gave to David when he fled.

He gave a wink to the woman and thanked her.

The flight had been emotionally agonizing. David got off the plane wary that an assassin might be waiting at the gate. His apprehension heightened to new levels. Despite airport security measures, he was relieved when he stepped from the ramp to the terminal that no bullets were fired. A pilot, standing with his carry-on against the wall, reached into the breast pocket of his blazer. "Here we go!" David thought, preparing to duck and dive. But the pilot merely extracted his smart phone.

David walked head down through the concourse. Airport security eyed the modest swarm of travelers, and fortunately did not seem to pay special attention to him. David exited past the security gate, searching for JW. Panic set in as he didn't see him. *Keep moving.* David's heart rate rose. While there were many people walking in the same direction, a man wearing a black jacket and khakis seemed to be tailing David, rushing to catch up to him. He followed the sign for the taxi stand, as did the man in khakis. Further from the gate, a clean-shaven college kid with a hoodie pulled over his head sat on the floor along the wall playing a video game on his phone. As David walked by, the kid called to him in a hoarse whisper.

"David!"

David looked, quizzically, and kept walking. The kid stood up, his six-foot-three frame bulkier than David first imagined. He approached David, carrying a small backpack.

"Doofus! It's me."

Only then did David recognize his buddy, James Gomez. It was the hoodie, and the clean-shaven face that threw him off.

"Didn't you understand my texts? We're in danger. You got to take this serious. I'm being followed," David scolded him.

"Well hello to you, too. Nice greeting from a friend I haven't seen in awhile," JW responded.

"Sorry, but I'm in no mood for goofing around. We need to get out of here. Now!" David said as he picked up his pace.

JW lagged a few steps behind David as they got to the exit doors of Terminal 2. David spotted the man in the khaki pants, and while he was not overtly watching David, he was talking on his cell phone and heading in the same direction.

"Walk faster!" David instructed JW. "Where did you park?"

"Follow me, David." JW doubled his pace and led David to his car in hourly parking just outside the terminal. David was now hunted prey. Powerful forces, be it the government or Steinman or Marty Martin's thugs, sought to eliminate him because of what he knew about Heaven Ride and his intentions to shut it down. He could hear Holly's voice uttering the words "Martin is 10 times as bad and he will take you out."

"That guy in the black jacket. Is he the one?"

"Yes," David answered.

"Okay. Now, run!" JW said, darting between parked cars. David tried to keep up, carrying his bag. A second time, JW cut a sharp corner between a van and a tall pick-up truck. They reached JW's Mercedes SUV David threw his carry-on in the back seat. JW backed up and headed for the pay gate. In the rear-view mirror, he saw the man in the black jacket recognize that they were getting away. A tan sedan screeched to a halt near him, and the man got in.

"I'm pretty sure that we're being followed so you'll need to find the fastest way to your house," David warned JW.

Just after JW paid the parking toll and exited onto the airport connector, the tan sedan changed three lanes quickly and was just two cars back on the Mercedes' tail.

"Who the hell is tailing us and what do they want?" JW asked.

"Whoever it is wants me dead, if Holly was telling the truth," David said. He cringed as JW drove close to the bumper of the car in front of them.

JW quickly responded, "Dead?"

"Yeah, one of the last things Holly told me was that Marty is ten times as ruthless as Steinman. He blew up the headquarters of *Servare Caeli*, killing who knows how many. And he'll stop at nothing to protect Heaven Ride." David's reference was to a radical group of priests and religious zealots who vandalized Heaven Ride centers and targeted key players with acts of violence. The car in front of them moved over.

"Do you think Steinman's in the car? I still can't believe that dick is alive," JW said as he punched the gas.

"I doubt Steinman's in the car, but um, a, can we lose these guys before I get into this? I don't want a 'holy shit' to turn into a high-speed roll-over," David requested.

JW made an illegal U-turn, followed by a few quick turns down one-way side streets and sped onto I-15 North with no sight of the tan car.

David exhaled for the first time in several minutes.

"I'm impressed, JW, maybe it's all those action movies you've watched have paid off."

"Naw, I'd say video games," JW corrected. "That was definitely a Gran Turismo move."

David regained his serious posture.

"Listen, JW, as I told you on the phone from DC, Steinman being alive is just the tip of the iceberg. Holly spilled her guts to me in the five minutes I had before the feds showed up at her apartment. Not only is Steinman back, he's teamed with Marty. This whole Heaven Ride business – it's not what it seems. We were duped! Duped big time, JW. It's all controlled by the government and has been from the beginning.

"You know how you always talked about government conspiracies and cover-ups? Well, my friend, you and I are right in the middle of the biggest one. Yep, nothing about our great venture is without the U.S. Government's big thumbprint at every turn."

"I'm not sure what you're talking about. Jesus, just cut to the chase; enough with the set- up. What do you mean that we've been duped, and government's involved?" JW demanded.

"Okay, you'd better brace yourself and don't drive off the road," David continued.

"I'm good," JW assured him. "Just keeping an eye out for the thug in the Members Only jacket."

"Everything that's Heaven Ride," David said, "and that led up to you and I discovering it and bringing it public – it's all been a facade. The technology, the people, the financing; all of it. Holly moved back to Washington. But it had nothing to do with her sister with breast cancer. Hell, I don't even know if she had a sister. She moved back to be a fucking communications agent for the president. Her father is not Marty Martin. And her name isn't even Holly!"

"You've said that. Three times already."

"I know. I can't wrap my head around it. From what Holly said, or Alison – hell, I don't even know what to call her." David slammed his fist on the dashboard.

"Don't do that," JW said calmly. "You might set off the air bag."

"Alison said Heaven Ride was discovered over a decade ago by scientists at NASA – Ames Laboratory to be specific. At Mountain View, right near where we lived in San Fran. We were duped from the beginning. They auditioned us to play the main roles and we didn't even know. They made you think you discovered the heaven wave, and the ability to eject souls. When you didn't figure out how to track it, they gave me the infinity reader. We thought we found all the answers. But JW, they planted all those discoveries, and the people around us – Holly, Kelly and others, so that we would find them and know what to do with the technology. You and I, we were just rats in their maze. Now all that's left are questions. A huge, stinking heap of questions."

JW grew silent, letting the shock spread across every synapse of his brain. David continued his rant.

"Everything we did over the last three years, everyone we trusted, they were all in on it. What they're doing is peeling off that energy from heaven, and using it, or storing it somehow."

JW was not fully paying attention. All his thoughts went directly to Trish, and Tommy.

David continued in rapid speak about the urgency to shut down Heaven Ride and do it without being killed.

JW pulled over his Mercedes near the darkened woods.

"Why are you stopping, JW?" David said anxiously. "There's nothing here."

JW sat stunned and didn't answer.

"How far are we from – what did you call it, Five Rings Ranch?" David asked.

"Yeah," JW answered quietly. "Tommy named it Five Rings Ranch, after the Olympic symbol on the iron gate. It's paradise. And we're safe there."

JW turned to David a question burning through his brow. David knew what JW was going to ask before he voiced the words.

"If Holly isn't Holly, and is an actor, then who the hell's Trish? And Tommy. Am I going home to a movie set where my lovely not-girlfriend and her make-believe son greet me with open arms and smiles, hugs and kisses?"

David could see that JW was upset, heartbroken and on the verge of tears. He also got swept in the emotion, and did not reply right away.

"Give it to me straight, D, is Trish in on the gig?"

David contemplated his reply a second longer.

"No, my friend," he said. "The good news is Trish is Trish and your relationship is real. Yes, she did work for Marty but Alison told me directly that she got out of the ordeal to protect Tommy. He's her real son, and she got out so she could be with you. No strings attached. She loves you, and don't doubt your feelings for her. Alison wouldn't have lied about this knowing how important you are to me."

JW listened intently. He wanted to believe David's words, but his mind still raced. Could he trust Trish completely and get back to a place with her before hearing David's news?

"Okay," JW said. "Let's go."

Just a few miles further, JW pulled his Mercedes up the mountain drive that led to the massive stone wall and iron gates that kept out unwanted visitors. An unmanned guard tower flanked the left side of the entrance.

"Damn, I'm glad you can see the road. It's pretty dark," David commented.

"Given our situation, I'm going to hire a security guard for the gate."

"I don't want to put you and Trish and Tommy in danger. I need to find a hotel or someplace to stay."

"No way! You're staying here, my friend. Believe me this place is secured in many ways, and tomorrow I'll make it ten-fold more if I have to. It's obvious Martin knows this house because he occasionally calls Trish, which means Steinman knows, too. And probably anyone in this entire covert operation for that matter."

"She's still in contact with Martin?! Aw, crap!" David said.

"Don't worry about it. Trish has certain security privileges. We'll all be safe here."

Now David was the one with agita.

"You have your choice of eight bedrooms. There're others, but you'll have to get Tommy's permission. He's got forts and games set up in some of the others. Aren't you tired?"

"Eh. The adrenaline. I'll probably be up all night."

The Mercedes wound uphill, and around a bend at the Five Rings Compound, the trees opened to a clearing. A huge mansion of reddish stone, the same color of the sandstone used in the great Mormon temples, became visible, its walls illuminated by floodlights. JW pulled up toward the garage, and the door automatically lifted.

"Pretty cool, eh?" JW said.

"What?"

"I don't have to even hit a button to open the garage doors. There's a chip in the car and it automatically opens when I'm about 24 feet away."

"And you've got seven garage doors to choose from. I see you being a geek hasn't changed," David said.

"Right. You should talk."

"Yeah, I guess we're both geeks," David said. "But we're two of the richest geeks in the world!"

As both men exited the vehicle and began walking from the garage, JW grabbed David's arm to stop him.

"Hey, before we go in could we not get into this with Trish, at least not initially? I need some time to process what you told me, and I don't want Tommy to hear any of this discussion. Okay?"

"Sure, I think that's a good call. But I think Trish knows what's going on already. We'll find the time to discuss it. Maybe tomorrow."

JW opened the door, and they both spilled into the house together like college buddies. Trish stood at the top of the stairs, excited to see JW and David's smiling faces. Tommy pushed past Trish and ran down the stairs to hug JW and David. David hustled up the stairs to hug Trish. She didn't seem to want to let go.

"It's so good to see you, David. Welcome to our home. I know JW is so excited you're here. It'll be good for him having his best friend around."

Trish walked downstairs and hugged JW. She kissed him on the cheek and whispered in his ear, "I'm glad you made it home safe. I was worried."

As she finished her embrace, JW pulled her closer, tighter and whispered, "Just tell me this is real."

Trish squinched her eyes, thinking JW's comment a bit strange. "It is, and I truly love you, JW."

Not another word was spoken about the situation.

"We need to crack that bottle of Redbreast Irish Whiskey and toast my best friend on his visit to Five Rings," exclaimed JW.

After a few drinks JW told Trish that he and David were going downstairs to the game room. Guy time, ya know?"

"Oh, all right," Trish said, sadly. "But don't stay down there all night. It's nearly 10 and I want to see David, too."

David followed JW across the spacious great room and down a wide staircase to the basement. Motion-sensitive lights above the baseboard lit the way, and very faint ceiling lights illuminated the hallway. JW led David halfway down, and then down three steps into a home theatre. Again, dim lights turned on triggered by their motion, and brightened slightly after five seconds.

David soaked it all in. The room was outfitted with a distinct University of Utah décor. One entire wall was red, and in the center hung a massive Utes' flag, red with a block "U" inside a white circle bearing two feathers. Farthest from the door was a black wall furnished with a huge Ultra High Definition screen, flanked by two

50-inch monitors. In front of that were two rows of plush, leather recliners. In the back was the bar, mahogany with blue velvet cubbyholes, where scores of premium liquors made their residence. In the center of the back counter was a familiar fixture to David. JW called it by name.

"Barmaster. Two Redbreast. Neat."

David interrupted. "I prefer mine on the rocks with a pinch of water."

JW frowned at him, his eyebrows sloping in annoyance. "You're a wuss. Barmaster, cancel that. Two Redbreast, one neat, one on the rocks with a splash of water." The latter instruction was said with disdain, for JW felt putting ice in a fine distilled spirit destroyed the essence intended by the originator. He glided behind the bar and placed two rocks glasses on the bar mat, and Barmaster dispensed the single-pot still whiskey as proscribed.

"Where did you get that?" David asked, admiring his first invention that may have started his current business spiral. Or it may have just been a convenient excuse for Thomas Steinman to recruit David for Dynamic Technologies.

"Don't be offended," JW offered. "I bought it for a fraction of the retail price online."

"The voice-activated mechanism... nice touch."

"What can I say? I have too much time on my hands." JW handed David the drink, the reddish-amber liquid sloshing over square cubes. They touched glasses and sipped. "Welcome to your new home, brother."

"Thanks," David said. "Thanks for taking in a freeloader."

"C'mon, you're no freeloader. Dude, you're my friend. Besides, you let me freeload at your place in San Francisco for years."

David smiled sheepishly. He really was not a freeloader. At last count, the money David no longer had direct access to totaled $82 billion, net worth greater than almost any other man who ever lived. But he did possess an envelope with $10,000 in cash.

"And don't be afraid to use the big screen TV. We're subscribed to almost all the streaming video services."

"So why didn't you want Trish to be with us?" David asked.

"Is everything okay between you and Trish, I mean before what I told you?"

"Oh, yeah. Yeah. Yeah, we're good."

After quaffing the quality whiskey, JW gave David a giddy tour of the vast house that was the fruit of his partnership with David. At the far end of the basement hall was a workout room, modest in size, but furnished with top-of-the-line equipment. A television and stereo speakers were mounted high on one wall, and a walk-in closet had been converted to a dry sauna.

"Tell me the truth, JW," David said. "You haven't even used any of this."

"Yes, I have," JW argued. "I just fell out of a regular routine with it."

David slapped JW's belly playfully. "We'll keep that between us. Nobody will ever guess. Okay for me to keep it from rusting?"

"You are welcome to it, brother. I'm glad you're here."

The room across the hall was sparsely furnished with just a bed and a dresser. A few folded cardboard moving boxes were stacked on the floor. Through one door was a bathroom and shower, and another door was a small closet.

"This room will do fine for me," David said.

"But it's so far away from us, and the kitchen," JW protested. "And our media room. I haven't even shown you that yet. We've got a terrific stereo system."

"That's okay. For now, I want some quiet time. Being close to the fitness room will suit me fine."

"Alright. We can bring your bag down here. It gets chilly down here so I'll let you borrow my Utes hoodie." JW pulled it over his head and threw it to David. David let it fall to the ground. "I'm not putting on that oversized smelly thing, nonetheless a Utah Ute, blah."

"Suit yourself, wimp." JW signaled to David to head back upstairs to talk with Trish.

Trish was in the enormous kitchen and joined JW and David in the living room. A wood fire licked the limbs in the fireplace, providing added heat in the cavernous open rooms where the kitchen met the living room. The smooth lambskin sofa enveloped David. His visit to Five Rings so far was like a massive welcome home party, even though he had never been to JW's Olympic ski house before.

Trish had put Tommy to bed on the third floor so the three of them could talk. The conversation was catch-up on the past, reminiscing and stories about the house, Tommy and Utah in general. Not one word was spoken about Heaven Ride and the dangerous level of their current situation.

Chapter 2: What Really Was Is Not

The bright Utah sunshine filled the house of stone and glass. There was a bowl of milk in the sink and a cereal box on the counter. Trish was in the kitchen alone drinking coffee when David sleepy-eyed and tousled hair made his way up the stairs.

"Good morning, sleepy head," Trish said.

"What time is it?" David asked.

Trish looked up from her iPad and pointed at the clock, which read 10:47.

"Oh, wow! Good morning. Where's JW and Tommy? I expected the house would be full of noise and chatter."

Trish responded, "There was some earlier. I'm glad it didn't wake you. JW took Tommy to his mother's in Layton. He should be back any minute."

David grabbed a mug from near the coffee maker and poured a cup.

"Trish, look," David said, very businesslike. "JW asked me not to talk to you last night about what went on in Washington with Holly, I mean Alison, as I'm sure you know her true name. But I'm glad JW left. We need to do a lot of talking this morning. I want to hear every detail. I know you know every detail."

"Okay, but JW asked that I wait to get into it 'til he got back, if you don't mind."

"I respect that but before JW does get back I need to ask you directly are you really in love with him? Is this thing real between you and JW?"

Trish was taken back with his question, but she understood why David asked it.

"What do you think? You think I'd put my son in this situation after what we went through with him almost being kidnapped? Hell no. I love Tommy and I love JW. We have a real life together, and going to make sure that doesn't change," Trish said in a rapid curt voice.

"Holly told me it was real, and that when you got out it was for good. I did tell this to JW last night on our way home. I think he believes me but you're going to have to work this through with him. He has to hear it and see it from you. You don't owe me anything, but you have to come clean with JW and not keep anything from him."

Just as David was going to continue speaking about Marty's threat, Trish jumped up and headed for the front door. "JW's back."

JW opened the door and was greeted with a big hug and kiss from Trish. He hugged and kissed her again and walked toward the kitchen.

"You're up," JW said. "You guys been talking?

David answered, "No, not really. I just made it up here 5 minutes ago and grabbed a cup of Joe," and he quickly changed the subject. "Hey, how's your mother? I can't wait to see her."

JW didn't answer David and turned to Trish and the conversation began.

"David, why don't you go first?" Trish said.

David declined and responded to Trish. "I think I'd rather you tell us what you know so I'll know how it compares to what Alison said about all of this."

"Fair enough," replied Trish and went over to JW and put her hands on his knees and looked straight into JW's eyes. "I know David told you everything that Alison told him, including that what we have is real and I'm not some scripted performer. I love you, J. I felt that way pretty much ever since you walked into my life at my Parkmerced condo nearly three years ago. This is the life I want and I want for Tommy. I know what you heard and what I'm going to tell you will confuse you and make you wonder, but don't. Please, believe me, I'm going to convince you otherwise. I hope you give me that chance."

JW didn't say anything but put his large hands on hers. Trish whispered again, "I love you."

Trish stood up and turned to David. "I know what happened in New York with Marty. I know you know that Steinman's alive and Alison called me about your conversation in her apartment. Truth is she shouldn't have told you what she told you, David. No one knows this other than you and me. I suggest we keep it between us so Alison will remain safe. Marty is really a sweet guy, deep down. But – when the job requires, he can be ruthless. When it comes to Heaven Ride, the ante is that high. He's not about to mess around. You saw it with *Servare Caeli*. He is capable of ordering a hit, and that includes one on you if you continue your shutdown efforts."

"That's not very comforting," David said.

Trish continued, "I have a special exemption that goes back to my days working with Marty Martin. Wherever I go, and Tommy, and husband, boyfriend, significant other, we are protected. Our home is sanctuary. We are completely safe here. You will be completely safe here, too."

David asked Trish to explain her special security privileges.

"Well," she started, choosing her words cautiously, "Before Marty, I was recruited to the CIA as an information officer. It was my job to take messy situations, some with national security at stake, and smooth them over for the general public, or for international diplomacy purposes."

"Such as?" David asked.

"It's best if I don't give you specifics. Some – most – of what I did is still classified. I did some things to prove my loyalty, and – I did a number of things I'm not proud to admit. Let's just say that there are a lot of *heroes* dead in the ground who were just poor souls who got in the way of essential operations, or they were obstructions to the greater good." She accented the critical word with finger quotes, leaving little to David's imagination.

"So, when I needed to bow out for maternity leave for Tommy, I negotiated a package deal. I never felt safe there, as occasionally it was in vogue for political rivals to release the identities of CIA operatives. They – I should say Marty – gave me a blanket security pact to provide protection for me and Tommy and anyone under my roof."

She saw doubt in David's eyes, so she repeated, "This is a sanctuary."

David squinted, thinking. "Then how was it possible that Tommy was almost kidnapped?"

"That's why I was so freaked out! That should never have happened with the layers of security we had. But it goes to show you that you have to be vigilant. Always."

JW piped in, "Mind blown. My girlfriend is CIA or ex-CIA and what did you say, 'did some things to prove your loyalty, things you're not proud of. And, what might these be? Should I worry you might be Marty or Steinman's secret assassin? What's up next?"

"You have nothing to worry about, JW, I'm done killing people," Trish said laughing to add levity to the conversation.

"How confident are you that me being here keeps this a sanctuary? I mean, I'm sitting here as we speak with a big X on my back. Does this negate your former bosses' agreements? I'm sure he knows I'm here. The fricking CIA knows everything."

Trish said a CIA bond cannot be broken or betrayed unless you become a double agent. I suggest you not become one."

JW piped into again, "David, I have a high school friend who runs a security company. We talked about hiring him before but didn't see the need. Now? Maybe an extra layer of security is a good idea. His name is Randy Anderson and I'll call him this afternoon. He's ex-Air Force in special ops so he would be up for the challenge since I'll let him know he may be up against CIA operatives. He'll love that."

Trish changed the subject. "David, your bank transfer went through. That was generous for you to put all of that in a trust fund for your sister."

"Seemed like the only thing I could do," David said. "I mean, all this work, and JW and I really did work hard, along with you and Karl and Kelly. But to come out of it with nothing is wrong. At least there's the money."

"Speaking of which, dude," JW interjected. "You got none. How does it feel to be broke?" David just shrugged. "Mi casa, su casa. Mi pesos, su pesos. Anything you need, you got it, okay?"

"I've got some cash."

Trish added, "I take care of the books, even though he's the brains of the operation. Sort of. Yeah, you need anything at all, I will get it. Or I will get you access to money. I would advise you to stay put. Don't need the CIA on your tail."

"Again?" JW joked.

"David, your Heaven Ride money is still there – nearly $100 billion. You just don't have access to it now. Eventually, that will change. So what more do you need? You don't need anything more. As I said before, be like JW and put Heaven Ride behind you. Be done with it for good."

David felt defensive and heard Marty's voice come through in Trish's; David shot back "Trish, you don't get it. It's not about the money. It's about fraud, deceit and deception. It's about robbing people of their souls, their lives on this planet, with no possibility to return to heaven when they perish. I know you were CIA and maybe you could put all you've done behind you and move on like it never happened. I'm not like that. I know you were doing your job, but I have a different moral integrity than that. When I ran H2H I didn't know what I know now. If I did I would've never opened that door. "

Trish's face cringed with alarm. "I'm trying to advise you for your own good, David. Knowing what I know, the entire Heaven Ride system is so highly protected with impenetrable security there is no way you could get in the door let alone into the computer system. I suggest you lay low here and focus on something else."

David shook his head and stayed silent. JW became animated, his voice tinged with angst.

"What I want to know is how and why that Stein-prick faked his own death and killed Karl in the plane crash," JW demanded. "And, why was he is in with Marty. I want the details on how we were selected by the government and how all of this was staged. When did it begin and how did you get all of those people to play their parts. I mean Kelly, Bridget, Professor McNutty, all of them. This was a regular Truman Show and I was Jim Carrey. Three years of my life was a goddamn movie set."

"Calm down, J, your life was real and is real. None of the folks were actors. They all worked and continue to work for various government agencies. Not all had clearance to know everything that was happening. Most were aware of the Heaven Ride technology but nothing beyond that. As for Steinman, he is probably the most gifted pilot ever, and sky diver, a real-life James Bond meets Tom Cruise in Mission Impossible. Karl unfortunately betrayed Steinman, and the entire operation. He was secretly feeding Heaven Ride data and secrets to foreign agents. We were not sure if they were German or Russian or from somewhere else. Steinman gave Karl several chances to stop but after he crossed the line the third time he was sent to heaven in that plane. Steinman bailed out at the last minute and left Karl strapped in to crash into the Idaho mountainside."

"Were Steinman and Karl having an intimate relationship or was that part of the script," David asked. Trish looked perplexed.

"I saw them kissing just before they left on their ski trip and I followed them to the airport. Maybe Steinman offed Karl because he didn't want to be blackmailed as being a homosexual."

She never had heard this about Thomas. She didn't answer David but instead went on to tell JW and David the full story behind Heaven Ride and how and why they were chosen.

During the late 1990s and early 2000s, Russia and the U.S. collaborated on the International Space Station (ISS). NASA's Chandra X-ray Observatory, in conjunction with the giant radio telescopes at the Arecibo Observatory in Puerto Rico and Greenbelt in West Virginia were focused on extraterrestrials, dark matter and gravitational waves. The project, code named MUSIC, detected a new wavelength of the highest frequency levels in 2003. This wave was like no other and was traced to the circumference of Earth's troposphere into one invisible wave to the nearest black hole called V616 Monocerotis. The wavelength was moving data or invisible matter at light speed. The scientists hypothesized it was sucking some form of energy from the Earth and speeding it through the exosphere to outer space and disappearing into V616 Monocerotis.

NASA's Ames Research Center at Moffett Field, California, took the frequency data and started to study what it was feeding on; what was it transmitting from Earth. Scientists predicted it might be energy from dying human beings. The day after Christmas in 2004, a tsunami in the Indian Ocean off the coast of Sumatra took more than 220,000 lives. The energy spike following that disaster confirmed the researchers' theory. Two years later Ames scientists perfected the ability to bring healthy individuals to a near the death state and release the energy and noticed when they processed was reversed an additional amount of energy entered the body. All participation subjects in the experiments were enlisted U.S. military personnel. Post-experiment the military noticed these individuals had increased their mental capacity and well as their physical abilities almost 2- or 3-fold. Most of the subjects described their "trip" as an out-of-body experience and gave vivid details of visiting what they described as heaven or similar and interacting with people who were deceased. Ames shared the top secret highly classified findings with U.S. Military Brass and the CIA, and a lower-level less classified report with ISS members Canada, Japan and Russia. Not satisfied with the report, Russian officials from the Kremlin filed a complaint asking for full details of the project, including tests performed at Ames.

"Jesus, no wonder it only took us only six months to figure it out," JW said, interrupting Trish's story. "They worked years and probably hundreds of subjects and millions of dollars to invent the real Heaven Ride."

David piped in, "So did they give into the Russians? And why did we need to be involved if this was already a military operation by now?"

Trish continued, answering David's questions.

"The Russians were very adamant and threatened to pull out of the ISS altogether, which NASA was planning back then to end its Space Shuttle missions and would have to rely solely on Russia for ISS space transportation of our astronauts. The U.S. compromised and shared more but not the top-secret findings about the energy transfer. There was a rumor that the Russian's tried to steal the entire program and technology. But we know that wasn't the case.

"As for the two of you. I have to say you aced your auditions. More than 30 JWs and more than 50 Davids from all over the country were identified, screened and put through rigorous tests and interviews. JW, your process began with Dr. Redmond at the University of Utah Medical School and continued through medical school at UC Berkeley, and, David, yours began when Thomas Steinman hired you at Dynamic Technologies, as did Karl Mann's training. Everything you did there was preparing you for your big discovery and ultimately to bring Heaven Ride to market and operate it successfully."

"What about the others?" JW asked.

"You really want to hear this?" Trish asked with a bit of a chuckle in her voice. "Jonah was focused on the data analysis. Steinman became aware that this energy transfer had potential in a variety of ways. He consulted with Dr. Cheryl Redmond at the University of Utah. It was Dr. Redmond who helped make the connection between the energy boost and the possibility to harvest that, or strip it for other uses. Dr. Redmond had just graduated a star pupil – JW. He had already begun his PhD. curriculum at Berkeley. When Steinman began his search for the scientific entrepreneur, JW became one of four candidates. As Steinman's plan developed, he realized there would be an equally strong business component. He read about a college kid who sold a bartending invention for millions, so David became one of three prospects. But David seemed intent on doing his grad studies at Wharton."

"I was pretty hot on Wharton," David said. "But Berkeley made me an offer I couldn't refuse."

"I had a hand in that," Trish said. "The Thomas Anderson Fellowship. Totally fabricated."

"No, it was a real thing," David insisted. "It had a history that was pretty impressive."

"It had a history, all right," Trish said. "On a website. I remember creating that little history. I named it after the creator of MySpace – remember that? And then I sent leaflet after leaflet to your home to spur your interest in Berkeley, in California, in the Bay Area. Steinman thought it would be too difficult to mesh two people together if one was on the West Coast, and the other was in Pennsylvania. If David chose to stay back East, neither one of you would have been selected. Steinman prodded some of David's key influencers to join Dynamic Technology."

"Who else was in the running?" JW asked.

"Oh, I can't tell you that."

"C'mon!" JW pleaded. "Who do you think we're going to tell?"

"I don't remember their names," Trish said. JW flashed a look of incredulity. "Okay, okay. One was actually a professor at Purdue at their Institute for Integrative Neuroscience, and some business whiz at Michigan State."

"I wonder what happened to them," JW said.

"The Michigan State guy is probably in prison," David said. The other two looked at him for explanation. "We played them in the Frozen Four hockey tournament. They had some dirty players."

JW got a kick out of the comment.

"Oh, so all Spartans are destined for jail time!"

"At the time, I thought so," David said. "What about the others, Trish?"

"Well, the frontrunners were a neuroscience woman from MIT and a finance guy from Harvard grad who went to work at the Federal Reserve Bank of Boston."

"You mean there was somebody more highly regarded than me? And David?" JW intoned.

"Isn't that unbelievable?" Trish answered with sarcasm. "Yeah. Silly Steinman. But the Fed guy got married and his wife got preg-o immediately, so Steinman believed he lost a degree of control."

"How did Steinman find the others?"

"Alison was an interesting story. Steinman wanted eyes and ears on you all the time. He had a researcher locate photos of every girl you ever dated. They performed facial recognition on the photographic data and developed a composite drawing. Thomas was looking at it in Jonah's office, looked at it closely, then looked up and saw a picture of Alison on Jonah's credenza. He knew Alison was the one. He didn't want anyone to trace her lineage back to her famous grandfather, so they changed her name to Holly. And Marty Martin had a role in getting this off the ground so it made sense for him to be positioned as her father."

"I always thought Martin was a little too old to be her father," JW said.

"Uh, well – you know, guys can father children at almost any age," Trish said. "It worked. Fooled David."

"Did they do facial recognition for my girlfriends?" JW inquired.

"JW, you were the master of one-and-done relationships. They tried, but your tastes were all over the board. They picked a sweet, young girl, I think her name was Amy."

"Amy Gamble. Very petite. Big boobs," JW said.

"Apparently that was one of the preferences they identified," Trish said. JW smiled sheepishly.

"Guilty," he said.

"Amy was supposed to be your girlfriend. But no. JW, you were so buried in your research that you totally ignored her. She didn't leave because she was freaked out by dead bodies. She was fired because she couldn't seduce you. Steinman almost brought Dr. Redmond into the picture, because it seemed apparent that you had a big crush on her. I guess you always went for older women." She paused to take in JW's reaction. "That was way too complicated and Cheryl didn't want to step down in Utah. So Kelly Bryant was brought in because she actually has a scientific background, plus she was a much stronger personality than Amy."

"What did McNulty have to do with this? I mean. He approved Kelly."

"Professor McNulty wanted money for the department. He was told to bring in Kelly. McNulty did everything he was told because he didn't want to lose any funding."

"The others?" David asked.

"Referred by the CIA," Trish said. "They applied for different job descriptions, but they were vetted and checked out. Everywhere you two went and everything you did was somehow monitored and manipulated. Steinman wasn't completely sure until David came to work for him at Dynamic Technologies. Thomas knew then that he could use your loyalty to him against you."

"That raises the question, what about Karl?" David said.

"God, I miss that big guy," JW said.

"Karl was authentic," Trish said. "He wasn't recruited. And, he posed some problems for Steinman. He almost cost Steinman his job by sharing information with his friends back in Bremen, in Germany. Steinman went so far as to pose as, to become Karl's bi-sexual lover, to try to rein him in. He couldn't do it, so he had Karl killed."

"Why did Steinman fake his own death?" JW asked.

"Thomas was reassigned by the government," Trish explained. "They felt the operation might be in danger if they couldn't quash the investigation into the plane crash and a few other costly missteps. The situations never blew up, and Steinman's new assignment was defunded, so they brought him back in. I will tell you this. Steinman was pissed! He and Marty were friends for years. He came back and Marty had assumed the leadership role. Steinman was completely paranoid and directed his anger at Marty."

"You said 'they.'" David observed. "Do you know exactly who *they* are?"

"It goes pretty far up the chain of command," Trish said. "There's a Congressional Committee on Commerce, Science and Transportation. Senator Bob Sanders is the chair of that one. They oversee a subcommittee on Space. That's like a secret society within a secret society. Anything they put out is classified."

"But here's the thing. Once Marty and Steinman were put in charge, who knows what they reported back to these committees? The whole thing is a clandestine cluster-you-know-what."

David looked at the ceiling to absorb the information and try to connect the dots.

"But why go through elaborate scheme and process? The time, people and money wasted," David asked. "The government could've been light years ahead without us, H2H and the Heaven Ride Centers."

Trish responded, "Some of what you say is true, but it would have never worked."

She continued, there were less than 1.4 million active-duty troops back then and those numbers are still dropping today. Even if you counted in the 20,000-plus CIA employees and other high security agencies you'd not even hit 1.5 million people. The government needed tens of millions of people to ride Heaven Ride in order to meet its goals. So, the powers to be decided it needed to be a public enterprise founded by a group of highly gifted entrepreneurs and that's where you came in. The House Appropriations Committee approved $100 million to cover initially expenses with the caveat that Heaven Ride would be self-funding within three years. Congratulations, you and JW did it within 12 months. This made all involved very happy, and you both were handsomely rewarded. David, when you were in Washington, DC, you saw the President at the Justice Department meeting with Marty and Thomas. This would be the first time that POTUS would be informed that Heaven Ride is a really a covert government operation and what the real intent and importance of the Heaven Ride operation. Rest assured, David, you'll now see the President and Congress be pro-Heaven Ride and counter any calls to have it shut down. Not only do you have Marty and Thomas to contend with, now you'll be facing the entire U.S. government should you pursue your Heaven Ride shut down plans. Again, I suggest you put it behind you starting today."

Chapter 3: Souped-Up Security

On the third day of David's stay, Trish got a message that a FedEx package for David Brownington was waiting for pickup. On his first night at Five Rings, David called Paul Graham, a hockey buddy in San Francisco, to go to his Pine Street house and retrieve a file from his bedroom marked in fat, Sharpie letters: Bridget. He also requested his coveted Buffalo Sabres' jersey. But when Trish picked it up and David saw the box, it was much bigger than he expected. Graham took upon himself to fill the box with much more including David's hockey skates and equipment, along with his high school and college yearbooks. Graham sent other mementos and a note saying that he gathered his photos, computer, tools, suits and other items that he would store for David.

Since Trish revealed to David and JW the back-story of Heaven Ride and what he was now up against to stop it, David barricaded himself in his room, alone to make sense of what was real and what was scripted for him in his life. For hours, he sat staring at his iPhone, the backpack, the skates and the files with Bridget's odd correspondence. Then, there was the JW's red Utah University hoodie that was hanging from the closet doorknob. That and the few outfits he had in his overnight bag was all that he possessed. He did not feel loss for his other possessions. He felt free.

But he was not happy.

David pulled from the box sheaf of pages tied with a purple

ribbon. The ribbon was a reminder to David that he was forever tied to Bridget Moynihan, a friend to JW's lab assistant, Kelly Bryant. David took Bridget out on one date, and determined that she was highly sensitive and not his type. Bridget was smitten by David, and interpreted his polite demeanor as a romantic advance. Kelly invited her to the lab for a Heaven Ride demonstration, and Bridget volunteered as a participant. She returned from the ride shaken and chilled, literally and figuratively. After days and nights of mental torment, Bridget jumped from the Golden Gate Bridge wearing only a pair of costume angel wings.

These pages were drawings Bridget left to David before she committed suicide. By depositing these in his room, she implicated him in her insanity. As much as he tried to shirk the guilt of her bridge jump, he felt responsible. She viewed him as more than a friend. Their one and only date cemented, in David's mind, that they were incompatible. Bridget felt convinced they should be together.

The oversized pages were from an artist's sketch pad, yellowed with tattered edges. She used a variety of markers, paint pens and colored pencils to generate the hieroglyphs. Initially, the drawings struck David as infantile. After weeks of wrestling with them, his vision became clear. Like those stereo-optic 3D pictures, David learned to see past the limitations of pen on paper. His mind adapted, fleshing out symbols and representations of deep, dark intelligence that spoke to the unholy terrors Bridget experienced on her Heaven Ride. Each simplistic drawing captivated David for hours with in-depth interpretations that added breadth to David's talent that he simply called "The Gift."

He became mesmerized by the story she told. He recalled his Heaven Ride trip and the silver cord that guided him to and from a spiritual nirvana. Bridget's words and pictures were other-worldly, from the other side. Bridget described her tormented trip, which contrasted sharply with David's blissful journey. She detailed the loss of her soul upon arrival, and that for the return trip, a celestial being, possibly an angel, bestowed upon her a "gift." This is what enabled her to return. That return turned terrifying, as mechanical thieves pursued her in an attempt to steal that gift. It was a pure energy, and a supreme knowledge. The marauders knocked her off course. She was lost, struggling to find her way back to a life that was joyless and tinged with sadness. She knew that she was the steward of a divine gift, and her obligation was to protect it. Its strength might save her and protect her, she thought. Instead, it ended up being that which destroyed her.

David absorbed her emotional story. Internally, his "gift" grew. From beyond, Bridget changed him, enlightened him and gilded the golden knowledge bequeathed to him. It was an inner strength, a superhuman power that provided an almost godly insight. The ancients called it hermetic knowledge. The scope of this insight extended beyond his own framework of knowledge into that of all human knowledge, and all universal knowledge. He was strong enough to bear the responsibility, unlike Bridget, who became overwhelmed by it. Lamenting the responsibility, she jumped from the Golden Gate Bridge, wearing wings symbolic of her desire to return the gift to the angels.

The vast majority of millions taking Heaven Ride did not know they needed to fight to retain the gift, and forfeited their souls. David poured over her drawings again and again, each time gleaning another aspect of the treasure that had been stolen from the millions. He yearned to understand why.

Bridget wrote that she was to find other bearers of the gift. There would be thirteen. Each would provide a key that would unlock even more secrets of heaven. She claimed that together, these keys would unlock a great truth that could be used to defeat the source of the evil.

Occasionally, JW would venture over to see if David wanted to join him and Trish for lunch or dinner or to watch a movie. David declined choosing to stay engrossed in the mysterious manuscripts that bore a peephole to a celestial wilderness that he did not know existed. In these revelations, he found direction, as if from a heavenly mentor. They provided a roadmap for what was to follow.

David found a calling. He knew that the knowledge he possessed would pose a danger to others. With the curious documents rolling through his brain, he worked out in JW's fitness room twice a day. These workouts intensified each day, releasing the fury from his past failures. He pushed himself, knowing that his physical host needed to be as strong as his brain. The pain from these torturous workouts reminded him that he was mortal. The endorphins obfuscated his paradox.

Less than three years ago, JW and I took a trip to heaven. Now, I'm one of the richest men in the world, but I'm forced to live alone in exile, detached from my family and unable to enjoy any of the wealth that I earned. This isn't heaven. This is hell.

Any calm that came over him was masked in urgency as the weeks passed. The miracle they created was no miracle at all. It was robbing people of their souls. Already, a growing number of violent events and dangerous behavior were being attributed to Heaven Ride. He began to connect the dots. He was ready.

A tap on the door preceded JW's hand reaching through and firing a super ball that whizzed just above David's head, and careened off the walls and floor.

"I've hardly seen you in a week. What's new in Camp Brownington?" JW asked playfully.

He got a dead serious response.

"Somebody's got to bring this mother-fucking Heaven Ride down. Are you ready to help me?"

"Dude, you heard what Trish said; Martin and Steinman will kill to protect Heaven Ride. It's not the money they're after it is the power. The Gift shit that you have. They want it all. I don't know for what, and I don't even think Trish knows, but to them, this mind power is worth the souls of millions.

"That's right," David said, pausing to frame it just right. "We're going to have to fight fire with fire. JW, would you kill somebody to achieve our mission?"

JW answered without delay.

"If it's that prick, Steinman. Oh, yeah. In a heartbeat," JW responded. "But I told you, this isn't my mission." Knowing that David grew up with a more religious background than he did, he threw the question back at him. "Could you?"

David wiped his hand over his eyes.

"I've been wrestling with that," he said. "But, yeah, I could. I saw a quotation from a speech by Martin Luther King. He said, 'You have a dual citizenry. You live both in time and eternity; both in heaven and earth. Therefore, your ultimate allegiance is not to the government, not to the state, not to nation, not to any man-made institution. The Christian owes his allegiance to God, and if any earthly institution conflicts with God's will, it is your Christian duty to take a stand against it. You must never allow the transitory, evanescent demands of man-made institutions to take precedence over the eternal demands of the Almighty God.'"

"Yeah. I agree," JW said haltingly. "I just want to know how you remembered that whole quote. Pretty impressive, Mr. Brownington."

"It's that Gift shit," David said. "So, I'm asking you – you're in?"

"I'm in. But just between you and me. I'll help in any way 'cause I know how important is to you but nothing that will impact Trish or Tommy. Trish cannot know," JW said." And, you really need to lay low around her about shutting down Heaven Ride. Let's play it cool. It's not that I don't trust her, but I think we could keep Stein-ass and M&M at bay by keeping stealth about what we are doing. "Oh, and about that dual citizenry you just recited; given my heritage, I could probably get dual citizenship in Mexico, as well. Heaven. Earth. Mexico. The paperwork would be brutal, dude."

He made David laugh out loud. David let the laughter roll before turning serious once again.

"We've got to find a way to identify the people who escaped with the gift. If we could use their brain power if may help us outsmart Steinman and at least confuse him. Any bright ideas, JW?"

"David, it just so happens that I might. I built a remote code into the program that can allow me to access the data from a different computer. Actually, I had three different codes. If Johansson hasn't shut them down, I can view certain fields from anywhere."

"Wasn't your password deleted?"

"Yes," JW said in a pouty tone. "But I don't think I need a password for this."

"Why," David said, piqued, "you are a genius. Tell me more."

"I can access it and check record sizes. In this case, we'll be looking for records with huge amounts of data for the return trip."

"Will that get people from any of the Heaven Ride centers, or do you have to access them individually?"

"No, it accesses the central record base. It'll do all of them."

"Can you get on this today?" David asked.

"I'd rather not risk screwing up Trish's security deal. While you've been sequestered at Camp Brownington, I've been busy in my lair working on several things. In another day or two, I can show you. Then, we'll have access to a computer that isn't linked to this house."

"Whose house is it linked to?"

"The University of San Francisco Medical Center," JW said.

David laughed again. "And they only have about ten thousand computers there? Man, oh man, JW! You are on top of it today."

"Well, Johansson may have screwed us, so don't be too hopeful. But I'm pretty sure I disguised one of the access codes pretty well. I can't wait to show you our new toy."

"Our new toy? As in you and me new toy?"

"No, it's my new toy. But I might let you use it. No hints. You'll have to see it to believe it."

David spent that evening down in his room, looking at the final sections of Bridget's hieroglyphs. Though timid throughout her life, Bridget was brash, direct and detailed in chronicling her Heaven Ride nightmare. It put him in a virtual reality trance, dreamlike, and he was with Bridget. It was a guided tour of her mind. From beyond, she was able to show him what her Heaven Ride return was like. The terrifying journey included Bridget being chased by "soul-robbers." David followed her trail, descending the silver cord, descending faster, being pursued, plummeting and then – the silver cord was gone. She was no longer on the path back to consciousness, and David quickly equated that to the time they spent wondering if Bridget was going to regain consciousness. In the lab in the basement of the UCSF Medical Center, her body lay motionless in the pod. David could recall the expressions on all the faces. JW was as concerned as David. Holly looked frightened. Kelly looked out from the control booth, searching for JW, and shrugged. The only one not worried was Steinman. He looked annoyed, likely because he did not want his turn on Heaven Ride delayed any further. But wait! As the scene replayed through his mind, Kelly was not shrugging trying to find JW. She looked straight at Steinman. Kelly was aware that something had gone amiss.

Meanwhile, in oblivion, Bridget was hiding from the soul robbers. They appeared mechanical, with toothy jaws. They chomped in every direction, but Bridget evaded their notice. After they passed, she wandered, trying to find her way back. She found the severed cord. It seemed to be a lost cause. What were mere minutes in the lab lasted an eternity in oblivion. Glimmering in the distance, the cord! David followed her, and she struggled to get there. Something grabbed her from behind, trying to pull her back. He experienced her pain.

Reality interrupted David's excursion with Bridget in the form a loud scream. It was JW. It took David a moment to discern whether it was part of Bridget's vision, a dream or reality. It was reality, and the screams grew more intense. David threw himself toward the door, and ran up the hallway, and up the stairs. JW screamed as though he was being attacked. Could it be Trish?

Once upstairs, David reacted like a firefighter, barreling through the bedroom door. His eyes met Trish's as she calmly tried to massage JW's chest. His legs were kicking under the sheets, and his shoulders twisted from side to side as if her were trying to throw a huge weight. JW pushed her hands away and thrashed in the bed. David swept in, but Trish told him, "Don't. It's best not to wake him."

David ignored her. He grabbed a half-empty cup of water from the night table and threw it in JW's face. The screaming stopped. JW's thrashing continued.

Trish put her finger to her lips and pointed to the door. David met her in the hallway and followed her to the kitchen. David whispered, upset, "What's going on?"

Trish poured water into the Keurig machine. "Tea? Coffee?"

David felt distracted by her nonchalance. "Tea. Please. And what's going on?"

She sorted through a rack for the tea and set a second one on the counter for herself. "I should have told you," she said. "JW's been having these night terrors the past month or two. They've gotten worse the past few weeks."

"Is this the worst it has been?"

"One of the worst," she said. Tommy walked into the kitchen rubbing his eyes.

"Mom, is that JW? Is he okay?"

"Yes. It was. He's going to be fine, Tommy."

"He was yelling really loud."

"Yes, he was. But he's okay now. It was just a nightmare. You go to bed. Go on!" Tommy began to protest, but Trish cut him off. The boy trudged back to his bedroom.

"We went to see a psychiatrist in Provo two weeks ago. He was baffled by this, but said he had a few other patients exhibiting the early stages of these night frights. I tried to stop you because Dr. Michener said it might be dangerous to wake him suddenly from these nightmares he is having."

"I'm sorry. I'm really sorry," David said. "We need to try to figure out the cause of this. It never happened when we were roommates."

"He's probably fine. The doctor prescribed some pills and suggested we keep a close eye on the situation."

"Does he remember it the next day?"

"No. I tell him about it but he doesn't remember."

"Okay. I won't say anything. It might make him angry."

The following day, during David's morning workout, JW burst through the outside door and called for him.

"Gotta come out here and see this! This is really cool!"

David grabbed the red hoodie and followed his friend out the door. JW was excited like a five-year-old at Christmas. JW stopped at the edge of the driveway.

"There she is!"

David looked and saw nothing. He heard a car engine running but did not see the vehicle that was idling.

"I don't see anything," David said.

JW moved over a bit and began pointing out an outline of an SUV. Then, David could see a faint outline of the vehicle, and when JW opened the passenger door, the interior was clear.

"What the hell?" David asked.

JW went around to the driver's side, opened the door an pushed a button. The SUV came into full view.

"It's a Mercedes GL, a twin to my other one, except a year newer. This one has Ghost Cloaking Technology."

"Ghost cloaking?"

"Military technology. It's got dozens of cameras, and its paint is thousands of tiny receptors that depict what the camera sees on the opposite side. It creates an aura of invisibility," JW said, beaming.

"It's the only SUV with it in the world. I figured this was more practical than a tank."

David shared his enthusiasm. "Turn it on again!"

JW pushed a button and the Mercedes seemed to vanish. They both reacted with glee.

"How the hell did you get access to this type of military technology?" David asked.

"David, David, David," JW said. "When you have as much money as I have – as we have – no technology is out of reach."

"Does it work at night?" David asked.

"For what I paid, it better work 24-7, every day, Sundays and holidays," JW said. "Just because we have stone walls and iron gates to keep other people out doesn't mean they have to keep us in. Get in!"

With the ghost cloak on, JW pulled onto the back-country road.

"I'm not sure how this is going to work in city traffic," JW said. "This will be a challenge."

"Is all of this legal?" David asked.

"What do you think?" JW replied with sarcasm. Noting David's uncertain expression, he added, "No way *any* of this is legal. The technology is classified by the military. Driving around with no plates visible would probably cost me my license. This probably breaks a half dozen traffic laws."

"Not to mention that the other drivers can't see you flip them the bird," David joked.

"Right," JW said. "Sometimes we get government cars sitting across the street from our driveway. I'm going to build a bat cave under the barn, with a secret driveway out to the road."

"You do know you are insane," David opined.

"Haven't you always wanted a bat cave? Tell the truth."

"Alright. I always thought it would be cool to have a bat cave." "It's even going to have a huge turntable," JW explained. "Pull straight in, then the car will spin on the turntable so that you can pull straight out. The underground tunnel extends to the edge of the property onto a dirt road that leads out to the county road. This baby will escape surveillance like nothing else in the civilian world." "Impressive. So how far away is the monastery?" David asked. "Wait, is this the same monastery that makes that incredible hearth-baked bread?" David's mind quickly drifted to the first dinner Holly made for him. She served him the delicious monk-made bread with hand churned butter, a jar of organic mountain honey.

JW feigned ignorance, surprised at David's intuition. "What do you mean?"

"That's where you're taking me, right?" JW offered no answer. "What's there? Are we picking up bread, I hope."

"You'll see when we get there."

JW could not remember ever telling David about the monastery but he did remember providing the bread to Holly for her dinner. JW navigated down the back road and turned onto Main Street, where traffic was building. "I think you should turn at the next intersection JW and left on Aspen Grove," David said.

"How do you where the monastery is located and that I was planning to go this way?" JW asked perplexingly.

"I envisioned it a few days ago. It's part of the gift. I envisioned you taking me there. And today, as soon as we turned onto the road, I knew that was where you were taking me."

"But you don't know what's there?" JW inquired.

"If I thought about it enough, I could read your mind and figure it out. I don't want to wreck the surprise, so I filled my head with hot hearth-baked bread with butter and honey."

"The gift lets you do that?"

"Yeah. It's a lot like a Vulcan mind meld," David explained.

"Does it work with people in the same --"

"No, it works over distances, too. For example, my little sister, Katie. She's head over heels for a jock at her school. Brett. She wants to have sex with him, but she's afraid my parents will find out."

"Doesn't that creep you out a little?" JW asked. "I mean, knowing personal details about your sister?"

"Yeah, it does. By the way, she's more terrified of my parents than anything, so she's not going to do it with Brett anytime soon. But I can also tell you what Marty Martin is working on."

"Really. Do tell."

Before David could answer, a blue Honda made a right on red into JW's path. JW slammed on the brakes. In the rear-view mirror, he could see a truck closing in on him. He accelerated, and spun the steering wheel to the right, guiding the Mercedes into a space next to a fire hydrant. Again, he slammed on the brakes. Glass bottles in the SUV's mini refrigerator clanked and shattered. Frazzled, JW put the vehicle in park without turning off the engine. Passersby on the sidewalk reacted to the sound of the screeching brakes, looking curiously through the outline of the SUV. JW turned to David.

"So much for driving through traffic with smart camo on."

He flipped the switch to turn it off. Several of the onlookers jumped back, not believing their eyes.

"Yeah," David said with false surprise. "That's not going to draw any attention to us."

"At least it gets us off the ranch."

With new-found visibility, JW pulled into traffic and they continued on their way. JW showed off the features of the souped up stereo with XM satellite reception.

Stopped at a red light, David blurted out, "I can tell every person who has been on Heaven Ride."

JW, caught up in singing the Rolling Stones' tune "She's So Cold," turned down the radio. "How can you tell?"

"Just by looking. They – aw, this is gonna sound really crazy but a certain feeling, a vibe, hits me just by seeing a person who has taken Heaven Ride," David vague-splained.

"Is it a happy vibe? Is it like a secret society thing? You're not going to do that VW "punch-bug" thing every time you see one, are you?"

"No to all three. Your arm would get very sore. No, it's like a feeling of dread. I'm sympathetic for their loss."

"Hmm," JW acknowledged. "That's weird. But you can pick them out of a crowd?"

"Yeah," David said. "They give off a negative energy."

"Do I give off a negative energy?" JW asked.

"Yeah, you do," David said.

JW sniffed his armpit, and joked that he thought he showered. Then he grew thoughtful. "How do you know Heaven Ride is the reason?"

"I just do. Bridget told me I would know. She saw it, too. She called them shadow people." David pointed out a few shadow people at the intersection. He stopped, "Bridget said I had a diamond glow that was more pronounced. She said Steinman had it, too. The strange thing, she said" –

David looked at JW to make sure he was listening.

"Steinman had the glow before he took the Ride."

* * *

They passed a humble steel ranch gate archway, under which was a suspended sign denoting the Abbey of Our Lady of the Holy Trinity.

"You're full of surprises," David said. "A monastery?"

David crossed the parking lot to view the surroundings. The buildings were simple, post-WWII barracks and Quonset huts, save for one three-story brick building. The chapel was an elongated cylindrical shape bisected by an arched entry. The grounds consisted of a vast field, and at the far end, David thought he could see a herd of sheep. Looking across, David recognized the mountainside Snowbasin Ski Resort far in the distance. The entire setting evoked a modest, rural community.

JW opened the refrigerator in the back of the vehicle to survey the damage.

"Two bottles broken. Two unscathed." he reported.

"A beer fridge? It's 10:44 in the morning," David said. "Not sure I'm ready for a Belgian dubbel at this hour."

"Your liver tells time? These are for later, David. Abbott Brennan will have some cleaning supplies for the fridge. Follow me."

JW led David toward the three-story residence, then down the stairs to the end of the hall. The room was as JW left it nearly six months ago, on his last visit. His desk seemed overtaken by a keyboard and flat screen monitor, the surface strewn with magazines and articles printed from the internet. The coffee maker still contained some brown liquid, covered by a foamy white and green mold. Books pulled from the shelf, an open toolbox on the floor. In the corner, to David's surprise, was the original pod from the University of California at Berkeley project at the San Francisco Medical Center lab, the one which started the Heaven Ride adventure.

David approached it with wonderment, as if it were a saint's relic. He remembered Steinman's words that it looked like a bobsled trying to finish third in a race. That drew his attention to the dents, dings and scratches on the surface, before he became enthralled with the wired connections and dangling cathodes. The San Fran lab genesis of Heaven Ride evolved less than three years ago, yet it seemed like a lifetime for David.

"So this is what Steinman meant," David said. "Before he faked his death, when I met him at One Market Restaurant in San Francisco, he threatened to blow us in for property stolen from the hospital. You never told me you stole the pod!"

"C'mon, David. 'Stole' is a kinda harsh word for it. Bought is more like it. I made so many adaptations to it that it really became mine. I couldn't leave it behind. After we made our first fifty million, I wrote a big, anonymous check to the SF Med Center Hospital to be allocated to the UB program and Dr. McNumbnuts. It more than made up for the cost of the pod."

David corrected him. "Dr. McNulty is no longer there."

JW winked. "God, I hope I spelled his name right in that letter!" After a pause, he added, "Not there? How do you know?"

"I saw a news article. He disappeared mysteriously. Remains never found. He just disappeared, and nobody knows if he's dead or alive."

"Didn't Trish say he was part of the government scheme? Hell, one step out of line and you're taken out. Maybe they did know I stole, I mean bought the pod."

JW let that sink in for a moment, then resumed a cheerier tone. "So, what do you think?"

David cogitated the prospects. "We can work out of here? In secrecy?"

"A monastery is maybe one of the last places on earth where secrecy is still valued. Do you want me to bring in a desk?"

"No. I think you should just put a couch in over there, opposite the pod."

*   *   *

Over the next several weeks, JW's barn was erected and the

ground below excavated deep below the surface, invisible to surveillance from above. His longtime buddy, John Hoover, whose company built the Heaven's Gate roller coaster outside San Francisco, supervised the project. When it was completed, the boys had a barn with an escalator leading to a garage with an SUV-size turntable. The security door would open only with an automatic sensor built into the frame of the Mercedes. The subterranean tunnel ran beneath the fence to within a thousand feet of the road. In that stretch, a dirt road cut through the tall snakebark maples.

From that day forward, the duo began keeping regular office hours. This necessitated that JW tell Trish that he had set up an office in town. They both knew that any communications from the house would be monitored by the government. Trish never pressed him for details, except to inquire if the office was above a strip club. JW neither confirmed nor denied, and it became a running joke between the three of them.

Every month, Trish would bring David into her home office and swap out his burner phone. The procedure was more of a hassle than either would like, but David knew the necessity of the ritual. Each cell phone has a particular alpha-numeric identity, and certain common apps will broadcast that ID within a short radius of the phone's location. Police routinely keep tabs on suspects and have located criminals tapping into these broadcasted IDs. If cops can use it to their advantage, so can the bad guys.

The nature of their work became rather routine. JW scoured millions of Heaven Ride data records while David formulated plans to take down Heaven Ride. He was going to need information from the 13 Riders. According to Bridget, there would be one glaring concept or theme that they could share.

JW groused about not building search filters into the records that would make the job easier.

"The bad news is that I didn't foresee a need to retrieve that data remotely. The data is there. It's just hard to get to."

"It would almost be easier to hack into the computer system of every Heaven Ride center," David suggested.

"Right," JW said sarcastically. "Heaven Ride centers with security designed by the number one cloud computer security guru in the world, Jonah Johansson."

"I didn't say it would be easy. Maybe easier. I would love to outwit the best in the business. There is no victory as sweet as beating the best. Sooner or later, every #1 has to get toppled."

"Like your Sabres?"

"Hey, don't go there!"

"They lost again to the Bruins last night. Last year's champs are in third place in their division."

"Wait 'til the playoffs."

JW exulted. "Found one! The Los Angeles center. Wouldn't you know? The city of angels. Brian Givens. The data flow is off the charts!"

David's phone rang. This came as a shock because one of the two people in the world who had this number was in front of him in the room. The caller ID was not from Trish, but from a caller in Miami, Florida.

"David is that you?"

"Who is this?"

"You don't know me yet. My name is Clark."

"How did you get this number?"

"Well, I thought about it real hard, and it came – "

"How did you get this number?"

"As I was saying, I thought about it. I have The Gift."

David's jaw dropped. Words failed him.

"I have The Gift. It's incredible. The things I know now and what I see that I never saw before. But there's a bad thing. One really bad thing."

"What's that?" David asked.

"They're trying to kill me."

David was astonished with the revelation. He was concerned by the panic in Clark's voice.

"Are they after you right now?"

"No, I gave them the slip."

"Clark don't call me from your phone. Go get a cheap TracFone that they can't trace."

"Alright." Click.

About twenty minutes later, a soft tapping on the door interrupted JW's presentation of the data he was able to pull on Brian Givens.

"It's probably Fr. Brennan."

JW opened the door, expecting the monk with a plate of warm bread and fresh creamery honey butter. Instead, it was a sturdy man in his late twenties, with tattoos crawling up his neck underneath the collar of his thin coat. His flat top, close-cropped blond hair sparkled with particles of melting snow.

"Hi, JW. I'm Clark. Can I talk with David?"

JW stepped to the side, noticing that Clark was similar in height and build to himself. Clark wasted no time entering and extending his hand to David. Not only could David see the sparkling snowflakes, but there was an almost blinding aura about Clark's head. He hadn't noticed this with anyone else before.

"I thought you were going to call," David said.

"Naw. I was right down the road. I ditched my phone, like you said," Clark explained. "I'm one of the thirteen."

"The thirteen keys?" David asked.

"You were friends with Bridget? She leaves messages for me in my dreams. That's how I found you. And no, JW, I wasn't followed. But it's stupid for me to stay very long. I'm heading north to Seattle. My sister lives there, and I got a baby niece that I haven't met yet."

"Is that the only coat you have?"

"Yeah. We don't get lots of snow in Miami." Just when neither of them had much to say, Clark blurted out, "Kratos."

"Pardon me?"

"Kratos. The Greek god of power. That's my key."

They chatted briefly, but Clark insisted on hitting the road. He was going on foot to the train station, then ride the rails up to Seattle.

Before he left, David gave him the red hoodie to wear under his coat. JW gave him one of the Belgian beers, just in case he had a long wait for the train. Clark stopped in the doorway.

"What's going to happen when this gets shut down? What's going to happen to me?"

David replied honestly that he did not know.

"I think you'll always have the Gift," David said. "Maybe then you will be safe. After you visit your niece, you should maybe get out of the country."

"To where?" Clark asked.

David was uncertain. "Italy, perhaps. Somewhere near the Alps, away from the cities."

Clark agreed that might be a good idea. David and JW watched him leave, hoping the daylight would hold out for him to get to the station.

Later, under the cover of night, JW and David left the monastery. The ride home was punctuated by JW screaming, over and again, "I love this truck!"

*   *   *

Back at the Five Rings compound, JW checked in the new security guard for the first time. He needed to explain about the invisibility of the Mercedes GL, and the skeptical guard opened the gate. Inside, Trish made a stew. They ate during the local news. The third story of the broadcast caught their attention.

"A Florida man identified as Clark Meyers was the victim of a hit-and-run accident on Hewitt Road late this afternoon. Meyers, 29, is believed to be a drifter without a family. He was on foot when a car hit him on the shoulder of the road. The driver of the vehicle left the scene. Police say there are no leads, but they are asking any possible witnesses to report any clues that might lead to the capture of the driver."

David and JW looked at each other. Neither needed to speak a word.

*   *   *

Over dinner, JW shared the story of the Ghost Cloaking with Trish, ending with the admonition to always turn the feature off when driving in a crowd. Trish never asked where the guys went, nor was the information volunteered. After dinner, David excused himself to go to his room.

He spent the evening opening his mind to the many opportunities open to him because of the Gift. The process was draining. He felt as though he were nodding off, and changed into some shorts and a long-sleeved shirt. It was not long before he fell asleep.

It was a sound sleep. He felt cradled by the innocence of sleep.

The Gift shut down. Quiet.

Hours later, with the entire household sleeping, a scream pierced the silence.

* * *

October passed into November, and snow became a regular occurrence. JW located seven of the 13 Riders. Finding the rest of the gifted Riders was his obsession. He woke up trying to shake the cobwebs from an unsettling sleep. He heard soft music playing in Trish's office, and the coffee pot was nearly full.

"I just made some fresh coffee," Trish called to him.

"I see that," JW said, pouring a cup. "Thanks. Whatcha working on?"

"I'm going to apply to teach marketing at the community college. They asked for a preliminary lesson plan."

"Oh, cool," JW said.

As he drank his morning coffee, JW heard a high-pitched whoop of joy fracture the wintry air. It was Tommy. It was Tuesday morning. The 11-year-old was supposed to be in school.

JW fetched his coat and put it on as he walked to the pond. A few inches of snow had fallen overnight, but the ice on the pond was immaculately shoveled in the shape of a hockey rink. Tommy skated, and he was not alone.

"Tommy! Why aren't you in school?" JW worked hard on his authoritative "dad-like" voice, but he rarely had a chance to use it with Trish's well-behaved boy.

"I am in school, JW. David is teaching me some pro stickhandling moves. Look!"

Tommy demonstrated a slightly flawed technique, faltering but recovering to flawlessly maneuver a puck around three stationary pucks on the ice in front of him.

JW used the same authoritative voice with David. It was something just shy of anger. "David, did you make Tommy skip school?"

"No, sir. I did not," David said in mock seriousness. "I – let's say, I encouraged Tommy to attend a different school today."

"Trish is going to freak out when she hears that Tommy is

playing hooky."

"I'm not playing hooky, JW. I'm playing hockey," Tommy said in an innocent tone. "And mom doesn't have to know."

David tilted his head and opened his eyes wide, his unspoken words indicating that the kid had a point.

JW frowned at David.

"You shut up!" David said.

"I didn't say anything."

"Yeah, you did. With your head."

"Ninety percent of what we learn in life happens outside the classroom," David said, citing his personal encyclopedia of facts. "I might add, we have a very structured lesson plan here at the David Brownington School of the Icy Oval. Here, we have the morning skate, and stickhandling drills, which now must be extended due to your interruption. Then, we're going to have hot cocoa and history – the history of the game and its importance to civilization. After that, geography, and the locations of the NHL franchises and where some of the great players learned to play. We'll need to have a lunch break. I might have to sneak some food out of the kitchen. After lunch, it's science. Tommy was curious about how to lift the puck, so we're going to tackle some basic principles of physics as they relate to getting elevation and control on a wrist shot. I might have to sneak some plates out of the kitchen. Just kidding, I'm not going to break any plates. Then, it's time for the afternoon skate, where we'll practice pivoting and quick turns, and maybe work in some more practice on those wristers."

"Okay, stop!" JW pleaded.

"Wait," David cautioned. "Tonight, there's homework. I've downloaded a bunch of hockey biographies. I'll let Tommy choose which one he wants to read."

"I want to read the Bobby Orr story!" Tommy said with unbridled enthusiasm.

"You mean 'Dynamite on Ice,' isn't that right, David? Okay! I get it! How long have you been planning this?"

"Since yesterday," David answered without shame. "And Tommy promised he would get his homework assignments from Billy Mandell. Um... I could use an assistant professor out here. Why don't you grab your skates from the barn and lace 'em up?"

JW muttered, "Trish is gonna kill me." Silently, he followed David's advice, collecting his skates, stick and gloves from the barn. The lessons proceeded according to plan. Shortly after noon, David crept into the house and took a bag of frozen chicken nuggets and a bottle of barbecue sauce from the kitchen. On the way out, he poked his head into Trish's office.

"Hi," he said, sheepishly.

"Hi," she said. "It sounds like you guys are having a blast."

"We are. I just want you to know this was all my idea."

"That's fine," she said. "Tommy's getting good grades in school. One day off won't set him back."

David was taken aback by her agreeable reaction. "Okay. Just one thing. Will you give JW a hard time, anyway? We don't want the big kid to enjoy this more than the little one."

Trish laughed. "Good idea. Oh, and take the carrot sticks and orange slices. Also, I made hot chocolate – it's on the stove. And a Thermos on the counter."

David smiled, and left.

The guys heated up the chicken nuggets in the microwave in the new Mercedes and ate them rink side.

"This is the best lunch I ever had," Tommy said, munching on a carrot stick.

JW smiled at David. "Yeah, kid, it's pretty good. Welcome to the hockey life."

As they cleaned up their plastic plates and cups, the sound of helicopter rotors grew louder. A lone helicopter approached.

JW's concern etched his face. "Hey, Bucko. Leave your skates here. Head on up to the house."

Tommy saw the helicopter and the look on JW's countenance and did not question the order.

"Run," JW said. "We got you on the stopwatch!" Tommy ran, his boots crunching through the snow.

The black helicopter approached, then hovered fifty feet above the pond. David could see the pilot and another man in the cockpit. They did not appear to be military. The passenger raised binoculars to his eyes. "Let's go," David said. "Leave the stuff here."

The wind whipped, creating gusts at their backs as they walked to the house. David and JW glanced over their shoulders every few yards. The helicopter hovered lower, close enough that they could see the faces of the two men inside After they disappeared into the house, the helicopter peeled off.

As David and JW removed their outer garments, they heard Tommy telling his mom about his "best day ever." JW squeezed David on the shoulder and whispered, "Thanks. It was one of my better days, too."

David stopped JW before he joined Trish and Tommy.

"You know what that was about, right?"

"I think so."

"They are letting us know they're keeping tabs on us. If they wanted to kill us now, they would have shot at us."

"I know. But who is 'they'?"

"Probably Steinman. Martin. I don't think the IRS uses helicopters yet. Just in case, make sure you file on time this year, so they don't have an excuse to open fire."

Chapter 4: Operation Special K

DATELINE: ODESSA, UKRAINE. October 5, 2009.

Valentin Karmalov closed the fat binder, ending the briefing with the two Americans.

"What do you think?" he asked. There was no immediate answer. The Americans were pensive. "Commander Gomez?"

Vincente Gomez stared for a second at the black, Navy-issued diving watch on his wrist. He looked up at Valentin.

"What if it's a trap," he said. Vincente was never one to mince words. Karmalov, captain of the National Space Agency of Ukraine. Commander Gomez' words slashed a wound in his pride. To him, these Americans, Gomez and Sanders, were larger than life. He looked to this joint Ukrainian-U.S. mission to get back what the Russians stole from U.S. government some three years earlier and destroy the Russian project. By assisting the Americans, the Ukraine Space Agency would finally get access to ISS.

"Capt. Karmalov, how do you know this is where the target is located if you don't know what the target is," Gomez asked.

"We have people who have been there in person and have seen American documents about some type of intergalactic space travel, interterrestial," Capt. Karmalov responded.

Vincente rubbed his chin. "I want to observe their security first-hand. Boots on the ground. Can you get Simon and I into Rostov undetected?"

"Oh, yes. But then, what?" Valentin asked, with a note of desperation.

"If it's a go, we'll carry out the mission within 24 hours. If we smell a rat, we back off. Fair?"

The two Navy SEALS watched Valentin's reaction, checking for signs of deceit.

"I stand by our intelligence," Capt. Karmalov said. "We believe your skills will allow you to get in, get the target and get out. It's an old building and even though it is a premier Russian research facility, it lacks sophisticated security systems."

Gomez and Sanders said nothing.

"Listen, you want this technology. We want ISS access, plus more U.S. defense aid against the Russians. This is going to be a win-win for our countries," Karmalov summarized.

"Let us look at those schematic drawings again," Gomez demanded.

* * *

The Russian Academy of Rocket Forces in Rostov Oblast posed few problems for the two Black Ops soldiers. Getting in would be easy. Getting out? Not as simple as Karmalov painted.

Within weeks, the Americans received their wish for boots on the ground. They drove a black Mercedes SUV, very common to the region, from Odessa to Rostov-on-Don. Following Karmalov's instructions, they landed at a cafe near the RARF operated by a mustachioed, portly Ukrainian ex-pat, Yuri. They took a shadowy booth in the back, sipping tea and lingering long past closing time.

Darkness overtook Rostov, but traffic illuminated the streets.

Built in 1957, the Russian Academy featured a rooftop emergency exit with an archaic lock and an unsophisticated security system throughout the building that had not been updated in years. Vincente wanted assurances that Yuri was coming through on his end of the deal – the escape. Yuri provided them with security clearances that would get them in the building, which looked official to Gomez' trained eye. He and Sanders grilled Yuri until the wee hours on the logistics, particularly the escape. It was deemed too risky for future operations for Yuri to drive, so Yuri's 22-year-old son, Aleksander, would wait out front in a Hyundai SUV, then take the Americans to Taganrog, a port city that was neither Russian nor Ukrainian. There, a U.S. boat sailing under Norwegian flags would depart at 11:40 a.m. sharp for Odessa, where a navy airship would fly them to the NASA's Ames Research Center in California. Once the details were meticulously laid out, Gomez and Sanders bunked down in a back room for a few hours.

* * *

The October sky showed signs of brightening early, even though the sunrise came nearly two hours later. Gomez and Sanders donned attire that is usually reserved for painters, although they embellished the gear with some gadgets, sensors and tools supplied by Uncle Sam. Yuri left food for them in the refrigerator. They reheated *valenyky*, a doughy pouch filled with a creamy potato and cabbage filling, and *kutia*, a porridge-like sweet wheat mixture eaten cold. Simon complained, but ate it anyway. They left through the back door. Sanders lugged a duffel bag rigged with brushes, scrapers and near-empty paint cans to carry out the ruse.

Rostov was primed for a gray day. Luckily, there would be no precipitation, just clouds that would fill in as the day wore on. The city woke slowly, and as the Americans walked the few blocks to the Russian Academy of Rocket Forces, the streets were mostly deserted aside from a few taxis, buses and night workers getting off their shifts at hotels and all-night pool halls.

The Academy building stretched over two square blocks, its white walls with many windows festooned near the roof with ornate scrollwork. Like most academic buildings, it featured a wide stairway in front as the main entrance. Other entries in the rear were downward stairways leading to steel doors in the basement.

The guard at the front chastised them roundly, telling them they needed to enter through the workers' entrance in the back. *You idiots can't go through here with all your tools. Is it your first time here?*

Gomez understood only a few words – "idiot" and "tools." Sanders answered in flawless Russian. *It is our first time. Which door do we go to in the back?*

The third door. But there is no guard there until 9 o'clock.

Without delay, Sanders retorted, *Then I am not such an idiot.*

They told us to come here because they want our work completed before 9 o'clock.

The guard looked at them, a blank expression shielding his uncertainty. He asked to see their credentials, and after inspecting the flawless replicas, he let the painters in, bypassing the standard security scan. The guard gave them instructions to get to the roof. The Americans did not converse from this point forward. They took an elevator, as instructed by the guard, up to the top floor, and exited onto the graveled rooftop after propping the door open. The mechanized scaffold was in place on the southeast corner of the ten-story building. Each of the men inserted an earbud and clipped a transmitter on their collars. It contained a tiny button that emitted a high-pitched beep on the Bluetooth earpiece: two beeps if someone was coming, three to abort the mission and run like hell. Gomez opened one of the paint cans. Inside, under an oily liquid that resembled white paint, he extracted two nylon guns and bullets of a similar synthetic material. Once each of the men was armed, they loaded their bags onto the scaffold and dropped to the seventh floor. Using a Dremel-like cutting saw, Sanders severed the casing and locking bolts in the bottom corners of a wide window. Gomez pushed, and the window swung inward, allowing him to slide into Room 714-A, a restricted research lab which was in the briefing document provided by Valentin Karmalov in Odessa. Sanders handed him a gym bag filled with some tools, and a matchbook-sized high-res digital camera. Sanders opened a paint can, stirred the paint and actually began painting the outside of the building. All the while, he watched, and listened for possible interruptions through highly sensitive receivers within the equipment bag. Gomez oriented himself to the room, which contained eight empty desks in an open-office configuration, and one cubicle in the corner with a larger desk and office accoutrements such as a stapler, a paper clip dispenser and a computer. He identified the file cabinet containing the target documents in that cubicle.

Distracted by an odd set-up with a cot surrounded by various medical devices, Vincente snapped a series of photos. He took a few close ups of the monitoring devices that seemed out of the ordinary. He crossed the room to a partly partitioned cubicle in the corner bearing the file cabinet. He opened the drawer, and then received a two-beep warning from Sanders. He left the cubicle, file drawer still open, and knelt behind the closest of the desks.

The door to Room 714-A opened, and a professorial-type man wearing a white lab coat entered. He peered quizzically at the open drawer, shut it, and pulled a file from the front of the middle drawer. He sat down, inspecting the information at length. Vincente rolled his eyes and pointed to his watch, a specially designed black multi-function watch made exclusively for Navy SEALs. Simon hand-signaled Gomez to sit tight. The professor leaned back in his chair, reading, and Gomez bent as low as he could, peeked around the corner of the desk and silently snapped a picture of the man. Momentarily, the professor opened the desk drawer, picking a memory card from a plastic sleeve, rose and walked to the opposite corner with the monitoring devices. He inserted a memory card in one of them, punched a few buttons and downloaded some data. He returned the data card to a plastic jacket, and put it back in the desk drawer. Then, he took the folder and left the room.

Gomez looked to the window, and Sanders gave him an all clear signal. Nimbly, Vincente opened the cabinet and located several files of interest. There were blueprints and charts showing the development of the technology, some in Russian and others in English. Out of curiosity, he opened the middle drawer, which contained about a dozen files bearing names. Gomez randomly selected one and took photos of the documents inside. He double-checked one of the design documents, and returned all the files to their places. He doubled back across the room, ignoring signals from Sanders to leave. Gomez noticed a mini refrigerator against the wall. He opened the door, and inside were hundreds of neatly packed vials of a blackish brown liquid, about 2 ounces in each one. They were sealed with a rubber stopper, and Gomez then noticed a box of syringes on a stainless-steel table within arm's reach. He unzipped a compartment on his sleeve and pocketed three of the vials. Then, he visually inspected the machine that was of interest to the professor. He yanked the cord from the outlet and removed all the connecting cables with a few tugs. He wrapped the power cord around it and tucked it under his arm. Gomez placed seven plastic explosives throughout the room, each with a 3-minute timer and containing U.S. military grade Octanitrocubane, known to virtually turn everything to ash. A smile crossed his face as he saw Sanders' panicked expression. Before reaching the window, an afterthought occurred to Gomez. He retraced his steps to the cubicle, opened the drawer and took the plastic sleeve with the memory card, tucking it into a pocket. Two beeps signaled an intruder. Gomez made a dash toward the window. The door opened, and the professor entered, just as Gomez was opening his portal of escape.

"Hey! What are you doing?" the professor called in Russian after the fleeing saboteur. He watched Gomez climb onto the scaffold with Sanders. Eyes wide open, the Russian professor, Gogol, raced to his phone and dialed a three-digit extension to notify security.

Within seconds, an alarm sounded, piercing the morning air in the academy and in the streets outside the perimeter of the campus. The scaffolding dropped at a pace designed for safety, and not for escaping a burglary. To the sixth floor. Twenty seconds later, the fifth. Those seconds ticked like an eternity. Sanders jettisoned the paint can, and it spattered white paint on the lawn and shrubbery below. Gomez stuffed his stash inside the equipment bag. He placed the camera into a small, customized pocket sewn into the waistband of his pants.

"You weren't supposed to disrupt the equipment, Commander," Sanders said.

"I've never seen anything like this before," Vincente replied. "I needed this to complete the mission."

"We have our work cut out for us now."

A second siren blared, this one from the street. A military security unit pulled up beside the building. Third floor.

"Let's ditch this piece of shit!" Gomez shouted. Clutching the bag, he dove over the edge, plummeting about thirty feet. He landed on his feet, then rolled to a safe stop. Gunfire commenced, as Sanders viewed the steep drop from the slow-moving scaffold. A bullet pinged off the metal nearby. All in white, Sanders fell toward the splatter marks he just made with the paint.

Gomez was already on the run when Sanders hit the ground. He felt a piercing pain in his left leg when he hit, and the jolt jarred his teeth. He ran, despite the pain in his leg, following Gomez across the campus lawn toward the rendezvous point with Aleksander.

Gomez reached the street and stopped. Aleksander wasn't there. The first security car sped across the lawn towards them as a second pulled around the southeast corner of the building. Simon arrived, breathless. Frantic, Gomez scanned the street looking for their getaway car.

"Goddamn traitor!" Sanders said, voicing Gomez' thoughts at that moment.

Sanders ran into the stopped traffic and opened the door of a brown Volkswagen SUV. He pulled a young woman out, despite her effort to cling to the wheel, and flung her to the ground.

"Get in!" he yelled to Gomez. Gomez opened the door, threw his sack in the vehicle and jumped in as Sanders gunned the engine. A bullet pinged off the door just as Vincente was closing it shut.

"This fucking country!" Sanders ranted. "You can't trust any of them."

Simon cut across two lanes to make a left turn, leaving a wake of screeching autos behind. The security vehicle was stuck in the civilian traffic. Next, they heard a huge explosion that shattered store windows on the street. Smoke, fire and fallen debris rained down.

"Jesus, Gomez, do you think you over did it?" Sanders said.

"That'll keep them busy for awhile. They'll need a new paint job," chuckled Gomez.

"I hope I remember how to get to the M14," Sanders said.

"Stay true," Gomez said, a calm voice that belied the situation. "About a mile up the road, the entrance will be on the left."

New sirens blared in the background.

"You been here before?" Sanders asked.

"No. But I studied the map last night." He exhaled the excitement from the chase. "Yuri's not a traitor. Aleks is an agent, too. I'll bet he was detained."

"Well, call me a cynic," Sanders complained.

The Americans blazed through traffic, pursued nearly the entire way to Taganrog Bay by Russian police. The police discontinued their chase as the stolen SUV crossed what was formerly the Ukrainian border. Before long, Sanders and Gomez were dodging industrial vehicles at the port. The Norwegian flag stiffened in the breeze over a speedy yacht that was dwarfed by the frigates and freight ships.

* * *

Jonah Johansson finished shaving and trimmed his Van Dyke beard, looking more like a GQ model than the chief administrator of a space research lab. Although he was far more MIT than Hollywood, Johansson carried movie-star good-looks into his 60s. He patted his face with a towel, removing all leftover traces of shaving cream. It was all rote behavior, while his mind churned complex formulas and sophisticated language for new patent applications.

It all came to an end with his phone's ringtone, "Uptown Girl" in the next room. It was his granddaughter, Alison. He smiled.

"Good morning, Angel! Why are you calling me so early in the morning?"

"Were you asleep? I'm sorry."

"Hell no! I've got inventions to invent and worlds to conquer. Been up for hours. What's going on?"

"Papa, I'm so excited!" Alison gushed. "I just got a new internship."

"Congratulations, Angel. D.C. or West Coast?"

"No, D.C." she clarified. "I will be interning in Senator Bob Thomas' office."

"Bob Thomas of California? Does that mean my pretty granddaughter will be coming out to northern California to visit her old granddad?"

"You betcha! In fact, I'm scheduled to come out there next month. The details have to be confirmed, but I wanted you to be the first to know."

Jonah's phone buzzed twice. Call waiting.

"Hey, Alison. I've got another call. Can I catch up with you tonight?"

"Sure."

"Congratulations on the internship. Gotta go." He clicked twice on his phone, and was connected to an incoming call from Bryce Patton, a research administrator at Ames.

"Bryce. What's up?"

"Jonah, you're not going to believe what just came through."

"Operation Kratos?"

"Yeah. Commander Gomez uploaded a portion of the intelligence. He's got some hard materiel, too."

"Material? He was instructed to – "

"Jonah. He sent pictures of what he has. We need an order to bring Gomez in for debriefing. Can I issue that?"

"Yes. Sure. I am eager to see what he's got. And if it was worth it. Write up that order and I'll sign it when I get in."

*   *   *

The transport plane touched down at Moffat Airfield the following day. Bryce Patton, wearing a civilian suit, walked briskly across the windy tarmac. A ladder was wheeled over the hatch of the plane. A smirk crossed Vincente's face as he carried the electronic device and vials off the plane. Getting one over on the Russians pleased him, and his gut told him this bounty was of incredible importance.

In the aftermath of the heist, Russia issued several veiled threats, not directed at anyone because they didn't know for certain who perpetrated the deed.

Patton was an eager Stanford grad, whose degree in public policy gave Jonah reason to hire him as his personal secretary. That, and a recommendation from Bob Thomas, the chairman of the Senate Armed Forces Committee. When a position opened as a research admin, Jonah promoted the young man. His baby face appeared older with a close-cropped haircut and a stocky physique. His job was about to get a lot bigger.

Patton graciously welcomed the Navy SEALs stateside and offered to carry Vincente's precious cargo.

Commander Gomez refused to give it up until he reached Johansson's office. Instead, he handed Patton the three vials of dark liquid. Patton squinted at the test tubes and shook his head.

Patton led the Navy SEALs inside, knocked once on Johansson's door and opened the door to the awaiting administrator of the complex. He performed a cursory introduction, and then departed.

Gomez scanned the sparse surroundings in Johansson's office. It was almost bare, save for an easel-back photo of his deceased wife, a photo of his daughter, Elle, with his son-in-law, and a larger, more glamorous framed photo of his granddaughter, Alison. When she was a little girl, he called her Ally Angel, and they developed a bond closer than most grandparents are privileged to find.

Ally Angel was the inspiration for Johansson's newest area of investigation. He was always intrigued by the prospect of love. He broke it down scientifically, theorizing that it was based on nothing, no element, no physical building block, no genetic strand. Nothing but thin air, and an inexplicable energy. Over time, with shared experiences or memories nurtured by being apart, layers and layers of this energy strengthen and reinforce this bond. Away from the government office, Johansson was developing a powerful information stream, based on the same principles as love. There was no infrastructure, just encrypted data. Jonah called it "the cloud," and it was already being put into practice at Ames, and by the burgeoning online retailer, Amazon.com. He drew parallels between the two, and in his modest spiritual belief system, both were from God.

"Nice digs," Gomez said with mock earnestness.

Johansson choked slightly while chuckling at the unexpected joke.

"Hey, thirty-five years in the private sector giving birth to cloud computing, all vanished after 10 months with the government. Commander Gomez. Special Agent Sanders. My commendations for a job well done," Jonah said, accompanied by a hearty handshake. "What have you got for me?"

Gomez glanced at Sanders.

"Sir," he said, deliberating. "We don't rightly know what we have here. What I do know is that this is important to the Russians. Logic tells me this is a key piece of their technology."

Johansson took the box from Gomez and set it on his desk. The box itself was stainless steel. On the back was a series of three green-tinted, s-shaped rods, affixed in a parallel formation. The metal seemed unfamiliar to Johansson. He sat down, tilting the apparatus in every direction, his attention finally riveted on the slot for the memory card.

He wondered aloud, "Is this some sort of receiver? Or a transmitter?" Puzzled and intrigued, he looked up at Gomez, who then remembered to pull the card from his sleeve pocket. Johansson smiled.

"Aha! This may be what we need. Good job!"

"What next?" Vincente asked after handing the card over.

"Weren't you going to take some time off for vacation? And Special Agent, I think you've earned some R&R as well. I've got Patton and his crew translating and analyzing the documents that you uploaded to the cloud. And this memory card. This may tell us what this, this gizmo is."

"Gizmo, sir?" Sanders asked. "Is that the technical term for it?"

A series of hard knocks on the door startled them all. Jonah invited the caller to enter.

Patton opened the door and stepped in.

"Sir. It's Yuri Panatov, and his son Aleksander. They've disappeared," Patton disclosed.

Gomez looked concerned. "Yuri? The cafe owner in Rostov?"

"Yes, sir," Patton acknowledged. "The cafe kitchen, it was a bloodbath."

Johansson frowned. "If he or the son talk, the Russians will certainly seek retribution. Putin would like nothing better than to scandalize a U.S. intelligence effort."

"Not if what we have here is such a state secret that it would bring his national security into disrepute," Sanders offered.

"Right." Johansson stood, and peered through the blinds out the window into the California sunshine. "You both might be in peril. Do you still want those furloughs?"

"I have a girlfriend who hasn't seen me in a month. At least, I had one. I'd love a week off," Sanders said.

"Sir, we're trained to protect ourselves in every situation. I have some business to tend to," Gomez said.

"All right," Jonah said. "Be cautious. And all this. I don't have to remind you of the confidential nature of it all. But if you have any flashes of brilliance on what all this Russian magic is about, don't hesitate to contact me."

Patton reached for the door handle, then pulled back.

"One more thing," he said. "That brown substance? We analyzed that in a spectrometer. It's fish protein. Very highly concentrated protein. Crushed Beluga caviar and Black Sea

Lamprey."

Gomez shrugged. "I hope I didn't travel all the way to Russia to steal Professor Gogol's lunch from the fridge."

Chapter 5: Enter Steinman

Hours after Gomez and Sanders left the complex, Jonah pored over the report Gomez submitted, spelling out minute details of their heist and the Russian Space lab where it took place. After consuming the contents, he dashed through other mundane administrative paperwork. His brain worked on two levels, and the Operation Special K report still processed in his head while signing off on the lesser documents. His phone rang, temporarily halting his progress on both planes.

"Bearded Vulture is at the gate," Patton informed him.

Bearded Vulture was the code name given to a new, high-level liaison by the Secretary of Defense. Jonah never met Thomas Steinman before. When they finally met, Jonah noted that Steinman was neither bearded nor vulture-like based on appearance. Lean and wiry, Steinman stood a bit over six-foot-tall, looking comfortable in a blue suit, starched collar and striped red tie. His tousled hair was prematurely gray, and thinning. When his face was relaxed, as it was now, he bore a welcoming countenance and his pale blue eyes showed a hint of mirth, like he was stifling a joke. His mouth naturally curled into a smirk. While Johansson earned the pedigree of a genius, Steinman always looked like he knew something others in the room did not. But when troubled or angered, those eyes turned steely gray, inset in shadowy sockets, and the smirk appeared as a serpent-like sneer. Johansson had seen that aspect when Steinman was called to testify before a congressional panel on a DOD ethics charge.

After Patton left the office, Steinman perused the stark details of Johansson's office.

"Did you learn your interior decorating skills at the Russell Trust Association?" Steinman asked in jest.

Johansson was surprised by the random question. He was obligated to answer truthfully.

"As a matter of fact, I did." Steinman established himself at the outset as an ally that Johansson believed he could trust.

"Let's get down to brass tacks," Steinman told him. "The DOD suspects that the materiel confiscated in Operation Special K is essential to a covert Russian military operation. I anticipate that you will be able to support or refute that."

"I've begun looking over the reports and evidence Commander Gomez submitted," Johansson said. "Honestly, I think the Russians stole our technology to use it for military advantage. But as it began to play out, from what I could see, they weren't sure how to use it one way or another."

"Do the Russians know we have it," Steinman asked.

"My sources on the ground tell us that what the Russians know is that they don't have it. They're not certain exactly who took it. Gomez and Sanders did a good job covering their tracks. The explosion on the seventh floor of the Russian Academy of Rocket Forces will set them back months. But there's one wild card. You probably know, our agent, Yuri Panatov, was tortured and killed. We don't know if he kept quiet or not." Anticipating Steinman's next question, Jonah added, "We'll have to wait on that one."

"We will be on the lookout for any retribution. Meanwhile, I want to be kept in the loop for the smallest details. Secretary of Defense Bryant and Martin Martin from the CIA are all over this."

"I've applied for re-authorization to test this on human subjects," Johansson said.

"Screw the re-authorization! I'm authorizing this," Steinman bellowed.

"But Thomas, are you – ?"

"It will fall on my shoulders if anything goes wrong," Steinman said "We can't sit on our hands with this. How close are you to having the new hardware in place?"

"As far as we know, it's done. Going forward, we will modify the Russian prototype if there is any value to our existing technology and equipment."

"From now on, we don't call anything 'Russian,'" Steinman corrected. "It will just be the prototype."

"Roger that."

"Try to find three candidates to test this on. I'd like to be here when it happens."

Their meeting ended. Johansson used this to size up Steinman. He found him to be highly analytical, a shrewd judgmental type with a Machiavellian approach to all things under his sphere of influence. Johansson recognized that for Steinman, everything was under his domain.

A week later, the new prototype was able to be tested. Steinman was summoned to the Ames base. One room was devoted to the apparatus and a second one down the hall as a debriefing room. An empty office served as a waiting room. Johansson put out a call to find five subjects for a secretive test.

The test included five enlisted military personnel with level 2 security clearances.

The first subject, Sandy Singer, was a willowy researcher with the Air Force who came in on a scheduled day off. In her early 30s, Sandy was athletic and healthy, with years of tennis keeping her in fantastic shape. During the introduction, she hid her nervousness with laughter, joking with Dr. Dan Crosby, the Ames' medical doctor Johansson assigned to the project. Crosby told her that it was a non-invasive experiment, except for one shot of organic protein. He explained that the entire procedure would take about fifteen minutes but that she might sleep through a portion of it.

"If you are just giving me a shot of protein, why would I fall asleep?" she asked.

Dr. Crosby was hard-pressed for an answer. "We've seen data from similar tests," he offered. "Your body may experience a moving sensation, like it is traveling through space, and you might have visions that will cause a degree of hypertension." He could see his explanation wasn't striking a chord with her. "It may be like hypnosis, where you are still conscious, but in a dreamlike state." He explained that he would bring her back to consciousness after just a few minutes, and that he would monitor her biological functions every step of the way.

Sandy was directed to the procedure room. She wore a pullover blouse that made it difficult to apply the numerous sensors, and was asked to remove it. She reclined on a standard military-issue cot, and the doctor attached eleven different probes on her hands, arms, head and chest.

"Your hands are cold," Sandy told him. As an afterthought, she added, "I'm not complaining. It's warm in here."

The doctor completed the work with the electronic sensors and checked the monitors to make sure they worked properly. They did. Dr. Crosby checked with Jonah to get the go-ahead to begin.

"Mr. Steinman is not here yet," Jonah told him. "But I don't see any reason to hold this up. Go ahead and start the process. I'll be there in half a minute. I'd like to observe."

When he arrived, Jonah introduced himself to Sandy, then stood behind the computers that would be monitoring her trip. Dr. Crosby administered the protein shot and pushed a button that administered a 12-volt shock. Sandy jumped.

"I wasn't expecting that," she said. "Whoa!" she said. Her heart rate dropped, and her breathing slowed as she began entering a dreamlike coma. Dr. Crosby sat down behind the computers.,

Johansson's phone sounded. Steinman had arrived. "Bring him into the procedure room."

Steinman quietly entered before the journey was completed. He stood next to Johansson, peeking over the doctor's shoulder at the instruments.

The timer struck the three-minute mark. "Her brain-oxygen levels are depleting. I'm bringing her back," Dr. Crosby announced. He sent a second jolt into a sensor behind her ear, and a scattered array of monitors changed their patterns. The reader showed colorful activity that was far exaggerated from the original waves. The oscillations were at least three times the size, and in multiple colors.

"What is this chart monitoring?" Steinman asked, pointing to a different machine.

"Those are her brain waves, sir" Dr. Crosby said.

"It's going crazy!" Steinman observed. "Is that normal?"

"No, sir. Her brain activity is heightened astronomically. She's coming to."

Steinman stepped into the center of the room and took note of the test subject for the first time. He was instantly smitten as he watched Dr. Crosby remove the sensors by pressing gently against the fleshy part of her chest above her bra, then her arms and neck. Sandy sat up and craned her neck mildly to stretch. She noticed Steinman for the first time, and her eyes met his.

"What did you experience?" Dr. Crosby asked.

Sandy grinned, remaining silent for a moment. "I don't know if I can put it into words," she said. "But right now? I feel the best I've ever felt." Steinman took in the contours of her body and the ripples of her abs as she put her blouse back on.

"Your name?" Steinman asked.

"Sandy. Sandy Singer," she said.

She approached him, and he shook her hand. She watched his eyes, intently trying to read the inner workings of what was going on behind them. Dr. Crosby explained that he was going to take her down the hall to a comfortable room and ask a few questions about her journey.

Steinman butted in.

"And before Miss Singer leaves, I would like to ask her some questions, as well," he said.

Sandy smiled and thanked both Steinman and Johansson as she left the room with the doctor.

"I want to go next," Steinman said.

"Now, wait a minute, Thomas. Let's analyze the data and see what we've got here. The, uh, foreign tests were not entirely safe. We can't pick up where we left off before the Russians stole the technology."

Thomas took off his suit coat, carefully folding it over a chair back. He sat on the cot, unbuttoning his shirt.

"Let's do this now," Steinman said. "No more arguments."

Johansson summoned Dr. Crosby back to the procedure room, where he connected the sensors to Steinman. As he worked, he commented, "The young lady started telling me about her experience. She claims to have had an out-of-body experience."

"Really?" Johansson said. "What did she see?"

"We didn't get to the details yet. I'll finish debriefing her and we'll find out. Mr. Steinman, just lie back and I'll check these connections."

Steinman looked at Johansson. "I'm going to Disneyland!"

"That will be an interesting debriefing session," Johansson joked.

"As a precaution, you should remove your wristwatch," Dr. Crosby recommended. "The electrical impulses might cause that to burn you."

He then executed the sequence as he did before, verifying the steps with his notes. On the reader that Gomez confiscated, two distinct bands merged after the electrical surge interacted with the protein. The doctor let the experiment run nearly four minutes before bringing Steinman back. The bands separated into more than thirty wavelengths, even more than the previous test with Miss Singer. Steinman was jolted by the energy as it returned. His eyelids fluttered, then opened as a smile came across his lips.

"Fantastic! Absolutely fantastic!" Steinman enthused. "I think it was an out-of-body experience. Better than Disneyland. I visited the dead."

Dr. Crosby excused himself.

"I'm going to go debrief Miss Singer," he said.

"I want to speak with her before she goes," Steinman said.

*   *   *

In the debriefing room, Dr. Crosby had no difficulty eliciting fantastic details from Sandy, who also revealed she visited the dead. Given the time to gather her recollections, she described a slow ascension above her body, then a silver cord that appeared. When she reached for it, the cord pulled her along. She was fearful and let go. The cord was all she could see in the blackness, so she grasped it again, letting it pull her along. She explained how the cord pulled her swiftly through a frictionless atmosphere, sometimes undulating to provide intense exhilaration. It seemed like a very long time, before she was greeted by thousands of pinpoints of light. They moved toward her, each one emitting a different tone. Together, they sounded like a magnificent instrument playing a beautiful melody. One blinking pinprick of light approached her closely and spoke to her in an odd language.

"Miraculously," she explained, "I was able to understand. It was my first lover, Matt. I wasn't shocked then, but I am now. Matt died eleven years ago. In a motorcycle accident. I was heartbroken. But in this new form, he told me how much I was loved. This place evoked an infinite sense of love."

Miss Singer described the energy she felt when she returned, and was brought back to consciousness.

"Right now," she said, "It feels like everything is new. It's vibrant. My brain feels like it's processing information on so many levels all at once. Memories… new ideas… insights into people I know."

Steinman listened to the debriefing on an audio feed with Jonah in his office.

"This vibrant energy. Where do you suppose it comes from?" Steinman asked.

Johansson's eyes met Steinman's. "We don't know, yet. I have a crazy theory."

"Let's have it," Steinman said.

"Almost all out-of-body experiences include some element of celestial intervention. Many include a spiritual aspect, and many of those contain common denominators that stretch the boundaries of coincidence. I'm not a big religious guy, but I think this energy comes from God. This whole process seems steeped in a spiritual dimension."

Steinman paused to let those observations sink in.

"This energy is incredible, Jonah," Steinman said. "Is there any way to steal it?"

"What? You want us all to go to hell?"

"Maybe 'steal' was the wrong word. Can we strip it and – what's a nice way of putting it? Redirect. Then we can redirect this to a socially useful purpose. Maybe even one that might please the deity at the source of this energy."

"If we were to strip it," Johansson conjectured, "where would we put it? What would we do with this power to keep it intact?"

"You're the scientist," Steinman said. "Isn't there some sort of battery cell or something to store it until we're ready to use it?"

"With any energy transfer, there is a loss. It's a diminishing resource. I wonder if my cloud could be a receptacle."

"Your cloud?" Steinman asked, extremely puzzled.

"It's a development I've been trying to perfect, a place to store immense amounts of data that does not rely on man-made hardware. I'm not sure if it would contain energy instead of data. We would have lots of research ahead of us. Can we effectively separate the energy from the human carrier? Can we contain it in a thermodynamically stable environment that adheres to principles of Landau free energy? Then, how would we safely transfer this energy for what you call a socially useful purpose?"

"You lost me in the tall weeds, Dr. Johansson," Steinman admitted, his impatience rising. "Bottom line, what will it take to invent this technology?"

"Time. Expertise. Persistence. I think I know some people in the scientific community who can be helpful resources."

"Keep it on the QT," Steinman said. "Only bring in people we can trust. I'm going to seek top secret classification for this project."

"This completely changes the direction of my research, Thomas," Jonah stated.
"I know. This is the direction we need to explore."

Over the intercom, Dr. Crosby continued to query Sandy on her experience. She balked.

"Are we almost done?" Sandy asked. "I feel like there are so many things I need to do right now."

Steinman stood, concluding his meeting with Jonah.
"I'm going to go put that young lady out of her misery," he said. "Please, work on this concept and by all means, keep this in the strictest confidence."

Steinman walked down the hall to the debriefing room. He walked in, stopping the doctor in mid-question.

"Are you finished with Miss Singer?" Steinman asked. Not waiting for a reply, he said, "I think you have done a fine job, doctor. Now I'd like to ask a few questions and let her go on her way." Dr. Crosby sat back in his chair, expecting to be a witness to their interaction. Steinman glared at him until he picked up his notes and left. Without speaking, Thomas turned off the intercom microphone and sat.

"May I call you Sandy?" he asked. She smiled at him.
"Of course."

"You're feeling pretty phenomenal right now, aren't you?" he asked.

"Yeah," she said. "Yeah, I am."

"This is just the beginning," he said. "Sandy, I would like you to be involved in this project moving forward. I think that all you conveyed about your experience makes you uniquely qualified to assist our country in this important research. I can have you transferred with a pay grade increase."

"Really? I don't know all the details yet, but I'm interested."

"Good," Thomas said. "Perhaps we can discuss details in a less institutional setting. Will you join me for dinner?" Anticipating her response, he said, "Tonight."

She agreed.

Chapter 6: Honeymoon Surprise

David strained to finish his last set of bench presses. His phone rang in while he was on his last rep, forcing him to temporarily lose his concentration. Veins were popping in his head and neck as he exhaled, raising the barbell with full extension of his arms. He dropped it on the rack with a clatter and huffed for half a minute to catch his breath. Stretching his bulky arms and taut chest muscles, he got off the bench to pull his phone off the floor.

"Hey, JW! What's goin' on?"

"You sound out of breath, buddy! Tommy and I were just making some high-octane pancakes from scratch. Thought you might like to come up and join us."

"High-octane pancakes, huh?" David questioned.

"Yeah! Bananas, blueberries, honey and oats. You'll have enough fiber for a month. Potassium and antioxidants, too. We're just getting started. Come on up and watch JW's cooking show. Unless I caught you in the middle of doing something nasty, in which case make sure you wash your hands."

"Right, smartass! I just finished working out. New record bench press for the Big D! I'll be right up."

With Tommy's help, JW was lining up all the ingredients on the counter. As if a camera were rolling, he described each step in detail for David and an imaginary audience.

"Now, we have our flour, sugar, and crushed oats. Don't forget the eggs. Surprisingly, you need very little water. You're not making soup, you know. These are pancakes, so go easy. We'll use the mixer for this. You want this to be the consistency of Quikrete. And we can add more water if we need it."

"Concrete mix?" David asked. "That sounds delicious."

"Oh, just wait," JW promised. "Now, in a minute, Tommy is going to add the secret ingredients that will make our pancakes super nutritious."

"Looks like some sliced bananas, blueberries and honey," David added.

"Man, you suck at keeping secret ingredients secret," JW said. "Tommy, what is David forgetting?"

"I can't tell you," Tommy said. "It's supposed to be a secret."

JW gestured toward Tommy. "Look at that! A child, a young boy of eleven – an extremely bright child – and look at how Tommy protects the secret family recipe. Good job, Tommy. And for our viewers at home, you never want to pour the batter into a cold skillet."

David apologized, but JW was moving on, heating the skillet on the stove. Tommy added the fruit, honey and salt, and JW thoroughly enjoyed taking center stage making breakfast. David didn't mind being the foil for JW's kitchen comedy because he couldn't remember seeing him this happy in years.

Trish set the table and poured orange juice while JW expounded on the merits of pure maple syrup over the commercial brands with maple flavoring. It took David back to his childhood, and when he was about Tommy's age, his father drove him out to the country with his brother and sisters to Wildwind Farms, where Mr. McMath showed them his sugar shack and the sugaring operation for organic maple syrup. JW was enthralled.

"Tommy, some day, we'll have to go there," JW said. "And let me guess, David. Maple candy?"

"Oh, yeah!" he said, remembering with glee. "At the end of our tour, we got to sample the maple fudge."

"Yeah, we've got to go there," JW said softly.

"Wanna talk business?" David said.

"Yeah, let's go downstairs."

Tommy protested, and JW told him to go do his homework, with a promise that they would play a video game later.

In the mancave, David told JW that he needed to venture out to locate The Gifted and alert them to the dangers. "I think it's going to take both of us, J Dubbs. Are you game?"

"Yeah, I'm game."

"You realize that when we're away from Trish, you're in as much danger as I am?"

"Yeah, I guess. I hadn't thought about that, but, I really don't have to think about it. If you're going, I want to go with you. You will be the brains, and I will be the – "He looked at David's bulging biceps and muscular physique. "Well, you'll be the brawn, too. I'll just be the other brain."

"Do you need to clear it with Trish?"

"Naw. Well, I should, you know, just to be sure everything is cool."

They formulated a game plan for reaching out to The Gifted that JW identified so far, which was six. David recommended visits to those closest geographically first. JW argued against David going to San Francisco right off the bat. He suspected that Martin and Steinman would have people there looking for them to return home.

"One of the Gifted is in San Fran?"

"Yep. Another down in Orange County. One in Illinois, one near Rochester and two in New York City."

"Crap. New York will be a challenge, too. We should see how some of the others go first."

"Maybe we work up a disguise."

"What kind of information are we supposed to gather from these people?" JW asked.

"I haven't a clue. From Bridget's notes, I think they will tell us what's burning a hole in their brain."

"When do we start?"

"This week."

JW nodded, recognizing that this would be a race to reach the riders before Steinman or Martin's Teutonic team got to them.

"Yeah, Steinman has been on my mind, too?" David said. "How did you know I was thinking about Steinman?" JW asked.

"I thought you said something."

"No. But I was thinking about him. What creeps me out about

Stein-fink, even more than he faked his death, was the way he was saying things that I was thinking that time we had dinner. Kinda like what you just did."

"When he used to call me, and say, 'Davy boy...' you don't know how that made me cringe."

"Do you think he has the Gift? Do you think he took the ride and has the Gift?"

"He knew about Heaven Ride before we were even a part of the plan. I'm sure he did."

JW was thinking. David replied to his thoughts before he could ask.

"We have to be very careful not to telepathically broadcast our location to him."

"You've gotta cut that out! Do you think Martin went? Does he have it?"

"I don't know. I don't think so. but nothing would surprise me."

The news that followed that December day in the next week established that Heaven Ride was once again the largest corporation in the world, although Amazon and Apple had closed the gap. Construction of 10 foreign Heaven Ride Centers were delayed due to railway strikes in Great Britain and non-Heaven Ride terrorist attacks in France. In his quarterly performance speech, Jonah Johansson announced to shareholders that H2H would wait to open all 10 centers simultaneously. He also introduced a new security platform, which he named Pearly Gate sequestering, which allowed H2H to block incoming security attacks but also freeze the intrusion in limbo so that experts could better reveal the source. Johansson divulged that 17 internationally diverse attackers were identified and were being prosecuted for attempts the hack the Heaven Ride database.

In an informal questioning after the shareholders meeting, journalists asked about growing suicide rates. Jonah deflected the questions, saying they didn't have reliable numbers or definitive cause-effect data, but they were working on getting that. He was asked if Heaven Ride would bolster its screening criteria, he simply said, "We'll see."

Jonah scanned the gaggle of reporters, and pointed to Kat Welsh, the reporter and host of "The Big Story."

"David Brownington. He was the face of Heaven Ride. Do you foresee any challenges stepping in for such a visible and media-savvy predecessor?"

Other reporters nodded, and readied for Jonah's response.

"Personally, I have the utmost respect for Mr. Brownington," Jonah said. "As an organization, we appreciate the contributions made by Mr. Brownington as an entrepreneur and a very capable spokesman for Heaven Ride."

"I asked about the challenges," she asserted.

"Every leadership position poses new challenges. The Board of Directors selected me to lead the company through the challenges in the next phase."

Jonah sidled past the reporters, waving briefly before escaping onto an open elevator.

Following the report, Heaven Ride shares rose 13 percent to $303 per share. David heard the news and joked, "Oh, good! More money that I can't spend to take down the company."

He missed the day-to-day challenges of running Heaven Ride and making it better. Of course, now his efforts were directed at a campaign of destruction, to tear down that which he, and people like Johansson, Martin and Steinman, built to be indestructible.

Since early October, snow began to accumulate on the Wasatch Front, and JW coerced him into joining him to ski the pristine powder just outside the property wall. David took to it quickly, given his ice-skating prowess, but he was still no match for JW. It was fun and beautiful, but David was not keen on hiking back up the mountain after making a run. He felt stronger for it, and viewed the ski runs as a challenging workout that was different than what he could do inside.

Some days, Trish would join them, although she did not venture far down the mountain. She surprised the guys one day by decorating the house for Christmas. Many of the decorations were hung by the time they returned, and candles burned with Christmas scents. JW took some of this for granted, but for David, it was the first time in years that he enjoyed a family holiday with all the trappings. With Trish's help, he ordered gifts for his family online allowing merchants to ship them direct. He wondered how Alison would be spending the holiday.

Christmas in Utah made JW remember how mush his father loved Christmas, more than any other holiday. Vincente always made it special for him and his brother, Petey. He wondered if one day, his father might walk through his front door. A smile crossed JW's face.

Two days after Christmas, a married couple from Sacramento entered the Heaven Ride Center in San Francisco. Denise and Sam told the concierge that they had saved up their vacation money to celebrate their anniversary taking Heaven Ride.

They were escorted to the pre-ride counseling room and told precise details of the procedure. They kissed before leaving for their separate pod rooms. Denise was very talkative while the technician prepared her for the four-minute journey. The procedure had been streamlined over the last two years. It required the connection of 23 electrodes. Sixteen of those were now contained in a helmet that automatically conformed to the shape of the rider's head. The others were placed on meridian points on the chest, neck and wrists. The technician swabbed her arm with alcohol before injecting her arm with a protein-laced saline solution. After the shot, the electrodes began pulsing, each with a different rhythm based on the detected brainwaves and the heartbeat of the rider. These pulsations slowed the heartrate and brainwaves, inducing a coma.

For the riders, their cognitive function slowed, much like when they fell asleep. Once they drifted beyond the dream state, a series of sharp jolts mimicked the final energy expulsion that the body experiences before death, and this ejected the soul heaven-ward. From the time of the impulses, a countdown began because in this comatose state, the brain was now without oxygen transfer. In just under four minutes, the technician started a series of electrical jolts that stimulated the brain to revive, bringing the body back to a conscious state, retaining memories of the journey.

Denise regained consciousness. A broad smile crossed her face. It was one that she didn't think would ever go away. When she was disconnected and let out of the pod, she gave a fist pump and let out a yelp of excitement.

"Oh, wow! This was so awesome, way more beautiful than anything I could have ever imagined! I was free from my body. I felt pulled, like on an invisible conveyor belt, sometimes fast, sometimes slower. Then, I saw thousands of points of light. They came toward me, each one blinking with an individual music note that blended in with the others to create the most gorgeous song. The brightest of the lights approached me. It was my mom, who passed within the last year. It was as though we spent a whole day together in a park with a waterfall that was so tall you couldn't see where it came from. It seemed like a whole day and this angelic symphony played. I never really saw my mother, you know, her body and her face – but it was her. It wasn't awkward when it was time to leave. I remember her saying, 'Don't you worry, Denise. I'll keep you safe right here with me.' I wonder what she meant by that."

The technician shrugged, offering, "It sounds like your mother still wants to take care of you." She helped Denise gather her purse and belongings and took her down the hall to the post-ride lounge.

"We'll bring your husband down as soon as he returns. Glad you had such a pleasant experience."

Denise sat, the euphoric pleasure filling her entire body. She felt changed. She could not wait to see Sam and to just feel close to him. She waited another five minutes, wondering what was taking so long. Finally, she peeked out the door where she entered. Down the hallway, one of the pod rooms was illuminated by a rapidly flashing blue light above the door. Much activity started, with technicians scurrying frantically, and one of them pushing a medical crash cart down the carpeted hall. Denise heard a technician tell the EMT, "He's not coming back."

Denise's intuition told her they were speaking of her husband, and she ran down the hall. She burst into the room with all the activity and the flashing blue light, and positioned herself in the center of the room, so she could see into the pod. It was Sam, and his face was contorted with a horrific expression, His skin was pale pinkish-white, with blue veins showing through.

"Fourteen minutes and counting!" said one technician. She and others tried to pull Sam from the pod onto a gurney, eventually succeeding.

"We've got no bodily function," the EMT declared. "No brain waves. The body temperature has dropped below 70 degrees."

With the body on the gurney, the EMT and one other technician made a last-ditch effort to revive Sam.

"No!" Denise screamed, suddenly drawing attention to herself. She pushed past the technician to hug her husband. "Come back, Sam! Come back! God, let him come back!"

The technician pulled her away.

"Tell him to come back!" she screamed loudly. Reverting to her experience of just a few minutes before, she loudly pleaded, "Mom! Mom! Send him back. Send my Sam back to me!"

A cool, emotionless voice said, "Get her the hell out of here."

The EMT stepped back from Sam as Denise was being dragged from the room to a back door.

"Time of death, 3:27 p.m."

Denise was taken back to the debriefing room, her euphoria converted to anguish. She could not speak coherently.

"Muh-muh-muh-muh-my Huh-huh-huh-sband. Wha-wha-wha-what d-d-did you d-do to hi-him?" she stammered.

The technician tried to calm her. They had been trained for adversity, but how could anyone be trained for this.

"Muh-muh-mom told me," Denise said. "Mom told me... I'm pregnant. I wanted to tell Sam so we could check with the doctors."

The EMT entered the room.

"I'm sorry for your loss, Mrs. Romano."

Chapter 7: A Sandwich Packs a Punch

JW set up appointments with the first three of the Gifted. It was a quick flight to San Francisco, and then a puddle jumper to John Wayne Airport in Orange County. They met with one rider in the LA area, and spent a fair amount of time stuck in traffic. JW plugged his road trip playlist into the rental car radio, and they passed the time singing at the top of their lungs.

"I think you should audition for that TV singing competition," David told him.

"Really?" JW said, flattery oozing from his voice. "You mean 'The Voice?'"

"No, the other one," David said, setting him up. "The Throat. I think you be able to win against some of those musically challenged rejects."

"Oh, you're wrong," JW said. "I'm an awesome singer."

To punish David, JW purposely sang badly and butchered the words to the songs. David joined in the parody. They both burst out in laughter many times. The clues they gathered put them not further ahead than they were before, but David knew that they would add up to something when the last of the keys were collected. They flew to Chicago at night, so they could have a full day there.

It was a beautiful Chicago morning, and JW was able to arrange and early meeting with their Gifted one. David needed to prod her with questions a bit, because there wasn't one overriding "key" that she could identify. In talking with her, David and JW picked up on some frequently used phrases, all of which referred to "father." What David was unable to decipher was if the term meant an earthly father, the heavenly Father or a priest. When they left, they gave her the instruction they gave to all the Gifted.

"Be very careful because you are in serious danger. You should leave town, stay with friends or relatives for awhile, or invite them to come stay with you. Do not take your personal safety for granted."

She surprised them with her reply. "I'm sensing that you are in more danger than I am. Follow your own advice and be careful."

They left her downtown office, and JW took the wheel, heading to the south side. JW's glasses broke in LA, and since they had time to kill, he wanted to go to an optician to get them fixed.

"Why?" David asked. "You never use them."

"I've been needing them a lot more. Like right now, I'm practically blind without them."

"Oh, great. Maybe I should drive."

"Naw," JW said. "It's just a little ways from our favorite Italian beef place."

"Tony's? Good. Drop me off then. I don't want to drive around town, and certainly can't see myself sitting at an optician's office."

"If you went, maybe you could see that," JW said, laughing at his own pun. "I have no problem dropping you off. If I have time, I want to stop at a sporting goods store and get a Blackhawks' jersey for Tommy."

"Definitely drop me off," David said. "You maybe can't understand how nerve-wracking it is for me out on the road. I'd rather sit in a public place, like a restaurant, than drive around to a bunch of retail places."

"Suit yourself. It won't take me long."

David started to get excited when JW turned onto Pulaski Road, near one of his favorite meaty concoctions on the planet. He and JW found Tony's almost by accident when they were doing final checks on the Heaven Ride Center in downtown Chicago. Their hotel was near Chicago Midway Airport, and when they asked a hotel bellman about nearby pizza restaurants, he suggested Tony's, located in a non-descript brick building. That was the last time he and JW visited Chicago together, and it seemed logical that they go back to visit. JW dropped him off and went on his errands.

David grabbed the day's Tribune off the front counter on the
way to his seat. The narrow restaurant was equipped mostly for take-
out, and offered about a dozen stools at a long counter opposite the
cash registers. He enjoyed the distraction of a newspaper. He often
felt too isolated to stay on top of current events at the Five Rings
Compound. He sneaked a peak at the stock listings, pleased to see
that Heaven Ride was just over $305 a share. He also enjoyed the
daily word jumble puzzle. Ever since high school at Bishop Kearney,
his English teacher, Brother Richard, gave the class those word
puzzles each day. He timed their efforts. David became so adept at
them that he could usually solve the five words and word pun in less
than a minute. Today he was stumped by one word – ICLTGH. It
became GLITCH. JW called to say the glasses were taking a little
longer than expected but told David to order anyway.

Sitting, distracted by the news, he reached a point of relaxation
that he hadn't felt in months. The paper, the clatter of pots and pans
from the kitchen, the gentle din of voices and the tempting aromas of
Italian spices soothed and nurtured his spirit.

David ordered at the counter from a young man wearing a
nametag "Mike," who brought him two Clementine-flavored Izze
bottled sodas and a large cup of water. David put in the order for two
Italian beef sandwiches. JW texted that he was on his way, but was
delayed in traffic. David took a seat across the way and at the far end
from several other customers. Moments later, David's meditation
was interrupted by the arrival of his food. It was not delivered by
Mike, but by a scruffy, unkempt red-haired man wearing a plain
black T-shirt. He slid the plate in front of David, and across in JW's
spot, displaying neither care nor courtesy. Still, he brought two
heaping plates of delectable beef on a garlic-butter soaked roll. The
red-haired man wiped the counter, which already appeared to be
clean.

David balked at his sandwich.

"Whoa! Did somebody overdo it with the garlic?"

"I don't know," the redhead answered. "I don't make 'em, I just
deliver 'em. But a little extra garlic never hurt anything, right?"

"Good point," David said.

The first bite was as good as he remembered. The garlic was
more pronounced, but not totally unpleasant. He took a second bite

and dug in for more. He decided he was hungrier than he first thought. Despite the strong garlic flavor and scent, he chowed down half the sandwich. He took a swig of the drink, and had a hard time swallowing it. He took a break from the sandwich to rest and digest. He drank half the glass of water, but still felt thirsty. His throat tightened, and he began to wheeze.

He reached for the bottled soda but knocked it over. He felt like he was drunk. Sweat began to form on his brow, and his breathing became even more labored.

His face was visibly pinker. The red-haired man, and a burly man approached the table.

"Let me help you, David," Red said. "Come with us."

David tried to stand but got tangled with the chair legs. He kicked over the stool before falling to the floor.

"Folks, no problem. He's just having a medical issue," Red announced. "Come on, David. We'll get you to the bathroom."

David tried to speak but could not. His tongue felt three sizes too large for his mouth. The men picked him up off the floor and dragged him toward the men's room. David tried to keep up with his feet, but had trouble moving his legs. They barely got him into the men's room when David puked. Slightly incoherent, he was propped against the stall while Red locked the door.

"Aw, David," Red said, standing in front of him. "You have a widdle throw-up on your chin. Let me get that for you."

Red clobbered David on the jaw with a hard-right hand. Red stepped away, telling his cohort, "He's yours now."

As David grew too wobbly to stand on his own, the beefy thug held David up with his left hand while tattooing him with his powerful right. David's face bled and his eyes closed beneath rosy red eye sockets. The big guy finally let David fall to the floor and began kicking him in the ribs and legs

JW came into the restaurant and did not see David. He noted the toppled stool and the spilled beverage. One of the other patrons said, "He got sick. They took him to the restroom."

JW scanned the room, saw the sign and rushed to the bathroom. He tried the door, and then knocked frantically. "David! Are you okay? David! Can you hear me?"

David did hear him but could not speak to answer. He tried to speak with JW telepathically, but given the chaos of the moment, he couldn't get through to him.

JW tried to kick the bathroom door down but failed. The waiter, Mike, cautioned JW to stop.

"Get the key to the restroom. Fast!"

Red pulled his henchman away so that he could get in on the beating again. He stepped on David's head, then continued to kick at his ribs and abdomen. David turtled up, not giving him an easy target for his most vulnerable body parts.

Mike came back with the key and opened the door. JW burst through and surprised the assailants. Mike followed. The bathroom was barely big enough for the five men.

"Back off, chubbs!" he told the bigger one before clocking him with a sound punch that caused him to stumble and fall butt-first into the urinal and then to the floor. JW moved on to Red, and pulled him away from David. JW hit him quickly, hurting his hand with a powerful left.

Red called for help. "Beast! Come and get this guy."

As "Beast" tried to pull himself up, waiter Mike used some apparent martial arts training to land a kick to his head, keeping him on the ground momentarily. 'Beast' watched helplessly as JW unleashed the fury of hell on Red. "Beast' scrambled out of the room on all fours, and Mike watched the door so that he would not return.

JW stopped pummeling Red, shaking his left hand in pain. Red scrambled out of the bathroom, dazed, and Mike followed him through the crowded dining area and out the door. He then called 911 on the restaurant phone to summon an ambulance. Mike returned to the bathroom to find JW hunched over David, sobbing as he used toilet paper to wipe blood from his face.

"Buddy, I'm sorry. If I had gotten here sooner, this wouldn't have --"

David was able to muster a word. "Poison."

JW stopped, stunned. Mike looked on for a moment.

"Do those guys work here?" JW asked Mike.

"Never saw them before in my life," he answered. "I put the food up on the counter, and before I could get to it, they must have doctored it and took it to him."

David's phone rang.

David pulled it from his pocket and fumbled trying to use it. JW grabbed it from him and looked at the caller ID.

"It's not Trish," he said. He answered the phone.

It was Steinman.

"Ah, this must be the boy wonder, JW."

Still out of breath, JW asked "What do you want, Stein-wart?"

"Now, now. Must we call names JW? It's beneath you. Especially since I saved your friend's life. Come to think of it, JW, we haven't spoken since my return from the dead. And how is Davy Boy?"

JW looked at David, who was in rough shape and still struggling to breathe. He did not reply.

"Well, anyway," Steinman continued, "Your sandwiches were spiked with arsenic. It shouldn't kill him, but then again, it might. Martin wanted to give you both a fatal dose, but I convinced him that 80 micrograms would be enough to send a message. If you ate your sandwich, you would have been rolling in your own vomit, too."

"So what is that message, you sonofabitch?"

"Just stay home," Steinman warned. "Stay in your little palace in Utah where you'll both be safe. As much as I need a playmate, next time Martin will use lethal force." In a sinister voice, Steinman threatened him. "Heaven Ride will go on. If you try to mess with it again, you and my little friend will go down."

Steinman cut off the call. JW cussed. Mike raced back with water for David.

Shortly after that, the ambulance arrived.

Chapter 8: Solitude in the Slopes & HAARP

It had been nearly a week since David's near poisoning and pummeling in Chicago. His throat was still sore, and his ribs ached, but he would not be put down. David dragged himself up the stairs and found JW deep into his iPad on his comfy coach. The house was uncommonly quiet. David plopped down in a large worn brown leather chair across from JW.

"Whatcha looking at?" David asked.

"Oh, hey. How ya feelin'?" JW said, checking out David. The facial bruising was darker than in days past, and David was bent into a shape that was bearable for him to sit.

"Damn, the last time I felt like this was when Killer Koloski went psycho on me in the New York State high school hockey finals in Lake Placid. I ended up with a cracked rib, bruised esophagus and broken nose."

"Geez, I hope he got ejected. What did you do to him?"

"The sucky thing about it my coach said absolutely no fighting in the playoffs or get benched, even if the other guy starts it. So, I just took it. First a butt end to the ribs followed by a high stick to the throat, my helmet ripped off and a hard one to the nose. Koloski did get ejected and I ended up with a 10-minute major for cowering – served in the nearest hospital."

"Dude, there is no way I would've been able to hold back, championship or no championship. You gotta defend yourself."

"That's how I feel about Steinman's sucker punch in the restaurant. If I wasn't poisoned, I would have messed them up bad. But he ambushed me out of nowhere. There was no way I could fight back."

"I was a little late, but I did throw a few revenge punches to those dudes."

"Yeah, thanks again for coming to my rescue. Where were you a decade ago at the rink? My poor dad and mom had to spend their time at Lake Placid in a hospital room instead of an Olympic rink."

"Speaking of your mom and dad, have you had any success in speaking with them?" JW asked sincerely.

"I'm working on it but haven't been able to connect. I feel I'm getting closer, but I need to prove to them that I will shut down Heaven Ride for good. I'm communicating to them through my sister and that's the best I could do for now. Man, I wish my mother was here to nurse be back to health. I really miss her and my dad. This sucks not having them around."

"Did you tell them what happened to you through your sister?" JW asked.

"No way. I couldn't image giving them that scare of almost losing another son."

JW shut his iPad and stood up to take a giant stretch and a bear-size yawn.

"Did I tell you I almost tracked down my dad but missed him by maybe a week," JW asked David.

"No, bud, what happened and where?"

"About three months ago in Alaska," JW explained. "When my aunt told me that he didn't die in a fishing boat accident I set out to find him. She gave me some information about what she thought was his whereabouts in Alaska, so I hired the best private detective I could find, and we hightailed it to Valdez. I spent three weeks covering every little seaside town north and south of Valdez."

"Is that the same town the Exxon Valdez spilled tons of oil back in the 1980s?" David asked.

"Yes, it is. I guess we all read the same history books in high school. But, man, you'd never know that it was covered in oil at one point. It's incredibly beautiful. The whole area. A different kind of beautiful than Utah. I'm going back there for sure with Trish and

Tommy. You should join us."

"So, you came up empty," David asked.

JW started pacing, "I wouldn't say empty. Even though I didn't find my dad, I learned a lot about him, and I feel good that we're going to meet someday soon. It's just a weird feeling I have. Apparently, my dad did odd jobs but would disappear for days and weeks at a time. Some said they thought he was in the witness protection program and others said CIA or KGB. He's a very mysterious and elusive kind of guy, I guess.

"I hit the proverbial Alaskan gold mine in a dude I met just south of Valdez in a local restaurant. He's a Northern Californian transplant that works summers managing the bar there – good hearty food, local brews and plenty of Russian vodkas. His name is Tiger Yates. His real name is Bill. He reminded me of my dad, about the same age and same build. And, a lot smarter and interesting than you'd expect from a bartender type. Oh, he also attended the University of Utah. Can you believe that? Anyhow, my dad confided in him about a lot of things over the better part of a decade. He told Tiger about having a family in Utah – I think that's why they connected."

Tiger also knew my dad was military but didn't say what branch. He confirmed that he traveled out of state and country a lot and that he would frequently visit a place known as HAARP. That's an acronym for High Frequency Active Auroral Research Program. It's in Gakona, Alaska. It used to be the headquarters for an ionospheric research program jointly funded by the Air Force, Navy, the University of Alaska, and something called the DARPA – Defense Advanced Research Projects Agency.

Rich Duffy, my private detective dude, and I took a drive out to HAARP. Man, you haven't seen the middle of nowhere until you've seen the middle of nowhere in Alaska. It's was a two-and-a-half-hour drive from Valdez."

"I've heard of HAARP. I watched a YouTube video about it a few years ago and all the wild conspiracy theories of what goes on there. Things like UFO research and machines that control the world's weather. But I thought they shut it down a few years ago," David said.

"Shut down or not, we drove out there and couldn't get in or the time of day for that matter. It's enclosed by barbed wire-topped fences and the area is filled with all types of antennas and transmission equipment spread over about 40 acres. We could see a few buildings and vehicles but no people. There was only one entrance and the guard in military dress didn't even bother to come out to talk to us. He just sat in his little booth watching TV or something. We asked some of the town's people and most said since the Air Force abandoned it they haven't seen anyone go in or out. Like Willy Wonka's factory when it was closed it to outsiders."

"Maybe you'll find a golden ticket to get in," David said, chuckling.

"Yeah, that would be great. But would it come with chocolate?" as JW reached for a hand full of dark chocolate fall colored M&M's in a glass bowl in front of him.

"Want some?" he asked David, but David waved him off.

"The few people we spoke with who were non-military but worked at HAARP are convinced the technology being tested was able to control people's minds and altering the very fabric of reality. They refute that it's just all about the weather."

"Did they say why it was shut down? Did anyone say they knew your dad," David asked.

"A lot of speculation why it was closed but people are still working there, and maybe living there which explains no coming or going. None of them could identify my dad by name but said they saw a man once in and awhile that fit my dad's description. It seems they pretty much kept military separate from civilians," JW explained.

"So, what's next," David asked.

"I left my contact information with Tiger in case my dad stops in. Unfortunately, even after 10 years Tiger never had gotten my dad's cell number or address. Strange, but that seems to be my dad's M.O."

"Do you think your dad ever snuck back to Utah or Berkeley over the years to spy on you incognito," David inquired.

"Man stop reading my mind. I not only thought about this since he left over twenty years ago but after talking with Tiger I think it almost 24 / 7. In fact, sometimes I look out the windows wondering if my dad is the brush or perched in a tree scoping me out. When I fly, I always walk up and down the aisles to check out all the men hoping to find him."

David and JW talked for a few hours more about the what ifs and when they both reunited, JW with his dad, and David with his parents.

Over the next several weeks the two spent the majority of their days at the monastery plotting their strategy to take down Heaven Ride. Secrecy was paramount. When JW was bogged down in data, David would walk parts of the 1,800-acre habitat. He returned to perfect health and the time spent in nature allowed him to connect telepathically with friends and several of the other Gifted riders that JW pulled from the archived data. And with Bridget. He called the monastery ranch his "office without walls," and it was there that ideas crystallized and aided by the solitude and the daily loaf of fresh-baked bread and honey butter delivered by one of the aging monks, a plan emerged.

He tried to convince JW to join him for a trip to New York City.

"You do know that Trish thinks we've given up on the idea of stopping Martin and Stein-crook, and given up on the idea of traveling away from Five Rings. You know that, don't you?" JW asked.

"I know," David answered. "You'll need to be very delicate when you tell her."

"Me?!" JW said. "She'll never let me hear the end of it. What about 'We' instead of 'Me'?"

JW convinced David to join him in telling his girlfriend.

As expected, the idea met with the stern objection of Trish, who warned them against making any move outside of Utah. David's strong belief in the destruction of Heaven Ride significantly influenced JW, who gave impassioned arguments for continuing the quest. Reluctantly, Trish accepted his participation in the plan. She booked their travel arrangements for New York, using false names and virtual credit cards.

Chapter 9: The End in Sight

Vincente arrived at the Gramercy Park North residential building just after 7:30. He collected the key that was taped to the side of a newsstand a few blocks away.

He was exhausted. Even government charter flights can be delayed, and the plane sat on the tarmac for two hours before take-off. Arriving in the city after 2 a.m., he failed to find restful sleep. Today, he traveled lightly, carrying only a duffel bag.

He arrived at the address, nodded to the doorman and gained entry to the 17-story building. His destination was suite 1611, and the elevator climbed slowly enough that his eyes shut after the eighth floor, and he was startled back to consciousness by the bell that chimed his arrival on the 16th floor. He surveyed the hallway to locate the suite, set down the duffel bag and opened the door slowly. He never knew the circumstances he might be entering. In this case, the swanky room was vacant.

Vincente unlatched the gun case and extracted the sniper rifle that had served him well, earning him the nickname "The Grim Reaper" among his fellow SEALs. It was a Remington 700, meticulously tended, cleaned and polished, with a Nightforce Beast scope. Gomez had modified the rifle slightly, giving it even more power than the standard issue M-24. Today's mission would be standard – two man-size targets at 1,000 feet. Under ordinary circumstances, Gomez could hit a 4-inch plate 90 percent of the time. Splattering a man's head would be a cinch, although every mission brought its own set of quirky obstacles. His orders specified that under no circumstances could there be any civilian casualties. Targets Aries and Gemini, their code names, were classified as enemies of the state. Neither man learned in advance too much about their targets other than the body stats. Since there had been a heighten espionage of Russian agents in the U.S. especially in New York City they assumed the targets could be linked to that or the ongoing battle with radical Islam.

Urban shooting was a bit trickier, due to wind shear between buildings and residual heat from concrete and cement. For this distance, the lag time between squeezing the trigger and impact was about 0.8 seconds, and Gomez was well aware that anything can happen in that span of time.

Sanders called him by his code name on the radio. "Good morning sunshine."

Vince heard the walkie talkie through the canvas bag on the floor.

"A voice from the dead. How are you, Bullfrog?" Protocol dictated that only code names, no first or last names, be used on the radio. Vincente had a few he would have used for Simon Sanders, but it was more a code of gentlemanly behavior that protocol that kept him from calling him an asshole. Likewise, Sanders would have called Gomez a few choice names. There was bad blood between them. He still held a grudge dating back more than 12 years to Rostov-on-Don, when his commander, Gomez, reported Sanders for veering from the plan at a Russian space agency hack. Simon was the type to hold grudges.

"Life is good at the top, Grim Reaper," Sanders said. "You wouldn't know. Is the Wet Dog in position?" Wet Dog was code name given to Gomez's spotter for the day, Allan Hetzel.

"No sign of Wet Dog yet." Just as he spoke the words, Gomez spun toward the door. Allan entered, carrying two cups of Starbucks, raising one in a toast to Vincente. "Check that. Wet Dog is here, and he brought me a bone." Gomez nodded appreciation to his accomplice and accepted the coffee.

"You and Wet Dog jaw awhile. I need to set up this circus tent." Gomez told Sanders. He handed his radio to Allan.

Originally, Grim Reaper was assigned to take out a single target from a distance of about three city blocks. The order came down from Bullfrog the previous day that a second target was added. After the shots, a quick clean-up, pack and run to the basement, where Sanders had a sedan parked for their rapid departure. Hetzel finished his check-in with Sanders, who was in charge of this mission and recruited Gomez specifically for this job. Gomez was pleased to have the work, even if he was taking orders from the biggest crybaby he knew.

Grim Reaper and Wet Dog used the residence of a retired U.S. diplomat who recently moved to Boca Raton. The shots would be of concern to neighbors, so their escape needed to be fast and flawless.

Gomez paced the room in front of the window to find the optimal set-up position. Then, he fished in his bag for a glass cutter and suction cup, expertly scoring and removing a circular hole. He preferred to shoot from one knee, and the hole he cut was just a few inches above the ledge. The temperature was about 45 degrees. A slight gust of cooler air whistled slightly through the hole.

That was the only noise in the apartment, as Wet Dog methodically calibrated his electronic devices to measure distances, degrees and to communicate with an anemometer and barometric devices he placed midway between them and the hit site. Static broke the silence, from a two-way radio he set on the sill.

"Aries and Gemini are en route in a black livery Lincoln, license Sierra Echo Foxtrot 634. ETA equals 30," announced an expressionless voice.

"Roger," Wet Dog acknowledged.

Off radio, he told Vincente, "Plenty of time to enjoy your coffee while it's still hot. I'll pack up the remains.

"Right."

"So where you going after we complete this mission?" Wet Dog asked. I've got two glorious weeks in Hawaii with the ball and chain."

Vincente laughed. "I'll be off to Norman, Oklahoma. One of my buddies there has center-court seats for the Sooners and Jayhawks. Then, I don't know. Someplace warm." Tipping his cup, he added, "Thanks for the Ricky rocket." Vincente knew he was heading back to Alaska but his deployment there remained top secret even within the military ranks.

"You're welcome. Say something nice about me in your report. That should do it for all my gear," Wet Dog said. "All systems are operational. Is the Grim Reaper ready?"

"Time to kill," Gomez said, "before it's time to kill."

The minutes clicked past before the radio voice gave an update. "Come back, Wet Dog and Reaper."

Wet Dog acknowledged, followed by a reply from Sanders, "ETA equals five. Radio is dark and quiet."

Hetzel commented, "This is some top-secret shit. They're shutting down communications."

"Must be some important target. They're probably worried that they'll be listened in on," Gomez said. "We're just living up to our oath to take out the bad guys."

"Maybe they're government," Hetzel theorized. "You know, feds gone rogue. And they supposed they could be listening."

The two Black Ops men took their positions, with the Reaper on his knee, rifle in place, and Wet Dog to his immediate left with his electronic gauges and high-powered binoculars.

"Okay, we're looking at wind of just 4 mph from the east. Adjust for 6 degrees left. Make that 7. Downdraft is 3 degrees."

"Let's confirm that when the targets are in sight."

"Roger."

Per his custom, Gomez took in some deep breaths and regulated his breathing pattern. He steadied himself, watching for the target through his scope. A few minutes later, the black Lincoln Navigator slowed near the front door of the Inn.

"Confirm Jackpot," Wet Dog said calmly. "Right at the front door. Couldn't have planned this any better."

"Let's hope the bellman stays the hell out of the way," Gomez said as the Lincoln stopped. Its lights went out.

The driver was the first to exit the Navigator.

"Coordinates same as before," Wet Dog said. "Seven degrees left, downdraft 3 degrees."

Gomez drew a breath and prepared to fire two shots quickly at the two targets.

"Gemini is getting out on the sidewalk. Aries to follow," Wet Dog relayed.

The subject came into view for Gomez, but then bent down.

Gomez waited for a clear shot. He saw the back of Gemini's head as both subjects were now out of the vehicle. He squeezed the trigger slightly but flinched as the target turned. His rifle fired the assassin's bullet.

"Oscar Sierra!" Gomez exclaimed. "It's my son!"

With his rifle in hand, Vincente ran out the room and toward the stairwell. Surprised, Hetzel drew his pistol and followed into the hall. He called out a warning, and when Gomez did not stop, he fired. His shot pinged off the opening stairwell door. He stood momentarily, shaking his wrist, then went back in to retrieve all the equipment. Wet Dog used the radio.

"Come back, command! This is Wet Dog. The Reaper is AWOL! Repeat. The Reaper is AWOL!"

*　*　*

Blood poured out onto the sidewalk. The bellman reacted first, rushing to JW's side. David dropped to the pavement. A dozen or more pedestrians scattered in every direction, some into the street causing a momentary cacophony of screeching brakes and horns. The driver also scrambled around the back of the Lincoln to JW's side.

David rolled over to JW to assess the injury.

Vincente Gomez knew he was now a marked man. His priority was to see his son. He prayed his shot wasn't fatal. He burst out to the street, past the startled doorman, carrying his sniper rifle on one shoulder. Bystanders scattered. Some screamed at him to stop.

He cut across the modest traffic on Irving Place. Other pedestrians were running the other way. One man in a business suit who witnessed the shooting, then saw the gunman, tried to tackle Vincente. Gomez warded him off, pushing him to the ground.

"That's my son. I'm trying to get to my son!"

On the seat of his pants in the middle of the road, the businessman raised his hands. Vincente bolted toward the black Lincoln.

Wary for the potential for more shots, David tried to drag JW into the hotel.

"Give me a hand," he yelled at the bellman. "Pick up his feet."

The bellman refused.

"We should not move him," he said. The driver jumped in to grab JW's feet. They carried him toward the doorway, but the bellman stopped them.

"You can't go in there."

"Why not?" David asked.

"He's bleeding," the bellman said. "You can't bring a bleeding man into the Inn."

"Get the fuck out of my way!" David said. "This man's been shot, and there's a sniper out there who wants us both dead."

The bellman blocked the door. "I'm sorry. It's company policy."

David could not believe what was happening, but there was no time to argue. David and the driver gently set JW on the pavement.

Vincente arrived, and set the rifle on the sidewalk next to JW. He placed his hand on JW's neck, checking for a pulse. Vincente knelt over his son, breathing hard, telling JW he was going to be okay. A look of fear overcame the pained expression on JW's face.

"Who are you?" Seeing the rifle, his adrenaline level rose. "What the fuck?!" David yelled. "Get away!"

David reached a state of furious anxiety. He grabbed at Vincente's collar, trying to pull him away from JW. Vincente fended David off. Before David could land a blow with his fist, Vincente shouted, "Dammit, I'm his father."

David had never met JW's father. His fist remained cocked for a split second while David processed the information. Then, he relaxed his hand.

"C'mon, we've got to move quick!" Vincente said.

"Quick, let's get him in the car. If he bleeds on the seat, I'll buy you a new car," David told the driver. They carried JW to the Lincoln and put him in. David climbed in behind him.

"We've got to stop the bleeding!" JW's dad said. "Get him to a doctor!"

"Ow!" JW groaned.

"You're alive!" David said, with relief and concern dueling for his emotions. The driver climbed in and fumbled for the keys to start the vehicle.

David tried to close the car door but met with resistance. Through the opening, Vincente peered in, his rifle banging on the door frame.

"I'm coming with you," he said.

David looked at the would-be killer, and his own suspicions vanished when he saw the remorseful expression on Vincente's face.

"Get in the other side," David told him, pulling his door shut.

Vincente came around, placed his rifle on the floor and climbed in. He leaned JW toward David and pressed hard on JW's neck.

JW looked at the menacing figure. He struggled to focus.

"It's me, son. I'm your father."

"Dad!"

David instructed the driver to drive.

"I'm hurt pretty bad," JW said. "Can't feel my arm."

"Where to?" the driver asked.

"David, is my arm still there?" JW asked.

"Just go!" David said. "Take us to the closest hospital."

"No," Vincente said. "They'll be there waiting. Someplace else."

"Um... Take us to St. Francis Church on 31st Street," David instructed.

"Your arm is still there," Vincente answered. "Keep your head down. You, too," he said to David. "You're going to be all right, JW. I'm pressing on your neck so you don't lose any more blood. Okay? Why the church?"

"I know one of the Franciscans there. It might be a safe place to get help."

"If it's close, it sounds as good as any place," Vincente said. "Son, I can't see with your coat on. But we're going to wrap that up and get you the help you need. Driver, how far to the church?"

"Less than fifteen minutes. Is your friend gonna be okay?"

"Yes," David said. His eyes meeting Vincente's, he added, "I think he's gonna be just fine."

"But hurry!" Vincente added.

"I looked for you, Dad. I even went to Alaska and talked with one of your friends there. I knew you weren't dead. Petey told me you weren't dead when I went to heaven." Tears were streaming from JW's eyes and running down his cheeks.

"Petey? Heaven? What do you mean?" His father thought JW was sounding delusional but he didn't want to say that out loud. "Maybe we..."

"No, he's not delusional," David interrupted. "He really did communicate with Petey in heaven."

"Oh, that's right. The whole Heaven Ride thing. Of course, you saw Petey. I'm so sorry he's there." His voice trailed, and David could tell that a thousand thoughts were running through his guilt-ridden head.

"Petey told JW that he doesn't blame you," David said. Diverting the subject back to the present, he said, "We've got to figure out what to do. He's losing a lot of blood." To the driver, he explicated, "Not on your seat. He's bleeding on his dad."

"No worries," the driver said. "The seat can be cleaned up. Let's make sure your friend will be okay. It's horrible to think these things happen in our city."

"You don't know horrible," Vincente said softly.

"My head hurts," JW said. "I think I hit it when I fell."

Vincente turned JW's head toward him to get a better look.

"Yeah. It looks like you hit it pretty good."

JW continued to peer into his father's face. Tears poured, and his breathing labored. "Dad? I hurt really bad. But this is the best day of my life."

Vincente, hardened by years of military service of the most violent sort, felt involuntary tears fill his eyes. He pulled JW's face closer and hugged his neck, tears rolling down his cheeks.

"I'm glad, JW," he said. "I'm glad we are together again. I'm not going to let anything happen to you."

"I'm going to sleep now," JW said, drowsily.

"No, don't!" David said. "We're just about there. Fr. Brian will find a comfortable place for you to rest."

"I slept for five hours on the plane. You wouldn't think I'd be tired," JW mumbled.

"Yeah, you did sleep on the plane," David said. "And you drooled on yourself."

His comment elicited a muffled laugh from JW.

"Yeah, I do that."

The Lincoln stopped, and Vincente helped David pull JW from the car. The father wrapped JW's good arm around his neck and walked him toward the front door of the church. Although Trish already paid the car service, David instructed the driver to run his credit card, leaving him a $500 tip.

"Are you sure?" the driver asked.

"Yes. You may have saved a life today, my friend. Maybe two or three. Have a Merry Christmas."

* * *

"Wrong door," David hollered to Vincente. "Over here, to the left."

"Have you been here before?" Vincente asked. "How do you know where – "

"I just do," David said. "Trust me, and I'll tell you later."

They entered the church office. David asked for Fr. Brian. "My friend has been shot. We need to get proper medical attention."

"And I would like to give my confession," Vincente said. David was slightly amazed, particularly at the timing of his request.

The receptionist called Fr. Brian, and he brightened when he saw David. When the Franciscan saw JW's blood, it took his attention away from the reunion with his former student. Fr. Brian ordered the receptionist to find Mrs. Swanson, and ushered the trio into a room where they ordinarily held private conferences. David used scissors to cut the sleeve of JW's jacket lengthwise, while the priest and Vincente became acquainted.

"We hear confessions at 3:45. Is there some urgent reason why you need to confess sooner?"

"Because I won't be here at 3:45. We have people – murderers and government-sponsored assassins – chasing us, and if they catch us, well, I'd like to know I confessed my sins to God."

David peeled back JW's shirt and exposed his wound for all to see. They recoiled in horror, except Vincente. A large hole had been blown in JW's left arm near the shoulder. The bone was visible and shattered. Blood still gushed from it.

"These assassins. Did they do this?" Fr. Brian inquired.

"I did it," Vincente said.

The expressions of horror and disgust on the other's faces were all similar. They were afraid.

JW, wincing, spoke in a woozy tone. "You shot me?"

"I didn't know it was you!" Vincente snapped. "We were on

orders from a government agency. I don't know who gave his orders. Nobody was named. We had code names for our targets. Then, you turned, and I prayed that I pulled my shot enough that you would survive."

"We? There are others?" Fr. Brian asked.

"One other hired by my mission commander. He fired at me when I ran out of the building. Frankly, I don't know how he missed. But they will come after me. After us. We need to wrap this wound, get my son a painkiller, and get him to a hospital, preferably in New Jersey or in Connecticut."

"What's your commander's name? Can he help us," David asked.

"To Simon Sanders I'm as much of a target now as you both are, I'm afraid," Vincente said not caring he just violated code by revealing the other assassin's name – his partner Simon Sanders.

"Simon Sanders? Did you say Simon Sanders?" David asked incredulously.

Vincente was surprised by David's question. "Yes, Simon Sanders. Why do you ask?

"My, God, of course, it is. This is some weird shit. He's a Navy SEAL, right?" David replied.

"Not sure how you know this, but yes Sanders is an NS. Do you know him or something?"

"Sort of. He tried to kill me in my home a few years ago," David replied.

Vincente's face turned white and he was stunned by David's response, and could not utter a word.

The exchange ended abruptly as Fr. Brian returned with the church clerk Mrs. Swanson who had some bandages and brandy from the church commissary. Mrs. Swanson was a retired nurse and a volunteer at St. Francis.

"Vincente, come with me and I'll hear your confession," Fr. Brian said. The chapel is just down the hall. Vincente reached for his rifle, then, embarrassed, thought better of it. "I'll just leave this here with you, David." To the priest, he said, "Let's do this."

"I'll check on my iPhone for a hospital," David volunteered as they left the room. "How are you feeling, big guy? Up for a ride?"

"Is my dad coming?" JW asked. David answered in the

affirmative. "Okay, I'm up for it."

Mrs. Swanson cleaned JW's wound and packed it with gauze, then taped it. This resulted in many squeamish moments for JW, and several screams. Within a few minutes of the ordeal, he was asleep. David asked Mrs. Swanson to call his sister Diane in New Jersey and request that she come to pick up her brother and two passengers. David got on the phone and assured her he was okay, but that JW needed to be taken to the University Medical Center at Princeton. Diane agreed, and David asked her to hurry.

"JW, we're going to have to wait awhile, but we'll get you to the hospital as soon as we can," David said.

"Yeah, I figured my Dad would be in the confessional a long time."

David stifled a laugh. "No, that's not what's going to take time. Mrs. Swanson, have you got anything to take the pain down a notch?"

She thought a moment, and said, "Let me go get you some brandy. Will that be all right, JW?"

"Oh, yeah. That sounds good."

Diane arrived after about 90 minutes. David and Vincente helped make JW more comfortable in the back seat of Diane's SUV. She drove them to Princeton.

JW received the medical treatment he needed. Under these strained circumstances, David had a chance to visit with his sister, while Vincente was able to reunite with his son after two decades. A degree of bedlam ensued when David's nephews Tanner and Topher got home from school. They were just as excited to see JW's wound as they were their uncle. David cautioned them that this was a secret, and they couldn't tell their friends at school about it.

Over dinner, David asked Vincente where he would go next.

"I'm coming back to Utah. With you and JW." The news caught David by surprise but made sense. He was pleased, especially when he saw JW beaming at the other end of the table. "I don't know exactly what you two have done to piss people off, but you definitely need a degree of security. I promise I won't shoot at you anymore."

David and JW laughed, while Diane was amused just having them at the house. After dinner, David asked her to call his parents, and put them on speaker phone. He didn't say anything; he just wanted to hear their voices and laughter. The next day, Diane drove them all the way to Wilmington, so the three fugitives could catch a charter flight out of a small Delaware airport.

Chapter 10: Simon Says "Die!"

JW, Vincente and David returned to Salt Lake City on a chartered jet arranged by Trish. She was in a panic when David phoned her with the news, but later, a loopy JW had a Skype session with her and it calmed her down.

JW's initial shoulder surgery stopped the bleeding and closed the wound. He was required to wear an aluminum brace to immobilize his entire arm, which would have made a commercial flight implausible.

The plane landed in the early evening and taxied to the southeast corner of the airport complex for the charter jets. Trish and Tommy waited anxiously for JW.

"Do I look okay, Tommy?"

"You asked me that back at the house, mom," he said. "You look great."

"Thank you." After a moment, she explained to him, "I want to look good. I'm meeting JW's father for the first time."

Tommy smiled. "Me too, mom." They laughed and she hugged him.

"God, I hope JW's going to be okay," she said.

Vincente was the first to come down the stairs, followed by David. It took half a minute more for JW to come to the door of the plane and descend the steps. David stopped and waited for him.

Trish watched out the window, but her concentration was broken by the opening of the door. Vincente stepped through the door into the charter airline boarding center. He smiled. Vincente had strong, square facial features, and his body was powerful and fit, remarkably so for a man in his 50s. To Trish, he seemed larger than life. He crossed the room and she rushed to meet him halfway.

"Hi, I'm Vincente Gomez," he said. He extended his hand, and all Trish could think was that this was no ghost. He was alive, and JW must be thrilled. She extended her hand, and when Vincente raised it to his lips to kiss it, she melted just a little.

"I'm Trish," she said, blushing a little. "Trish Raines. Oh, and this is my son, Tommy."

Vincente shook Tommy's hand.
"Wow, that's quite a grip you've got, Tommy. I'm so glad to meet you."

"JW has said so much about you, Vincente. He admires you so much. I'm sure you two had great conversations on the way here," Trish said.

"Not so much," Vincente said. "JW's been out of it. The kid's had a rough experience."

David opened the door so JW could slide in sideways with his aluminum appendage.

"Look who's here!" David said. Tommy raced to him, and Trish followed.

"What on earth is this thing?" Tommy asked, eliciting laughter from everyone.

"This thing," JW said, "is holding my arm in place. They're going to do an operation and give me a bionic shoulder."

"Bionic?" Tommy asked.

"Yep. An artificial shoulder. They can rebuild me. I'll be stronger than before."

"Cool!" Tommy said.

Tears running down her face, Trish awkwardly navigated around the shoulder brace to give JW a hug. She didn't want to let go.

* * *

David spent hours doing research. After a few days on the ground, David asked his friend, "Any problem with taking another flight going the other way in a few weeks?"

JW answered in a low and slow manner. "If they can give me more of whatever they gave me this time, I would love to."

"That's all we need. An opioid addiction," David groused.

"It's not an addiction. I just can't imagine how much pain I'd feel if I didn't have them."

"Okay, well, I did a little online checking while we were on the ground. One of the best ortho surgeons for blast wounds is a doc at Johns Hopkins. Doctor William Mast. We're going to have a Skype session with him tomorrow afternoon. If we think he's the right guy, and by 'we' I mean Trish, then we'll get the reconstructive surgery underway."

"I can't wait to get rid of this thing," JW said, gesturing to the aluminum framework. "I feel like I'm wearing an Eddie Bauer tent. Will it be on for another week or two?"

"Three months before your next check-up. They may fit you with a smaller, titanium brace. But you'll have to be immobilized for six months after the surgery."

"We better get that done soon," JW said. "You know, so I don't miss ski season."

"I hate to be the bearer of bad news, JW," David said, but I don't think you'll be skiing next season. But I'll help keep you on track with your rehab."

The next day, they visited with Dr. Mast via Skype. He asked some probing questions, and the guys interviewed him about his experience with such wounds. His experience was extensive, and Dr. Mast mentioned that he used to be the ortho surgeon for the U.S. Ski Team. JW was sold, but there was one sticking point.

"How long do I have to wait to get this done?" he asked. Trish had forewarned him that non-life-threatening surgeries sometimes require a long lead time.

"You're in luck, sort of," the doctor said. "I'm semi-retired. So I'm available to meet with you anytime in the next week or two. The difficulty will be in booking the facility. I'll have my assistant look into that. But let's get you in for an in-person consult, and then work out those details. That is, if you decide on me, and Johns Hopkins for this procedure."

JW glanced at David, who seemed to share the same excitement.

"Dr. Mast, I'm sure you're the guy. I can be on a plane tomorrow."

The meeting was arranged for later that week, and the surgery was performed just twenty days later at Johns Hopkins outside Baltimore. JW was accompanied by Trish and his father. David had other business to transact.

* * *

Room 508 of the Latham Hotel offered no pleasant sightlines, merely a close view of an office building across the alley. To be safe, David closed the blinds. To his dismay, the Latham had shared showers. To avoid a waiting line and the risk of being recognized, he awoke at 5 a.m. to use the bathroom and shower. Even more disappointing, the water temperature fluctuated between cold and lukewarm. On his way back to the room, his shower sandals leeched water into the musty, brown carpet. He checked the door lock to convince himself that no assassin forced his or her way into his room.

Safe, he sat at the spindled desk to apply the mask that Trish commissioned for the occasion. The sheer, thin mask had been formed to a mold of David's face. He dabbed water on it with a makeup brush, and it clung to the contours of his face. He was careful not to tear the fragile, stretchy material. He brushed out the air pockets, checking it in a small, round mirror with an adjustable base.

The gauzy appliance tacked another ten years onto his life, adding a grayish five o'clock shadow, dark circles beneath the eyes and wrinkles. He dried his hair and used the hair blower on the mask. Like shrink-wrap, it conformed to his face in both movement and color. He sprinkled some talcum powder in his hair and combed it through until it matched the stubble color of the mask.

He wore a cap and a gray jumpsuit with the name of a heating and air conditioning firm. Up until now, his focus was called #10. He worked on attaching a name to her. Kathleen Mulhare was her name. Her apartment was about 11 blocks away from the Latham, in the Flatiron District, and David walked amid New York rush hour throngs. She buzzed him in, and he took the elevator to the 8th floor.

A queasiness came over him as the elevator climbed. *What if this is a set-up?* The feeling grew with each passing floor. He was on alert when the elevator door opened, and he cautiously looked both ways when stepping from the elevator. Nothing happened.

The hallway was dark. At either end, the windows were boarded up. He found Ms. Mulhare's apartment, number 811. He knocked. Glancing back toward the elevator, the nicely carpeted hall was too dark to see. He heard a woman's voice. It was not a physical voice from inside apartment 811. It was in his head, and it was urgent.

"Duck!" it said.

A shot rang out and David threw himself to the floor. A bullet whistled past him, lodging in the window frame. From the darkness, an attacker emerged, blocking David's path to the elevator. It was Simon Sanders.

Running would have been futile. David didn't want to take a bullet in the back. Another bullet fired, and it buried itself into the deep pile carpet near David's right hand. He used that hand to push his body upright, and with barely a delay, he rushed the shooter. Sanders was taken by surprise for an instant, as he failed to recognize his target.

"Who the hell are you?" Simon said, waving the pistol but not shooting.

David surged forward, taking two steps up the wall, then using a neighbor's door way to launch himself toward his assailant.

"I'm the AC repairman from hell!" David told him. He soared six feet through the air, his left shoulder finding its mark square in Simon's sternum, his right hand sweeping across to hammer Sanders' forearm. The force drove Sanders backward, with David on top of him. He dropped the gun. David threw a quick left-right combination, landing squarely to Simon's jaw with both. Sanders kicked up, trying to stand. David recovered his balance as Simon reached back to uncoil a right-hand punch. David was quicker, taking the opening Simon presented to karate chop the side of his neck. The blow hit hard and sudden on Sanders' vagus nerve. Sanders fell back on one knee, then collapsed.

David heaved, taking deep breaths.

"I didn't know that would work so well."

He picked up the pistol and removed the clip. He tossed the empty pistol down the hall. He stood over Simon for a moment, just to make sure his victim was incapacitated. Initially, he thought to take the elevator out of there, but thought he should first check to see if Kathleen Mulhare was in her apartment, possibly in peril. He stood at her door.

"Kathleen Mulhare, are you inside?"

"Yes. Help me."

David broke the door down with greater difficulty than it took to take out Sanders. Inside, he found a woman strapped to a chair, her hands and feet secured with zip-ties. Although she appeared like she had struggled, she had a magnificent diamond-shaped glow above her head. Using a utility knife that Vincente Gomez gave him, David freed Kathleen. She immediately launched into the abduction story, but David stopped her.

"Listen, just listen! We've got to get out of here, immediately. This Simon dude might not be out for long. Follow me!"

Kathleen found her purse and followed David. Out of habit, she paused to lock her door. With the key in her hand, she realized the door was shattered and stepped around Simon's body gingerly to meet David at the elevator.

They ran down New York sidewalks for a few blocks. On 8th Avenue, David stopped, waiting for Kathleen to catch up. They entered the lobby of The New Yorker hotel. 'They found a seating area in a public area. David asked Kathleen if she was all right. She nodded, and they introduced themselves more formally. Suddenly, the hotel staff began scurrying. One manager began locking the doors, except for one revolving door. Several other employees flanked the door. The manager used a remote to raise the volume on a TV in the lobby.

Reporters discussed the facts of a bombing in Chicago. It took place at a Wyndham Hotel, owners of The New Yorker. CNN's Mike Cardona reported that no motive had yet surfaced, but that a suspect had been taken into custody. The suspect had ties to a vigilante group called Teutonic, Inc. After dropping a gym bag near a meeting room, hotel security followed him outside the hotel. The blast occurred, a chase ensued and so far, the suspect refused to talk. Six people were killed in the blast, and as they were identified, David recognized one of them. It was #11 on David's list, Marty Bingham. Without the chance to get the key from Bingham, David had doubts that he could complete his mission.

"What's wrong?" Kathleen asked. She spoke with a touch of a British accent.

"Nothing. Well, it's something, but I need to worry about it later. You are going to have to get out of here. Do you have any family or friends out of state that you can visit for awhile?"

"Yes. I think I can go stay with my sister in Jersey. I'll go home and pack a bag."

"No. You can't go back. Call your landlord and tell them to barricade the door, but don't go back. Now, I need some information from you. On your return from the Heaven Ride, there was one thought or concept that repeated or became a theme. Do you remember this?"

"No, not really."

David was shocked. To this point, all his fellow riders with the Gift easily recognized a key. *What do I do now?*

"Okay. Just recount what you remember about the return trip. In your own words."

"It was all rather pleasant," she said. "Reunited with my mum, and then an old friend from college. I don't know that there was any theme, per se. But when it was time to leave, it became very sad. Ominous. My friend, Kitty, she told me, '… your path is made of tears. Tears of sadness, tears of joy. But your path is made of tears.'

"Is that word for word?"

"Pretty much," Kathleen said.

"That's what I was looking for," David said.

"Since I came back, I've had a lot of heartbreak and sorrow. Because of Heaven Ride, you know, seeing how beautiful it is there, I was able to deal with it all."

"There may be more tears if we don't get out of here," he told her. "Go as far away from here as you can because they'll be after both of us."

"My blouse is ripped," she said. "I'll just go to H&M, and – "

"No, you've got to go now! You have a Gift. Use it, Kathleen. Be aware if anyone is following you. Just, go now!"

He didn't wait for her to respond. David bolted down a hallway toward a street-level exit, and he was gone.

David ran to Penn Station, all the while feeling like his disguise was falling apart. He bought a ticket for the first train to leave. The lady behind the glass kept touching her lip, then told him, "You're losing your moustache, sir." He snatched the ticket and in the nearest restroom, saw the hanging facial hair. He ducked into a stall and tore off the phony mask and hair. He knew that with all the tightened security protocols that he might now be a target for Homeland Security marshals. He emerged from the men's room to see a long ticket line held up by two officials talking with the lady who sold him his ticket. Confident that his altered appearance would be enough protection, he followed the signs to the platform, where the train was now boarding riders. First stop, Harrisburg, Pa.

Chapter 11: Averting the Threatening Storm

Jonah Johansson worked from his California bungalow for a week. The beachfront cottage helped relieve pressure from the next challenge that would face him: finding a new job. Negative reaction to the growing number of suicides and violence attributed to Heaven Ride fell on his lap. In the computing field, he never had to deal with human collateral before. This was different. For now, the only decision he was making was which fruit to put on his morning granola.

He watched effortless sunsets in the evening and read a novel, and occasionally ventured into the water. He didn't have to work. Not for the money, anyway. On the fifth day, he grew stir-crazy. On day six, he visited the LA Heaven Ride Center, and the following day, he traveled home, up the coast on the high-speed rail line, which neatly deposited him at the TransBay Tower, San Francisco's newest skyline wonder. Some advertising posters directed newcomers to the 17th floor, where the Heaven Ride Center would take them away to a new experience that was out of this world.

Johansson entered the building, nodding to the security officer near the door. Jonah wore all black, which had become customary for him. He felt it accentuated his graying hair.

Jonah first entered the lobby of the building that housed the headquarters for Heaven Ride just more than three years ago at he invitation of David Brownington. JW Gomez just left the company to pursue a more peaceful life with his girlfriend, Trish, and her son

Tommy. Jonah was brought in to review the security policies of what was then the fastest growing business startup in history.

Brownington had no idea that the entire basis of the Heaven Ride procedure and security had initially been developed by Johansson a decade before. On that first day, Jonah came to the TransBay Tower with butterflies. He feared giving away information that might cause Brownington to question the source of his expertise. He mused about the possibility that he wouldn't get the job because David didn't think he was qualified.

He did land the job. David was prodded by Martin, who sent David an email: "You should contact Jonah Johansson about the SVP-Security job, to take the place of JW. That would be a PR coup for Heaven Ride, and I bet Johansson might jump at the chance to end his career with this type of visibility." David has already contacted Jonah at that point, and the chemistry between them in that meeting solidified his decision.

A few months later, David learned some horrific details about some of the dangers associated with Heaven Ride. As soon as Brownington made noise about hitting the pause button, Martin cut his ties with David. He quickly promoted Jonah to CEO, which had been Martin's masterplan all along. Whatever Marty Martin wants, Marty Martin gets, eventually.

The elevator chimed. As the elevator door opened, he witnessed the same sophisticated décor, smiling faces and crowded reception area that was customary at the San Francisco Heaven Ride Center. One face was missing.

"Is Melany here today?"

Melany Romero was the San Francisco center's director, and Johansson foresaw that one day she might be a major player with the executive team. The receptionist took Jonah aside and quietly told him Melany was resolving a Heaven Ride crisis.

"Well, I'm the crisis resolver in chief," Jonah said. "Let me see if I can help. Where is she?"

"She is back in the computer room."

The long, stark hallway ended at a door marked "NO ADMITTANCE." Jonah opened the door using a retinal scan. The room contained several workspaces. Melany sat at a desktop monitor, her long dark hair flowing down to the back of her seat. As she looked up, Jonah saw the consternation in her big brown eyes.

"We've been hacked," she told him.

"WHAT?!!"

"Our security is showing a breach at 4:10 this morning, and again at 7:39."

"That's not possible!" Jonah protested. "I built this system. It's hackproof. Let me take a look." He practically ousted her out of the seat. She leaned over his shoulder watching him review the reports she was reading. He opened a new login screen and looked up at her.

"Sorry. Secure password."

She understood immediately and turned away. Complete silence, permeated by the rapid tapping of the keyboard, created a tension she had never experienced. Jonah called up screen upon screen of data on pages Melany had never seen before.

"You were hacked before, just over a month ago," Jonah told her. "February 7. Did you know about that one?"

"No," Melany replied, fear in her voice. "There was no alert."

"This wasn't your fault, Melany," Johansson said to allay her fears. "I want to track the IP addresses to see where these infiltrations originated. It appears they disabled all of our warning systems. I'm trying to figure out what they wanted to find. They appear to be very precise. The breach on the 7th was pretty much to see if they could do it. Today, they wanted to mess things up and maybe retrieve something." Out loud, he muttered, "I have a suspect in mind."

"I feel awful," Melany said, tugging her hair to one side like she often did when she was stressed.

"Don't," Jonah told her. "This is a matter that goes several pay grades above yours."

Melany volunteered to get him a coffee from the lounge and left the room. He had a meltdown that was uncharacteristic for him. His impenetrable defense had been penetrated. He knew only one person with the mental capacity and motive to achieve this break-in. That was JW Gomez. His search for the origin would confirm if it was JW. None of the Heaven Ride infrastructure was damaged or destroyed. Jonah believed that if JW's mission was to tear down Heaven Ride, he would see more telltale signs. Johansson calmed down by the time Melany returned. But he was further puzzled by the results he was receiving. He delved further. JW was a long shot, unless he had moved. The hacker was in Russia. He pinged servers across the globe, but the origination point was a government server in St. Petersburg. They cleanly entered the "back office" of the databank as if they already knew the ultra-secret pass code.

Melany returned to the front desk. Jonah worked for several hours alone before trudging down the sterile hall toward the front reception area.

He asked Melany if she would call for a car service to take him to the airport.

"I'm getting off right about now. I can take you," she offered. "Don't you need to go back to LA?"

"No. I've got everything," Jonah said. "I need to get to New York. Something tells me I'll be back in LA soon. For good."

On the way to the airport, he turned the conversation toward Ms. Romero, but eventually, his troubles spilled into the conversation.

"In case I don't have a chance to talk with you in person, Melany, you have done a fantastic job here in San Francisco. "

"Why wouldn't you...?"

"I see the writing on the wall. Some things are brewing in New York that will leave me as the odd man out, I'm afraid. The suicides, the elder care issues, and now, the hacking. By the way, several other facilities were hacked without their knowledge – without OUR knowledge – so don't you feel bad." Under his breath, he whispered, "The Russians want it back."

Melany offered some befitting platitudes, but Johansson was not receptive to her kind words.

"No, I may have screwed up a few things, but something bigger is going down. For instance, with this incident today, I would ordinarily report back to Steinman, or worst case, to Marty. Steinman is off in Europe making launch preparations for new Heaven Ride Centers in Paris, London and Barcelona. But nobody can reach him. Ordinarily, as president and CEO, I would be a part of that trip. I have a meeting scheduled with Martin and Steinman on Monday. I've got to try and fix this thing between now and then."

"How can you fix it?" she asked. "I mean, it already occurred."

"I've changed all the pass codes. Right now, I'm the only one with access. And I've designed another layer of security. You have

Level 1 clearance. There were three levels higher, and only three people with complete access. Now, there are four. When David and JW opened San Francisco, it was one of three Heaven Ride Centers. Were you here then?"

"Been here since day one."

"Right. Back then, all three centers were on the same database. When they opened the next 10 centers, they did a smart thing and split them on two separate operating databases. But certain high-level functions are all merged into one pool, if you will. I was convinced I had it all safeguarded."

"What are they after? Names and credit card information?" Melany asked. "Do we notify Heaven Ride clients of the –"

"No, don't do anything. They're after much more than that. Way more than that. And don't say a word of this to anyone outside the center. Or inside."

"It sounds like there are pretty serious effects," she said.

"I could be out of a job. And my career could be shot."

"Well, Mr. Johansson, you are somewhat of a legend. I'm sure you could find a job anywhere. Or retire."

"Unfortunately," he said, drawing out the word to the fullest, "When you know as much as I do, I don't think you can retire from the H2H Corporation."

The airport came into view, much clearer than Jonah's future.

*   *   *

Jonah heard nothing from Martin or Steinman in the next three days. Instead of waiting, he called for a meeting with them, offsite at Peter Luger's in Brooklyn. He sent them a classified briefing on the security breach and informed them of the steps taken to temporarily safeguard the Heaven Ride databases and energy stores. He asked if H2H should postpone the launch of the ten European centers until extra layers of security could be employed.

"Postponement is not an option," Martin said. "Our government partners are eager for our centers to open."

"No, our centers are almost all ready to go," Steinman asserted. "Surprisingly, Athens is all set. London is just working on a few of the pleasantries. Paris and Barcelona are close. Dublin and Lisbon are almost there, as well."

"I was a little distressed when I couldn't reach you, Thomas," Jonah said.

"From Paris, I took a little side trip to Strasbourg and went skiing just south of there. I had little or no cell contact for two days. You have your ocean, Jonah, I have my ski slopes," Steinman said.

Over NY strip steaks and baked potatoes, Johansson told them about the breach, which affected only the clients from the San Francisco, Salt Lake City and Rochester centers. He told them about the Texas and Denver offices that were hacked but no data was stolen.

"They could have taken data if they wanted to. They were testing our defenses. I've installed new pass codes and an even more sophisticated security layer," Johansson explained.

"Are these layers built into our European systems," Martin asked.

"Not yet," Johansson admitted. "That was on my agenda when I met with our European directors. But Thomas took that trip without me. Is there a reason why I was excluded?"

"You were on vacation, Jonah," Steinman said.

"The trip could have been postponed a week," Jonah argued. "Or my vacation, for that matter."

"In retrospect, if you were in Europe, you may not have been able to react to our hacking incident as quickly as you did," Martin said.

"And I'm not sure if you enjoy skiing," Steinman said. "You're a beach person, right? And St. Petersburg is frightfully cold in March."

"St. Petersburg?" Jonah asked, looking at Martin to see if he caught the gaffe.

"Sorry, Strasbourg. The last thing we need is to be hacked," Steinman said, changing the subject. "Are you sure that our – assets – are safe?"

"Yes. No one got near it."

"Jonah, you've been a valuable asset to us," Martin said. We hope that relationship continues. But we think you may be overextended."

"Am I being fired?" Johansson asked, pushing his empty plate to the center of the table.

"No," Martin answered. "Again, we think you may be overextended. We would like you to stay on to repair the security wormholes. And to concentrate, really concentrate, on a completely unhackable network, for existing centers and for our new international facilities. We'll bring in someone to manage daily affairs, and until then, Thomas will become interim CEO. It's all for the better."

Johansson looked at Steinman. He felt as though Steinman was reading his mind, interpreting his doubt. Steinman was behind this change, even though Martin was the one voicing it.

"I'll think about it," Johansson said, standing to excuse himself from the meeting. "I believe our meeting is over." He departed.

Once Jonah was out of earshot, Steinman said, "He won't step down. But he'd be far better off just taking an academic position and riding that into the sunset."

"That complicates things," Martin said.

"No, it doesn't," Steinman countered. "I have an idea who might be able to step in. And Marty, I'm going to need to take some time off. Maybe a few weeks."

"Your leaving me with this mess?" Martin complained.

"Don't worry. It will handle itself."

"Just like you said about Brownington and instead you have your assassin nearly take out the Gomez kid," Martin said.

"JW and David Brownington are both major threats to the future of Heaven Ride," Steinman said. "Yes, I authorized a plot to take them out because I knew you wouldn't do it."

"As long as JW remains harmless to Heaven Ride and is with Trish and Tommy he's not a target. You don't even know the hell I paid because of your rogue mission. Do something like that again without me knowing, Thomas, and you'll be the sitting duck."

Steinman fired back, visibly perturbed by Marty's lecture and threat.

"Don't threaten me with your bullshit. I knew that woman and her son would be a thorn in your side. She could blackmail you any minute. You may outrank me, but I have nothing that prevents me from getting the job done. I just picked the wrong assassin, that's all."

"JW is off limits. Do you hear? But… if that punk Brownington continues his escapades, I'll have no choice but to put Teutonic on the case to stop him once and for all," Martin said. "And Teutonic never fails."

"I made David Brownington. Teutonic doesn't know him like I do. You should let me take care of it instead of bringing Teutonic into it."

"You seem intent on keeping your protégé on board."

"I did. The time wasn't right."

"The time is damn right now," Martin said, veins starting to pop in his neck.

"Fine. You want David Brownington dead? Call off your thugs, and I'll put him on ice. You want me to take out JW, too? I can do it."

"As I said, leave JW out of this unless he begins to stir things up with his friend. Besides I hear he's in a rapid decline with Heaven Ride Syndrome, which will do him in without our help," Martin chimed.

Steinman could see Marty was done with the conversation about Davy Boy and JW and instead switched back to Jonah Johansson.

"Assets," Steinman said. "Yes. Sir Jonah has been too squeamish about expanding this operation! Brother or not, he needs to go."

"Can we trust him?"

"We trusted him to bring him into this blessed event. Jonah's a brainiac. He won't ever put himself in harm's way. We never should have brought him into the inner circle."

"He gave us credibility after the IPO. When we cut loose Brownington, we needed someone like him."

"You're right. I'm struggling with the idea of cutting loose a fellow Bonesman."

"Okay, yeah. We can cut him loose, but no harm needs to come to JJ. Maybe we pull some strings to land him a cushy position with a government agency. Let's not talk about that here," Martin said. "So, our European Director, is he set?"

"Yes, Rodrigo Silva. Once, the most powerful man in Portugal. He lost his political clout in a sex scandal. He still has all the government connections we need, and for him, well, this is a rehabilitative step."

"And he gives us what we need outside his home country?" Martin asked.

"As long as the protests are minimal, the government agencies will turn a blind eye. And as long as the kickbacks are generous enough."

"How big of a payroll do we need to maintain in Europe?"

Steinman shrugged. "Rodrigo estimates that to be pretty large, by his standards. It will still only be about one-third of our payouts here in the States. I think that's reasonable."

"Okay. So now we need to find a new CEO here."

"I have an idea," Steinman proposed.

"That doesn't instill confidence," Martin complained. "So far, your ideas have been for shit."

"Really?" Steinman argued, offended. "I don't see any brilliance coming from your side of the table."

"We can't afford any more blunders," Martin said, adding sarcastically, "from your side of the table."

Steinman prepared to go to war with Martin, then thought better of it. "Okay, Martin. Let's pull the trigger on this Euro-launch. And there, we'll strip an extra third of the heavenly bounty."

"Won't that kill them?"

"Nah," Steinman said. "But what's the difference? We're not Europeans."

"I don't want any of this Heaven Ride Syndrome horseshit to shut us down."

"We'll just blame it on the Euros being more fanatical Christians than we are in America."

"You're way to blasé about this whole thing. Leave it the way it is. And after we kick ass in Europe, you'll take care of this David Brownington thing, right?"

"Right."

Chapter 12: JW's Descent

The morning news seemed to carry through the whole house, bringing David up from his basement quarters. "Thanks, Matt. Here in London, excitement builds for the grand opening of the first Heaven Ride Center in Europe. The ribbon cutting takes place in about a half hour, and later today, facilities will open in nine other European locations. This London center is being called the crown jewel of Heaven Ride spas. Even though it's not quite open to the public, we were able to get a sneak peek."

"I can't look at that anymore," David said. "Could you turn the sound down, Trish?"

"Sure. Mind if I ask why you're feeling this way? Is it because you wanted to be a part of this?"

"No! It's because of all the people who are going to get hurt. Where's JW? Sleeping?"

"No. He hardly sleeps anymore. He's out in the garage. He was up all night working on a project."

* * *

Alison Hill waited in line at Starbucks. *Where are you supposed to look? People sitting watch the people in line. The people in line are talking or staring vacantly at the menu board or looking wistfully at those waiting for their fancy coffee concoctions. Then, there's the camper in the corner, looking at me. He's kinda*

cute. Older. He must get here when they open. Same seat, every day.
Same glances, watching me, but trying not to stare. Too shy to say
anything. I never did go much for the shy guys.

"What can I get you today?"

Alison's thoughts were disrupted by the pretty young lady
with Elisa written in large letters on her green apron.

"Tall cappuccino. Low-fat. Please." She paid by scanning her
phone and the transaction was done. She walked to the other end of
the counter, working hard to not make eye contact with the guy in
the corner. After a short wait, the barista called her name.

"Alison, tall cappuccino, skinny."

She took the hot beverage. Her thoughts suddenly turned to
David. She stopped. It was as though he was right there, in front of
her, blocking her way to the coffee fixin's counter. She could almost
see him. Whenever he was going to ask her to do something, he got a
serious, pleading look in his eyes, and a slight smirk. That was the
look she saw. She called it his "Schoolboy Charm" look, and no
mortal woman could refuse him.

Alison? Alison, it's killing me not to be with you. I know this
is how it must be – for now. But there will be a day when we can be
together. I promise.

She took a step forward, but there was a force that prevented
her from taking another. Emotions welled inside her.

Neither one of us can put our lives on hold. But you've got to
know. I'm thinking of you now.

Involuntarily, tears started seeping from the corners of her
eyes.

When our day comes, I'll be there for you. Totally. You're the one,
Alison. I don't doubt that for a minute. I understand why we can't
talk, or write, or see each other. This is the best I can do. I can feel
what you're feeling. I'm glad you feel the same.

Alison began sobbing and dropped her coffee. She fell to her
knees in the wet spot and collapsed in a ball.

The man in the corner rushed over to check on her. He put his
arm around her and grabbed her arm to help her up.

"Are you okay? Is there something wrong? Hey, Elisa, get
her a water! C'mon, sit down..."

He kept talking. Alison listened for David's voice, but the

coffee house camper interfered with her concentration.

"Quiet!" she said sharply. She then peered into his kind, bewildered face and raised her index finger to her lips. "Shhhh! I'm listening."

She sat across from her admirer in the corner, smiling through the tears. David's voice returned.

Are you okay?

She greedily accepted the water from Elisa, and sipped from the straw.

Yes. I'm okay, she replied, through her thoughts. *You just, you caught me by surprise. Just like the first time.*

There was a pause, and she wondered if David was reading her thoughts and emotions, or if it was just her imaginings.

The first time?

She laughed, and her silenced admirer appeared perplexed.

The first time I knew I was in love with you.

"Are you better now?" the man asked.

"Yes," Alison said. "Yes … way better now. I know I've seen you here before. What's your name?"

"Pete."

"Well, Pete, I'm Alison. I've got to get to work, but thanks." Elisa brought her a freshly made cappuccino to replace the one that splattered on the floor. "Maybe next time we can talk a bit, Pete." She left, her heart buoyant.

* * *

Trish knocked on the frame of David's open door. "I'm going down the mountain. Need anything from town?"

David thought for a minute.

"I'm having a great freaking day. I just talked to Alison. Holly. Sort of. I still can't wrap my head around her name. No phone necessary. Cranium to cranium. To answer your question, I need a hobby. JW needs a hobby, too. Get us a home brewing kit. It will give us something to do in between saving the world."

"Where do I find that?" Trish asked. "Some kind of specialty store, obviously?"

"Yep. I can search for you if you want."

"I'm capable."

"Yes, you are. I'll email you a list of what we need to get started. By the way, where's JW hiding?"

'He's sleeping. Long periods of insomnia, followed by temper tantrums, then exhaustion. I'm worried about him, David."

"We all are."

"Would it be wrong to say I'm worried about me? And Tommy? Would that be selfish?"

"Not at all," David started. "I think..."

Just then, JW woke, launching into another screaming fit. At the top of his lungs, he yelled, as if being tortured by Satan himself. "No. No. No No don't do it! Save me. You've got to save me."

"I don't know what to do," David said. "Getting all these keys is important, but that's only going to help to shut Heaven Ride down. I don't think it will bring JW, or anybody, back."

*　　*　　*

JW's next outburst was louder and more violent than the one before. He had not slept for days, growing more irritable with each moment. When he finally did sleep, it was restless and uneasy. Trish huddled with Tommy, who was afraid of JW's behavior. The fit ran its course, and JW fell back to sleep as though nothing happened.

When the household quieted down, Trish convinced Tommy to close his eyes again, and she joined David and Vincente in the kitchen. Often the last to show emotion, Trish let her tears fall freely.

"I never thought JW could end up this way," she said. "David, you know how he was. Dedicated. Loving. Just plain fun. Now, he's... tortured."

"I know," David said. "I feel the same way. It's like losing a friend."

Vincente spoke up. "Both of you know JW from recent years. And you've been through a lot with him. He's my son. I – "The thought trailed off. "As a boy, you know, he used to tell me about his dreams and hopes. I can see it. He's become just a shell of himself. He's lost hope. His dreams are tormented. I never, ever thought of JW having – you know, mental illness."

David bristled.

"It's not mental illness," he argued, without fire. They looked to him to share some divine wisdom, but he found none. "I guess it really is."

"We need to look at ways of reacting differently," Trish said.

"No," David said. "We need to find a solution. Maybe it's in heaven. Maybe on earth. But I know there's a solution."

Trish, the most creative thinker in the room, squinched her face. "If we could replace the soul?"

"We don't have access, only God has access to it," David said. "I wonder if the process can be reversed."

"If anyone would know, it's you," Vincente said.

"Not necessarily," he answered. Looking at Trish, he said, "You were close to the original invention. Steinman. Martin. The one person who has a heart, out of all of them, is Johansson."

Trish frowned. "You're not completely right about that. Martin has. But you are right, I've known Jonah for years. Always a decent man. A moral man. I don't even know how he got tangled up in the current mess."

Vincente offered his opinion.

"I know Jonah," he said. "He's a stand-up guy. I always felt that he was open to ideas. And willing to help where he could."

"I do," David offered. "We – I mean, I brought him into it. When JW left. And I had no idea that Jonah had any previous dealings with Heaven Ride. Not only that, they're all Yalies."

"Is there a downside to talking with him?" Vincente asked.

"None at all, Vince. What do you think, David?"

"No, none. Do you want to make the call, or shall I?"

"I'll do it," Trish said. "No time like the present."

She took a minute to compose her thoughts, then scrolled through her phone for a number she hadn't called in years.

He answered, and they engaged in obligatory small talk. He made no mention of Heaven Ride, but told her much about his granddaughter, Alison. She asked Jonah to keep their talk confidential, and after he agreed, she told Jonah about JW's predicament. David slipped her a note: "Play up the inventor. He proved he could take Energy away. Jonah, prove you can put Energy back." Trish read it and nodded.

"I don't know if you're hearing me, Jonah," Trish said, her

tone still friendly. "You've made a huge scientific breakthrough. Maybe the biggest in human history. But you must admit that JW – and David – deserve some credit in bringing this to the world in the fantastic way they did. And you're reaping some of that success, right?"

"Yes."

"Jonah, JW's not doing well," she told him quietly. "I don't know if you put much stock in the Post Heaven Ride Syndrome."

"Not particularly."

"Believe me, it's real. He can't sleep, he's lost focus. He's paranoid. Jonah, he's suicidal."

The silence on the other end was Jonah's way of expressing sympathy. Finally, he said, "I'm not a doctor. I can't really do anything for him."

"JW doesn't need a doctor," Trish said. "He needs the energy that was stripped from him on his return from Heaven Ride. I'm pretty sure you know where and how that's being stored. And how to access it."

"I do, but, I can't."

"I also know you worked on a plan to instill it in military personal during early development stages," Trish said.

"Dammit, Trish," Johansson said. "Now you're getting into an area that puts me in a bad legal place. I might be tried for treason. You can't imagine how much weight the government has on this program."

"In all the years I've known you, you never turned your back on any idea by saying 'I can't.' Jonah, you always find a way."

"I'm not lying," Jonah said. "I can't." Once again, Trish was silent. "So what is it you are asking, Trish? You want me to peel away the aura, and somehow restore that to JW?"

"Yeah. Exactly. Put that energy back to heal his mind."

"It's never been done before."

"That's never stopped you before, Jonah. You invented the process to strip energy away. I'm sure that with your inventive power you can restore it. I know money isn't your sole motivation, Jonah. This restorative procedure is what history will remember you for."

"Damn, Trish, you know me too well," Jonah said allowing his conscience to speak. "Some of the information is classified. We don't know what form the energy evolves – or devolves – to when it is stored. We wouldn't know the exact method, or amount, to re-invest. We don't know so many things. We don't know the transport method from our storage depots to a human. Or if it would be lethal. So many things we don't know."

"But you have thought about it."

"Oh, yeah. But – "

"Then I trust you. You'll find the answers."

If Trish didn't know better, she might have imagined she heard mechanical whirring. No words followed for quite some time.

"I'm not able to help you at this time," Johansson said. "It was really good to talk and catch up with you."

Click.

Chapter 13: Post Heaven Ride Syndrome

For an entire week, CBS promoted an hour-long news special featuring an in-depth look at the topic everyone seemed to be afraid or unable to approach: Post Heaven Ride Syndrome (PHRS). CBS assigned its investigative journalists to the task, and over a three-month span, documented some of the devastating personal stories supporting claims that this was an actual psychosis, and interviewed experts and some not-so-expert authorities who debunked the story.

David, JW and Trish watched the program with interest. JW sat in a plush recliner chair that accommodated his shoulder elevation splint. For one more week, until his second surgery, he had to wear an apparatus that kept his left arm raised.

"Hey, Trish," JW said. "Turn up the volume."

"I'm sorry," she joked. "I see your hand is raised, but I didn't call on you."

"That is so funny the 330th time around," JW said with sarcasm. "You guys are lucky I can't bathe yet, so you can take in my manly scent. More sound, please. And can you move my drink a little closer? I may need it with this show."

"When is the second operation?" David asked.

"Let's see," JW said, "Six days, fourteen hours and, uh... thirty-three minutes away. It is to repair my proximal humerus and remove some shrapnel that came dangerously close to my subclavian artery."

"I always told you that you weren't very humorous. Dude, I won't even joke about that," David said. "Your shoulder looked like raw meatloaf with a chunk taken out. It was the third ugliest thing

I've ever seen."

Trish took the bait. "And the first two were...?"

"Head cheese, number one. Number two was JW's eighth-grade graduation mug."

JW took a sip from his cocktail. "Even with one hand, I can still mix one mean White Russian."

"You mean Barmaster X can," David said, deflating his ego.

"Shut up, it's starting," JW said.

The host and main investigator was Kat Welsh. David could tell she had taken Heaven Ride. Kat quoted statistics that surprised all three of them. To date, more than one in nine returnees had either committed suicide, murder or sought psychiatric treatment in the past 18 months. Further, nearly one in five adults diagnosed with alcohol or substance abuse problems cited PHRS as the major contributing factor for their illness. Several of the stories from sufferers were heart-wrenching, but the accounts of relatives of the suicide victims were especially taxing. Kat paid tribute to a CBS staffer who committed suicide months after taking Heaven Ride. Choked by emotion, she cut to a commercial in mid-sentence.

Welsh and a few of her associates interviewed several Heaven Ride advocates who denied the relevance of the death and mental illness statistics. They saw two familiar faces. Obviously, Jonah Johansson provided the company line. Sen. Bob Thomas was asked if there were any plans to legislate against Heaven Ride, given the amount of violence and potential psychological harm.

"Let's not jump to conclusions," Sen. Thomas said. "There's no reason to shut down a vibrant business based on conjecture. You wouldn't close down the auto industry because people get in car crashes."

Thomas went on to say he defended Heaven Ride mostly because it sprouted on his home turf. Kat went on to reveal his true interest in this deadly business.

"Are you currently on the payroll of Heaven Ride, H2H Corp. or Global Reach Partners" Are you a shareholder in the business?" she asked.

"No."

"Have you received any payments, goods or services from any fraternal organizations?"

"Stop the cameras! I don't like where this interview is going."

The senator got up, and before he could barge off, a technician blocked his path to retrieve the wireless microphone from his lapel. Sen. Thomas, thinking he was being accosted, cold-cocked the technician, starting a scuffle that was caught on camera.

On-air, in a more subdued studio setting, Kat explained that a sinister secret society seemed to have wrested control of Heaven Ride from its original owners.

"CBS attempted to reach David Brownington and JW Gomez for comment, but they declined to appear on this program."

"That's a lie," JW muttered. "I never was asked so how could I decline."

"I did for us," David said. "I saw a letter with the CBS News logo and addressed to you arrive here a few weeks ago. I opened it and it was invitation for both of us to come to New York to tell our side of the story. I sent a letter back saying no."

"Why? You're the media whore! This was a chance – we could have nailed these guys! Next time when something's addressed to me don't feel you can open it. Really, dude?"

"Okay. I know. At that time, I thought it was a trick by Martin to lure us out into an unsafe position. I am afraid to go to New York again. And, I know there's no way you were going."

"Yeah, I don't blame you," JW said. "New York sucks!"

"Hey, mister," Trish said. "New York was our first date."

"I didn't mean that. But I practically had my shoulder blown off. And if that bullet hit my subclavian artery, you would have been a widow."

"We're not married yet."

"A widow-to-be, then."

"Thank goodness I'm not grieving."

The report continued, and Kat wrapped up the program with a commentary.

"Heaven Ride burst into the public consciousness nearly three years ago and we embraced it like past voyages of discovery... Marco Polo, Columbus, Neil Armstrong. It jolted the imagination. To be able to go to heaven, leaving your body here on earth. It answered many theological questions about the existence of heaven, while raising others. Overwhelming evidence suggests that the riders actually do go to heaven. I did it. Like almost every other Heaven Rider, I did not see God. Only a handful of Heaven Ride travelers claim to have seen Jesus. I did not see any Biblical characters. So, what does that say about our religions? The inventors, JW Gomez and David Brownington, have been and should be celebrated for their contribution.

"But along the way, something went wrong. Perhaps people cannot handle this technology, perhaps we are too weak. Perhaps it's a flaw in the technology. Perhaps, and this is conjecture on my part, perhaps there was a flaw built into the technology on purpose, and the originators have created planned chaos.

"The numbers don't lie. Millions of participants, and nine percent of them come back damaged and self-destructive. After going to heaven, their life on earth is hell. "So, Gomez and Brownington bowed out of the company months ago. But they are cowardly in their silence. The new operation, headed by Jonah Johansson and controlled by Global Reach Partners, a big New York private equity firm that still owns a majority of Heaven Ride shares, is shut down tighter than any drum that reporters like me have ever encountered. You can get more information out of the Pentagon than from these characters. And even our elected officials are reticent to dig in to find answers. The company's limited shareholders only get the required SEC filings.

"I think there are forces in this universe conspiring to take something away from us, and to hide any and all evidence that will provide the answers. The cowards who know the answers won't come forward, while hundreds of thousands of people take their lives or die unexplainably. Last week, we endured our first day where more than a thousand Americans committed suicide. That included one of a beloved colleague right here on the set of The Big Story. These suicides and horrific killings are directly related to Heaven Ride. And now, Heaven Ride is expanding into Europe, South America and Asia. Every day, here in the United States, more and more people are taking Heaven Ride. What is this world coming to?

For The Big Story, I'm Kat Welsh. I hope tonight's program inspires you to seek the truth about Heaven Ride."

Trish turned the television off, and the three of them sat in silence for a moment.

"A coward? I don't feel like a coward," JW said. "Hours of research, nearly getting my arm blown off, living in seclusion for a year to avoid assassination... I don't feel like a coward."

"We're not cowards. But from her standpoint, and the public, it doesn't look good. All these issues with Heaven Ride, and we just disappear. It's part of the government plan to make us the scapegoat for all the killing and suicides."

"I bet millions were tuned in tonight, and more will see it on the internet in the next few days," Trish said.

Vincente came into the room, breathing heavily.

"Where have you been?" JW asked.

"I was horsing around with Tommy downstairs," Vincente said. "What's going on. Looks kinda serious in here."

"Well, David and I were just outed as cowards on national television. Nothing too serious," JW said.

"Ah, don't worry what other people say about you," Vincente said. "They say a lot of things just for ratings."

"Not this one, Vince," David said. "I see now that this is a very legitimate investigative report. I can tell she was asking the right questions but couldn't get any verification. I need to contact Kat and her crew for Part 2."

"Don't go to New York, David," JW advised. "That's their turf. It's not safe. According to my dad, his bullet was meant for you, too. I just happened to be the first out of the car. My father said his rifle could have taken us out from 2,000 yards away. Stay away from New York."

"I agree," David said. "I'm not going to New York. Neutral territory. I won't draw attention here, and I'll be away from their connections in New York."

"Let's do this!" JW said, impulsively.

"You're not doing this," David said. "You're having surgery. And a few weeks of rest and recovery. I'm doing this for both of us."

"Where?" Trish asked. "Why not just do the interview over Skype. I've seen a ton of interviews conducted on TV this way."

"Skype is a possibility, but I feel I need to see the reporter face-to-face," David said. He paused for a few seconds and then said, "Pick a number between say, 30 and a hundred."

JW called out 58.

"What's the 58th largest television market?" David asked.

Trish used her phone to search. "Tulsa, Oklahoma."

"Okay. I'm going to contact Kat Welsh and CBS to meet me for an interview in Tulsa."

* * *

A man in a black nylon shell jacket met David at the airport and drove him to the Hilton Tulsa. David had never been to Tulsa before. A freezing rain made it cold, but the chill made the hotel lobby that much warmer and more welcoming. David wore a disguise that consisted of long reddish-brown hair and sideburns with a beard, and even in a brief exposure to the elements, he had beads of ice forming on them.

He was ushered to an elevator, and up to the seventh floor.

The New York CBS Network news crew transformed the hotel suite into a makeshift studio. An editing area was set up in the bedroom. The large bathroom became a make-up salon, and two cameras were set up in the cleared dining and living room areas.

Kat Welsh was busy directing one of the cameramen to change the angle of his shot, and she told a technician to block a window where light was escaping through. A stranger entered the room in her periphery. She believed it must be David, and she stopped. She felt an immediate calm when she came over to him and extended her hand. Her blue eyes sparkled through porcelain skin. She smiled genuinely. The manic behavior, like rush hour on Broadway, came to a stop. Except her heart, which David sensed was still beating rapidly.

Then she laughed.

"I'm sorry. THIS is your disguise, David?" Her giggling was contagious, and David laughed with her.

"Hey, I told you'd I be wearing a disguise, and it got me here safely, didn't it?" He looked around at the crew, which consisted of six other people who were all focused on their tasks. "Who are all these people? Do they all work for the network?"

Kurt, the director, overheard and assured him they did.

"I thought this was surreptitious. I thought it would be just me, Kat and a cameraman."

"This is what it takes to pull off a network television interview," Kurt said. "We average six million viewers, so we can't cheap out."

"C'mon!" Kat said, and she led David into the bathroom to have her makeup person help him remove his facial hair and to apply some makeup for the taping.

"So, you liked the Heaven Ride story I aired last week?" Kat asked him, as the make-up artist washed some of the latex adhesive off his face.

"No. I hated it." He achieved the startled reaction he desired.

"Did I go too far bashing Heaven Ride and its safety record?" Kat asked.

"No. You didn't go far enough. You merely scratched the surface."

Kat watched the cosmetologist pick up a brush and apply some powder on his forehead.

"Why are you doing this to me?" David said in mock protest.

"This is merely to keep you from shining," Kat explained. "You don't want to look sweaty. It doesn't mean you have to turn in your Man Card. So, are you willing to talk on the record about the risks?"

"I most certainly am. That's why I'm here," David said. "How was your Heaven Ride? You said you went in your last broadcast but said nothing about your experience."

"How do you know I was telling the truth? Maybe I just said I went to let my viewers and the people interviewed that I to build credibility," she asked.

"I know. I can tell you took the ride."

"How can you tell? If indeed I did go."

"I'm not telling you. But I know. On the air, I want you to talk about your Heaven Ride experience."

"You mean, to fabricate an experience I never had?" She giggled with her childish teasing.

"Let's cut to the chase, David said. "If I can't trust you then why turn on the microphones? You're a rider and I'm going to ask you on air. Fair is fair."

"Are you my producer now?"

"No. But it will make for one hell of an interview." She sought truth in his eyes and found it. He wasn't bluffing and seemed to know things that he wanted to make public. He went to the rudimentary set, where two chairs were placed very close together at a 60-degree angle. Kurt attached a wireless microphone to his collar.

David was dressed casually. Today, it was jeans and a gray collared sweater. He caught Kat looking at him from the next room. David winked and nodded. He was on her wavelength, and this was going to be one hell of an interview because he knew that she would ask whatever questions he wanted her to ask.

Kat joined him of the set and each of the cameramen set their focus.

"You've done a lot of interviews," Kat said. "Do you get nervous in front of the camera?"

"No," David answered.

"I've done this a thousand times, and I still get butterflies until the signal comes for me to start talking," Kat said.

"Rolling camera one," a cameraman said.

"Rolling camera two," said the other.

Behind the sound board and monitor, Kurt showed three fingers, then two, then pointed to Kat.

"Good evening, I'm your host, Kat Welsh, and welcome to tonight's episode of The Big Story. If you're a regular viewer, you'll notice that this is not our regular set. We are videotaping this interview at an undisclosed location to protect tonight's guest from what he called "outside interference." Our guest is a co-inventor of Heaven Ride and former CEO of H2H Corporation. It's the first interview he's granted in six months, so we are excited and pleased to talk with David Brownington."

"Likewise, Kat."

She heard a voice in her ear directing her, but it was not her producer.

"So, David, we're here in a secret spot, and you arrived in disguise. It's not just paranoia, is it?"

"Actually, Kat, it is paranoia. It's the type of paranoia that comes with being stalked by paid assassins, poisoned, beat up and shot at and receiving threatening phone calls. I'm here with you because you called me and my partner JW Gomez cowards on national television. We have taken precautions to ensure the safety of you and your crew."

"My crew? Now, why would they be in danger?"

"It's the nature of this story. There are people who will do anything to stop this story from being told. Along the way, I'm sad to report, many people have been killed to silence me."

"Okay. Our crew is getting a little skittish. They didn't know what they were getting into. Some full disclosure here. David Brownington contacted my producer after we aired a recent story about Heaven Ride. Apparently, David, you were upset with our coverage of the rising suicide rates and thousands upon thousands of cases of Post-Heaven Ride Stress Disorder. In your estimation, did we go too far?"

"Not at all, Kat. You didn't go far enough." David let that sink in, then explained. "Of course, that's not your fault, or anyone's, because all of the facts weren't available to you. You, and the public, are victims of a massive cover up."

Kat was excited by his mention of a cover-up. The second voice that seemed to be coming from her earpiece became more dominant than Kurt's, who gave her instructions on the camera angles and other prompts.

"Cover-up? By you?"

"No, not me. By the government. The U.S government. I'll tell you how it works, Kat. Describe what the process was like when you took your Heaven Ride."

She started talking, and emotions got balled up in her throat. "Wow! It's still that emotional for me. First, they treated me like I was a V.I.P. at the spa before I went into the room. I was at the New York City center. Carol was the hospitality person who welcomed me."

"I know Carol White. I hired Carol when we opened the New York center. She's absolutely incredible!"

"Yes, she was," Kat continued. "After pampering me with a vitamin drink and a soothing video, she led me to the room, and the Pod. A technician there, Randy – also very nice – connected a dozen or more sensors to me and made sure all the biometrics were within range. That was the word I learned that day – biometrics! I felt a series of electrical impulses, oh, first, a little shot, injection of protein, and then electrical impulses. There was a rhythm to them, and in my head, they seemed to reflect the music played in the lounge earlier. I drifted into a dreamy state, and there was an explosion. Around me, I wasn't in it. It was like all the walls around me fell away, and I was alone in the universe. Not even in my body. I drifted toward a silver thread. Then I felt like I was moving, very quickly. I hope I'm not boring everyone!"

"No," David said. "This is all to prove a point. Go on."

"I moved very fast, a little herky-jerky, and then slowed. Very slow, and peaceful. Lights began to appear in the distance. Like little fireflies. One very bright light moved toward me. It reached me and just enveloped me. All the other light surrounded me. The best way to describe it – it was like a warm bubble bath. I felt very loved. And the one light, I heard a voice, and it was my father. My dad had passed a few years before from pancreatic cancer. And I – "

Kat became overcome with emotion. David reached over and held her hand, calming her. She raised her eyes to meet his, and she heard the voice, David's voice, telling her, "Be strong. Your father would want you to tell this." She felt an energy enter her, and a strength just as David released her hand.

"It was just wonderful. We were joined by, I guess you'd call it an energy source. It was Sammy, a boyfriend of mine who died in a car crash. And my Aunt Katherine, whom I was named after. They were all there to celebrate me. Nothing I had done here, on earth, mattered. They celebrated me, and how my soul had matured, the person for lack of a better word, that I had become."

"And then it ended," David said, coaxing the rest of the story.

Kat looked at David, and his face evoked the memory of her loved ones before she said goodbye. "Yes. Something came along and pushed all the other energy away, except my dad, and without words, I knew I wasn't meant to stay. Dad guided me back to a sort of entry point, and it wasn't sad in any way. It was just – part of the journey. He gave me something, like a ball of energy. He said I'd need it for the journey. I moved away from him, slowly at first and then faster. Then, I don't remember anything, except waking up in the pod with an incredible positive feeling."

"But you don't remember the trip back?"

"No."

"And did you have that ball of energy with you when you came to?"

"No."

"You see, the journey to Heaven, you remember every detail. But coming back?"

"Nothin'," she said, laughing.

"That's because – it was stolen from you."

"What do you mean, stolen? I was out, like in a trance."

"Yes. Every person who takes Heaven Ride is likely to have this gift stripped from them when they come back. It's a gift most people never knew they had. Every Heaven Ride Center uses software that was designed by my good buddy, JW Gomez. But, there's been some coding added to this program, unbeknownst to either of us. When I tell you who is responsible and who is stealing all this energy, it will blow your mind."

"Who is it?" Kat asked.

"Before I tell you that, I want everyone to know the detail that JW and I learned after Heaven Ride was already in thirteen cities. We put the pieces together but had the company stolen from us before we could do anything about it."

"What are you talking about, David?"

"Every person in those pods. We learned how to eject your souls and attach them to the Heaven Wavelength with your memory and conscience in tow. And because we located this amazing wavelength, we could bring you back just like you were before. Well, not quite. The price of admission to what we believe is heaven is your soul. With great pain and the loss of our friends, we've learned that your soul doesn't come back."

"What? How could... don't you need that to live?"

"Apparently not," David said. "Instead, our riders are blessed with this wonderful gift. We don't know all that it can do. It may be limitless. Whatever your talents were before, they're magnified a thousand-fold when you come back. Learning? It makes high school and colleges obsolete. You can tap into the consciousness of the universe. Basically, anything that was ever known is just absorbed into your being. Your brain function increases seven or eight-fold, to near capacity."

"Do you have this?" Kat asked.

"Yes, I have the Gift."

"Do I?" she asked.

"No. I'm sorry. We studied a few of the people who slipped

through with the Gift. Perhaps it was a glitch in the system. Or purposely. Some of them have met mysterious deaths or have been under attack. What happened is that some brilliant people, those who truly conceived the Heaven Ride technology, and they have inserted a malicious virus into the software code. We call this the Robber Virus. They are essentially brain mining as we come back to Earth from our trip."

"A Robber Virus? Brain mining? Mysterious deaths? It seems very scary to me!" she said.

"It is. The government is able to strip this gift from the return wave and divert it to a massive storage area. We don't know where it goes, but if it is ever weaponized, it will make the atomic bomb look like a child's toy. It's an energy form that is so powerful that it could be used for humanity's greatest good, or, despicable acts of evil."

"What happens to people after The Gift is taken away."

"Some people live normal productive lives. Others develop PHSD. And it's horrible."

"PHSD. Post-Heaven Ride Stress Disorder. The rash of crimes we're seeing. All the unthinkable acts. Are they caused by Heaven Ride?"

"They might be an after-effect. Everybody reacts differently to it. Throughout time, we always thought that the soul was equated with life. We now know it's not. We've got millions of people now who are living without their souls. But they are spiritual zombies. They – many of you watching – are caught between two worlds. And I'm sorry for my role in that. I just didn't know."

"Where does this energy go?"

"We aren't sure. We suspect it's being stockpiled, like data stored in cloud computers. We don't know where or for what purpose. We don't know enough about it to draw any conclusions. One thing is certain." He paused for dramatic effect. "Eventually, the people who did this will let us know. These people are very smart. They are very wealthy. And they are very powerful. They have a plan, and they will use it."

"What can we do to stop this from happening?"

"For most people, it has already happened. I've got people I'm working with to try to shut Heaven Ride down for good. But for everybody else out there, just stop taking Heaven Ride. Put it out of business."

"The business you founded – you want it to go out of business?"

"Absolutely. It was a huge mistake. It's got to end. After we end Heaven Ride, we can work on a solution. I just met you for the first time, Kat, but I can tell you are deathly afraid of the Post Heaven Ride Syndrome. Look what happened to your crew member who committed suicide. Many of the people out there are asking, can this happen to me? Yes it can. Yes – it has! I want to assure you that JW, me and our whole team are working on a cure."

"How close are you?"

"Honestly..." David looked straight into the camera. "Every time any of you take Heaven Ride, it negates the progress we make."

"There you have it. Stop taking Heaven Ride. This is more than we could tackle in just one interview. I'm sure David will be joining us again in the near future. Thank you, David Brownington, for bravely risking your personal safety to share these important thoughts with the public. And thanks to all of you for tuning in. Come back and see us again next week when we are destined to tell you... The Big Story."

Kat made eye contact with David, smiling and holding David's attention until they received the "Clear" prompt from Kurt.

"Damn. I feel like I have to throw up."

Are you going to be okay? Do you want my water?"

"No, I don't want your water. I want my soul back. All these years of doing the right thing, and sexual abstinence until I was 25, and not killing my co-anchor for his stupid on-set pranks. Ya know..." she didn't finish her thought.

David expressed his personal remorse, and the two chatted for 10 minutes or more. The crew struck the set, and had nearly packed everything up when Kurt came over to take their mics.

"That was one heluva show," Kurt said. "If that's not gonna be ratings bonanza, I don't know what is."

"Ratings bonanza. Yeah."

To David, she said, "You better triple your security wherever you live, because people are going to feel just like I do. They're going to throw up, and then they're going to be mad as hell. Are you done with us?" Kat asked. The answer was affirmative from her crew. "Let me show you your room, David." She led him a short distance down the hall and opened the door.

"So what's next?" David asked.

Kat took his question as an attempt to hit on her. She wasn't sure whether she felt offended or flattered until David clarified his question.

"I mean, with the segment."

"Oh," Kat said. "The piece will be edited. We'll add an intro and intersperse some background. Our marketing staff will put together some promo spots and probably promote the crap out of this between now and Thursday night. It's going to be good. I hope this is a safe place for you. The network never knew about the assassination attempt and poisonings."

"No worries. I brought my own security," David said. "Vincente Gomez. He's outside the lobby keeping an eye on things."

"Good. Do you mind if I come in?" she asked. "I have a favor to ask."

"Sure." What is it?

"Will you sit with me, and hold my hand like you did on set?" She bit her lower lip before continuing. "That was the closest I felt to the joy I experienced on Heaven Ride since I came back."

David sat with Kat and he could read her thoughts and helped her stay calm.

"You know there's one thing I failed to tell you on air," David said. "I learned from a very reliable source that after being ousted from Heaven Ride that JW and I didn't really invent Heaven Ride. We were merely hired by the government as parts to play in an elaborate scheme to bring the technology public by some idealistic young entrepreneurs. A real-life Truman Show and I was Jim Carrey."

Kat said nothing but shook her head in disbelief.

A tap came on the door. It was Kurt, who said Kat was needed on a conference call.

In disguise, David and Vincente flew back to Utah the next day. They found JW in excellent spirits, and reveling in the progress he was making two months after his shoulder surgery.

The following week, David, JW, Trish and Vincente eagerly awaited the airing of The Big Story with David's electrifying interview. When the show aired that Thursday night there was no interview with David. There was no Heaven Ride story. Instead, the network aired a repeat of the show discussing the dangers of scooters in urban cities.

Chapter 14: Undone in Odessa

Dusk's shadows did not dilute David's spidey-senses in any way.
He had visualized Odessa at dusk, or under severe cloud cover.
Nothing surprised him.

From the bus station, he trod mechanically down main streets
and alleys. Nobody bothered him; he bothered no one. Down an
alleyway, he saw a wooden sign over a door illuminated by a single
light bulb where two others burned out: *Plensky's Dine.* He opened
the heavy wooden door to go inside.

The interior was purposefully dim. Sturdy wooden tables had
borne the weight of heavy Eastern European meals – and
conversations – for more than a century, flanked by thickly
varnished benches.

The majority of the restaurant was vacant, but on one side,
groups of men clustered at three tables. Eight men filled the longest
table, barely sufficient to contain the multi-course family-style meal
and the elbows of the men. Wearing shirts that identified them with
the same company, they loudly argued about events that David could
not translate immediately but within minutes he understood every
word in Russian. Two men seemed more animated than the rest,
coaxing laughter from the group that dismissed any notion that they
might brawl at any moment. A second table of five men talked
quietly while demolishing the meals before them. A third table of
two men waited for their food, leaning in toward the center of the
table as if their conversation was a state secret. These men were

better dressed than the others, and David noticed that one had a briefcase on the floor next to his seat.

David took a seat at a small table in the middle of the restaurant, near the rowdy table. He sat facing the door. From that vantage point, he could see through a window to the other side of the wall, where a husky woman in a pink kerchief and blue dress toiled over greasy stainless-steel ovens and stoves. He tried to imagine her, just as he could see Odessa, but her image was somehow blocked from his mental gift. He surmised that she must be Aliona. Apparently, she ran the cafe herself, frantically chopping and carving, baking and boiling. For the moment, she was too busy to take David's order, but she called to him in Russian, acknowledging that she knew he was there. Her voice was loud enough to cause the rowdy men to look his way and take in the details of the stranger in their familiar dining spot. He pretended not to notice them looking.

The burly woman delivered two plates with starchy vegetables and slabs of meat to the two men. David could tell by the dull thud of the plates hitting the table that they were heavy, and probably very filling. He realized that he hadn't eaten in nearly a full day. The woman approached his table. She was aiming to smile, but it came across more as a look of disdain.

At first David did not feel comfortable ordering in Russian, and the woman offered no menu. What he really craved was information. He had practiced a bit of Russian before making the trip and attempted to speak it. Here, the Gift allowed him to understand the language as though it were his native tongue.

"Vy dolzhny byt Aliona." ("Are you Aliona?")

"Nyet."

David looked surprised, prompting an explanation from the woman.

"YA Natalya. Aliona poshel na rynok. Ona vernetsya v techeniye neskol'kikh minut." ("I'm Natalia. Aliona went to the market. She will return in a few minutes.")

David pointed to the table with the two gentlemen, and in English said "Same."

Natalya nodded, forcing a half smile that was less frown-like than before. She took a step away, then looked back at David. She spoke quietly, with her back to the rowdy men.

"Vse oni prikhodyat, chtoby uvidet' Aliona."

Natalya warned him that all the men had come to see Aliona.

A back door opened and closed. David saw a female figure whiz by quickly with a large paper bag, destined for the kitchen.

A clamor arose from several of the men at the rowdy table. The other men all followed the woman with their eyes. Several minutes later, Aliona made her way to the dining area, and surveyed the room. A few of the men hooted and called for Aliona. She upset them by going to David's table first. The diamond aura sparkled very brightly around her head. She extended her hand to David and shook it. Her strong grip surprised him.

"You must be David. I am Aliona. Call me Elena if you like."

"No, I like Aliona. It fits you. How did you know my name?"

"I've been waiting for you. For years, I knew that you would come looking for me. Or someone like you."

The rabble increased at the other table. Aliona scolded them to wait, promising her presence.

"You have quite a fan club."

"A fan club? Sorry. My English not so good."

"You are popular with those men."

"Ah, yes, now I see – fan club. Yes. Unfortunate, because I am pretty and have good fitness, they think they can easily get me into bed." She got up, and leaned toward David, giving him a flash of cleavage. "They are monsters. They don't realize that I choose very carefully. But I choose. They do not. Your food is almost ready. I'll bring you extra. You must try my specialty."

She went off to the rowdy table, graciously accepting their flirtations, looking back at David to roll her eyes. Aliona was teasing one of the quiet ones for not having a woman, then rebuffing one of the more loathsome for being a cad.

"Your talk is empty," she told him. "You could never keep a woman like me for more than one night."

Intentional or not, that fueled hope in his mind that there might be one night of bliss with Aliona. She had to backtrack and did so with a smile. David felt a strong attraction to her, much like the other men in the room. Her smile was infectious. She had a pale, unblemished complexion and seemingly perfect, white teeth. She wore a strawberry-colored shade of lipstick that was neither too dark or too red for her features. A thin layer of makeup concealed slight wrinkles at the corner of her eyes. Those pale blue eyes sparkled, even in the muted light.

Aliona wore a blue frock dress over a pair of skinny jeans. It hung over her body like a veil, and with every movement she made, David could tell that beneath the loose-fitting garment, she had a very athletic, well-toned body. Aliona had a certain swagger about her. The bright, diamond aura over her head made her even more attractive, an illusion of royalty in a pauper's den that only David could see. Her most noticeable concession to style was her boots, brown leather ringed with fur. They did not seem particularly functional for restaurant work but gave insight to her personal sense of fashion. As she cleared the heavy plates from the table, she looked over to David, aware that he was checking her out. She smiled, not seeming to mind.

She left for the kitchen, and after a long while, she returned with David's heaping plate, filled with meats and beets, cabbage and phyllo shells filled with tender lamb. David smiled at the special attention he garnered, and the pride with which Aliona delivered "her specialty."

"You know I'll never eat all of this," David said.

"Then don't," Aliona said. "You can have, how you call it, dog bag." He laughed at the way she said it. "What?" she asked in innocence. Maintaining her smile, her tone turned serious. "Pretend. Pretend you ask what all this is."

"I don't have to pretend. What am I eating here?" She ignored his question but pointed to each of the items on his plate as she talked.

"That man over there, the one with the briefcase – he's on phone, now. He's not regular. I think he's here to follow you. He's been here two hours. Waiting."

"Do you think he's a killer?"

"Maybe. Maybe just spy." She stopped pointing and leaned closer to David, close enough that he could smell her delicate perfume. "Eat. Enjoy. I'll keep you safe." There was that swagger again, following her back to the kitchen.

The rowdy table beckoned her, and she denied them the pleasure of her company. She told them, "Go home, boys. We are closing." A few of them got up immediately, and others sat to finish their drinks. Aliona sent Natalya out to clear their empty plates, and they took that as a sign to leave.

David did eat, and he enjoyed sampling each of the swarthy offerings on his plate. He barely made a dent in the meal before he was full. In his periphery, he kept tabs on the stranger on the phone. Aliona came out to deliver the check to the stranger, and David tried to eavesdrop on their conversation from where he sat.

"I'm closing early tonight," she told him. "Can I take your money now?"

The man raised no objection, and fished money from his pocket.

"Your friend? American?" he asked.

"Yes, he's a visitor. A friend of my brother," she explained in a lie.

"Is your brother here, too?" he asked.

"Not yet," she said. "He's traveling but is coming soon."

"Your visitor – "The man said it with derision. "Do you know him well?"

"No. I just met him," she said. "What is your obsession with him?"

"Can I meet him?" the man asked. Aliona quickly processed the request and decided it would be best to acquiesce.

"Certainly. We were just about to have a drink. Join us."

The stranger introduced himself as Maxim, and Aliona introduced David as William. Maxim told David, "I speak a little English."

David, who overheard their interaction, asked Aliona, "When is your brother supposed to return?"

"Andre? Not until tomorrow. You're early. Let me go get a liqueur and we can toast to your arrival." Gesturing to Maxim, she added, "And to new friendships."

David was baffled by Aliona's acceptance of the stranger. Unlike the others, he was less interested in her, but eager to invite himself to pry into David's identity. He decided to play along, for the moment.

Momentarily, Aliona returned with three heavy kiln-baked drinking vessels, slightly larger than a standard shot glass, and a jug filled halfway with a thick, maroon liquid. She unscrewed the cap, and poured into each of the glasses, setting one in front of Maxim, a second in front of David, and leaving the jug uncapped on the table. She lifted her glass and explained.

"Horilka," she said. "William, here in Ukraine, many old taverns make their own liquor, for special occasions. This is my own recipe. Horilka is especially strong libation. I make mine with sugar beets and currants, a little sweeter than most." She winked at Maxim, "Just like me!"

They laughed, and followed her lead in tapping the glass on the table and drinking the entire shot. David did not particularly enjoy the liquor, and it burned going down. The potency surprised him. Both Aliona and Maxim seemed gleeful with the concoction.

Natalya interrupted to tell Aliona she was going home. Aliona bade her goodbye, and the trio could hear the back door close behind Natalya. Maxim, perhaps feeling emboldened by her departure, loosened the buttons of his coat. David could see a pistol holstered underneath.

"Our lovely hostess tells me," Maxim started, interrupted with a cough. He cleared his throat to continue. "You are from New York, William?"

David felt uncomfortable answering questions from him but had committed to see this through. He was not afraid. After all, Aliona was there to protect him.

"Yes, I am. Born and raised in Queens. I work on Wall Street."

"Oh, Wall Street. In stocks and securities?"

"No. I run a small manufacturing firm for a very wealthy man." He tried to keep his answers vague, not knowing how long this interrogation might last. Aliona poured another round of shots, taking note of David's concerned expression. In his head, he heard her tell him, "Just one more." She had something up her sleeve, but he was not able to detect any aberration in her demeanor.

"Okay," she said with the giddy laughter of a young girl getting a little drunk. "Too much talk, not enough drinking." She tapped her glass, and drank another one down, nodding to David to follow suit. He did, and Maxim downed his.

"So, what do you manufashur?" Maxim asked, slurring. To Aliona, he said, "This horilka. Very strong."

David sensed Maxim was faltering.

"So, Maxim, you were telling me about your business here in Odessa. What do you do here?"

"Oh, I'm not – excuse me, I'm going to take off my coat. It's warm in here." He stood to remove his coat, revealing the holstered pistol, and stumbling slightly over the chair leg. Unable to properly drape his coat over the chair, it fell to the floor.

"I'm not from here," Maxim said. "I'm just here – to meet someone." He began coughing, gasping for air. Aliona watched him gagging with little concern.

"Have...?" Maxim started. "Water?" He choked on the last word. Aliona ignored his request.

"William, I didn't know you were born in Queens. Andre hasn't told enough about you."

"Obviously, Andre didn't tell me nearly enough about you, either," David said, trying to blot out the vision of Maxim, who was now thrashing in his chair.

"The second drink, it was more agreeable, no?" Aliona said.

"It grows on you," David said. "Sugar beets, you said?"

"Yes. Sugar beets. Currants. Nothing like it in America. Jägermeister closest. But this much stronger."

Maxim fell to the floor, unconscious.

"Apparently."

"Natalya!" Aliona called. She rose from her chair and went to Maxim's side. She extracted the pistol and rifled through his coat.

"Stetchkin pistol with silencer," Aliona said. "Issue of Russian Army," she explained to David. She found a red pack of Priluka cigarettes and used her own lighter to light one. Natalya emerged from the back room. She had never left. The two women dragged Maxim to the kitchen toward the back door.

"Let me help," David said.

"Non," Aliona bluntly, over the cigarette dangling from her lips. "You are guest."

Outside, she and Natalya lifted Maxim onto a heap of crates and refuse. She made a second trip to toss his coat on the ground beside him. Inside, she opened his briefcase and inspected documents in a foreign language. She revealed some to David, which bore photos of him.

"Russian," Aliona said. "I knew it. Orders to kill you. And me."

Natalya put on her coat and was leaving, this time for real.

Aliona closed the briefcase, stood on a chair and raised it onto a shelf out of sight.

"Is he dead?" David asked.

"Not yet. He might come to about six hours from now."

"Aren't you afraid he'll be waiting for you tomorrow?" David asked.

"No. Without pistol and valise, he is disgraced. He will be fired. He will run." She extinguished the cigarette. Motioning for David to follow, she put on her coat and they departed out the back door.

"What just happened in there?" David asked.

Aliona ran out to the main road, then turned back playfully.

"Come with me." She ran, her boots clattering on the sidewalk. David caught up and after a series of turns, Aliona led him down an alley and entered a back entrance to an apartment building. Inside, she wrapped her arm around his and directed him toward an elevator. The door closed, and without pushing a button, she gazed up at David, then leaned close.

"Midazolam," she said. Unsure of the reference, David was perplexed. "Maxim. I put Midazolam in cup before I served his drink. Very powerful sedative. Anesthesia."

"Will he be okay?" David asked.

Aliona shrugged. "I don't care." She pushed the elevator button and it jerked into motion. She put her arms around David's neck. "But you, David, you are okay. I told you I would keep you safe." She kissed him and let go just as the elevator door opened. "We have a lot to talk about, don't we?"

David allowed the kiss to mellow, like a fine red wine. "You need to tell me what you know," he told her.

"Oh, I will. But not now. We have better things to do." The elevator opened directly into Aliona's suite. She kissed him again, and he wanted more. She pulled away from him, and smiled and she looked into his eyes. Butterflies rippled down her taut abs. Aliona sighed, then encouraged David to make himself comfortable. David sat on a plush sofa. She lit a candle on a table. From a bookshelf, Aliona pulled a thick photo album and dropped it on his lap.

"For entertainment," she said. "I get cleaned up. Wait here."

She kicked off her boots, then stripped off her dress while

leaving the room. She was ripped, muscular in the right places. She was tattooed with a large, colorful yet masculine design on her left shoulder blade that appeared as an angel with wings folded and hands outstretched in greeting. A second, on her upper arm, featured a design almost like a corporate logo, appearing like a skewed red "A" without the crossbar, encircled partly by a blue swoosh. A third tattoo stretched across the small of her back. It was a nymph, like Tinkerbell, rising over a horizontal spray of flowers. He couldn't take his eyes off her until she vanished into the bathroom.

Her apartment was ultra-modern. It wasn't a style he gravitated toward, but he liked it. It suited Aliona, so far as he could tell. Independent. Original.

The dim light soothed him. Hearing the rush of the shower made him realize how tired he was. He approached his 24th hour without sleep. Tonight's intrusion by Maxim forced the issue: he would have to discuss the 13 keys with Aliona before leaving. She knew why he was here, and he expected this Ukrainian beauty would share a bombshell with him. He trusted her to tell him when she was ready. He paged through the photo album. Many were photos of architecture nearby. Then, modeling pictures, where Aliona made raincoats and rubber boots seem glamorous, and waiting for a bus seem fun. The signs in several of the photos indicated that they were taken in Rostov-on-Don, in Russia, not in the Ukraine. Further in were lingerie photos, and understandably, David spent more time scrutinizing the details.

The shower stopped. David felt completely relaxed. He fought the urge to close his eyes, anticipating Aliona's return. He was unsuccessful. But he snapped to when he sensed that Aliona was approaching. Her bare feet on the floor were enough to wake him.

She wore only a negligee. It was a fleshy peach color, and barely filmy enough to conceal her body. Her nipples showed through it, and again, David could not take his eyes off her. She smiled coyly at him, and made a detour to a credenza, where she poured a clear liquid from a decanter into a crystal glass. She took a sip, then approached him seductively, leaning over him, holding the glass near his lips. He took a whiff of the vodka, which mingled with a pale, floral perfume. Lilacs. Her breasts were within reach, and he could clearly see the musculature of her arms, legs and abs.

"Taste," she said softly, her accent making the word sound exotic.

She held the glass daintily, raising it near David's mouth, ready to feed him. David grew suspicious of its contents given the earlier incident with Maxim.

"You did mean the vodka, right?" he said, evoking a girl-like giggle from her.

He let the aroma fill his nostrils, searching for anything odd without giving an impression of distrust. She had already taken a sip, so he assumed it would be fine. He drank, letting the vodka flow slowly over his lips.

"For starters," Aliona said, surrendering the glass to David. She dropped down to the floor, leaning against his left leg while using his right knee to rest her elbow. She looked up at him admiring every aspect of his face. "What a man you are!" she said, her voice full of desire. She bit her lip, daring him to read her thoughts.

"You want me to speak Russian or English? Maybe English is sexier to you even though your understanding of Russian is superb for someone visiting for first time," Aliona whispered.

David could only think how wrong this would be if Alison knew. And, could Aliona read his thoughts. Aliona was the sexiest woman ever to seduce him, but Alison had set up shop in his heart.

"Before I leave, we should talk. You know, about heaven," David said. Aliona began tracing her finger on his leg, and it made him excited.

"Okay, but you stay here this night. It is safest choice for you," she said. He was about to argue, but she continued, "It is already decided." Her lips parted and formed a smile that was genuine. In his head, David was grateful for the invitation because he was too tired to find a hotel. He realized he left his bag at the restaurant.

"No worry," Aliona said, the smile still on her lips. "Natalya will bring here in the morning." She continued tracing on his pant leg and made note of the growing bulge in his pants. Her facial expression made them both laugh.

"Oh, look!" she said. "You're not ready for sleep after all."

She continued tracing on his pant leg, watching his reaction. Satisfied, she twisted her body toward him. From her knees, Aliona unbuttoned his shirt. She pulled it off him. Snake-like, she wriggled on top, kissing his bare chest. She moved down to his navel, and the sensation made him quake. He pulled her up from under her armpits, drawing her close to his face.

"We can't do this," he said, barely above a whisper. Something about his voice made her feel even more sexual. "I can't fall in love with you."

"Love," she sneered. "This is not love. This is negotiation. I want hot-bodied, athletic man, and you want hot-bodied, foreign woman." She pushed David onto his back and undressed him. They began making love. Conflicted, David was not in the negotiating frame of mind.

"C'mon, Davit! Put some muscle into it," she said, taunting him. "C'mon Davit!" She stopped, commanding his attention with her eyes. He wasn't sure if he liked her aggression, but she was certainly different from any American woman he had been with. She sensed his struggle in breaking some secret allegiance with the girlfriend who left him.

She nibbled his ear and whispered to him.
"I'll be your Holly tonight."

This angered David. He changed positions and became a dominant love machine, much to Aliona's pleasure. She howled in ecstasy as they both became mere animals for a short time, shedding the divine laurel bestowed on them. David's anger melted into another sensation unlike any he ever felt before. They both had orgasms and lay in an embrace catching their breath. After a few minutes, David returned to the question at hand.

"So now we will talk?" David said, more a demand than a question.

"Give me a minute," Aliona said. "My brain, it's like porridge right now. Oh, what you do to me, David Brownington." She kissed him and laid back to regain her senses for a few minutes.

"Okay, we talk," Aliona said, finally. "You need me to give the key. It is confused. The key, it is the 32nd book."

"What 32nd book?"

"I don't know. Maybe it make sense with other keys."

"It doesn't. Trust me. That's all you have for me? The 32nd book?"

"That's exactly why I make sex with you before telling. Now, you are thinking too hard." She laughed, and David chuckled. His mind was working overtime to figure out the clue. Soon, his weariness returned.

She beckoned David to follow her into her bedroom. As soon as he settled on Aliona's king-size mattress, he was asleep.

He awoke alone, still smelling Aliona's lilac scent on the sheets, and on him. He was naked and did not see his clothes. His senses took a moment to revive, and when they did, he ventured from the bedroom toward the aroma of hot coffee. In the kitchen, a clean, empty cup was next to a coffee maker. Remembering the way Maxim was disposed of, he smelled the coffee before pouring it. It smelled fine. If sexual chemistry was a factor at all, he was certain that Aliona would not off him.

He heard Aliona grunting from one of the rooms across the living room. Rhythmic. Like sex. He followed the sounds and found Aliona. She was pumping iron in a workout room. The weight on the bar was substantial, but she finished her reps with barely a struggle.

David leaned on the door jamb, naked, watching her.

"Training?" he asked.

"No. This is how I am," she said, smiling and flexing her bicep. "You come, naked boy, and give it a try."

She made it sound like a challenge. He had to do it. He swiped the towel from around her neck and laid it across the bench. He positioned himself under the bar and lifted. David struggled with the first rep but continued.

"Like I told you," Aliona jibed, "I will protect you."

He laughed out loud, and put the bar back on the rack after the fifth rep.

"Damn, woman! You're like iron."

"Yes," she acknowledged. "Only colder."

On the wall in the workout room was a badge with an inscription in a frame. It was from the Spetsnaz, the Security Service of Ukraine, Omega Unit. It looked very official.

"You like that?" she asked, putting her arms around him from behind.

"Yes. What is it?"

"It is my certificate. Ukrainian Special Forces. I'm retired now."

"Retired? At the ripe old age of...?"

"I'm thirty-five. Much older than you."

"That is hard to believe, looking at you."

"Do you like looking at me, Davit Brownington?"

He turned to face her. "Yeah, I do."

Aliona peeled off her athletic bra and rubbed against him.

"I need to take a shower and go," David said.

"Stay a few days. At least another day, when my imaginary brother comes home."

"No. I think I might be in danger."

"Danger? I told you, I will protect you."

"But who will protect me from you?" he asked. She smiled and moved her hand down his torso. "Where's your shower?"

"I think your little friend wants to stay."

"I try not to let my little friend make decisions for me. Your shower?"

"Next to the bedroom. You walked past it. Extra towels under the sink."

David left her, and ran the water in the shower, adjusting it to a warm temperature. He thought about the time when he and Alison showered together and made love for the first time. David's memories were interrupted by Aliona singing outside the door.

"Do you mind if I come in?" she asked, followed with a giggle.

He wondered if Aliona would join him and was torn between desire and betrayal. Making love in the shower would hit too close to home. The door never opened, and David dried off. He was perplexed given Aliona's forwardness about sex. David was convinced she read his thoughts and left him alone.

* * *

Aliona assured David it would be safe to return to the restaurant. He asked her about the photographs in her album, and why some appeared to be from Russia.

"I was born there," she said. "Father was Russian, mama was from Ukraine. I moved back fourteen years ago, and applied to Ukrainian Special Forces. One of first women admitted."

"Why did you move?"

"After what you call Heaven Ride, I was hunted by Russian

government. They did not want anybody to share any knowledge of it. They would have killed me, as they are prone to do."

They drew near to Plensky's Dine. "My government is doing the same."

There was no sign of Maxim in the alley. The restaurant was clean as any he could imagine. Natalya was on her knees scrubbing the floor in the dining area. David's bag was on the floor in the corner of the kitchen. Aliona gave him instructions on where to blend in at the airport. Before he could slide out the door, Aliona checked to see that Natalya was still scrubbing. She threw her arms around his neck, pulled herself close to him, and kissed him one more time.

"Do not forget me, Davit Brownington."

"I don't think that's possible, Aliona," he said. She had an uncanny pull on him, and he found it difficult to resist some of the thoughts she put into his head.

"Good answer. Because I can help you. We help each other."

"I'd better go," David told her. She did not loosen her grip on his neck. Aliona bit her lip, in seductive silence, looking David in the eyes.

She whispered, "You are amazing."

He broke from the gaze of her blue eyes and pecked her on the cheek. "You, too."

She let him go.

David hailed a taxi and made his way to the airport, very small for an international city. He found the one and only newsstand and picked up a few Ukrainian-language magazines and read, as Aliona instructed. He felt fully blended in, and in due time, his departure was announced. He boarded the plane without incident.

Chapter 15: Hell Ride

The Gift turned out to be a blessing and a curse some days. News reached David before it was reported. Kathleen Mulhare, the Gifted woman he met in New York after being rudely interrupted by Simon Sanders, was in a coma. It was reported that her car spun out in the Lincoln Tunnel and she suffered severe head injuries. When news did finally reach the internet, which was mostly focused on the two-hour delay to clear the wreckage, the article said that a first responder was at the site almost immediately, which saved her life, at least for now. Kathleen was the 8th Gifted Rider who suffered death or serious injury after providing David with the information he needed.

He strained to put together the clues, and he wasn't sure what they meant. He said a prayer. When he finished, it struck him that perhaps the keys he received has biblical significance. David read the Bible in its entirety as part of his Catholic education, and after saying his prayer for Ms. Mulhare, He immediately connected "the 32nd book" to the Bible and to Jonah Johansson. The 32nd book of the Old Testament was Jonah.

Just as David was able to communicate with others, he received a strong message. "You need to come back. I can help." It was Aliona communicating with him. He expressed doubt that he should travel halfway around the globe for information.

"It is only way. I must see you again in person," she told him. David had other priorities right now. He trusted Aliona saying she could help, but she would have to wait.

JW did not sleep for five days. Each time he began to drift off, his dreams took him back to the lab in the basement of the San Francisco Medical Center. Holcomb. JW re-lived his "experiment" where he electrocuted the old man. And Tanner, whom he executed with a bullet through the brain. And scads of John Does whom he dispatched by a variety of nefarious means. These had not surfaced in his conscious memory in years, but now, they overwhelmed his subconscious, returning and speaking to him. Waking him. Denying him the restful repose he needed to recuperate. Their revenge incinerated the peaceful existence he cherished, like their bodies in the hospital crematorium.

JW still wore a protective cuff over his shoulder, his head hurt, and he was easily agitated. Vincente tried to keep him occupied with some self-defense training, but JW's attention span was very short. In between, they played cards, and Vincente showed him how to play dominoes. Even that time together didn't spare Vincente from his son's rage when his mood shifted.

In those long periods of conscious annoyance, JW could not eat much. He went for walks within the compound, and Trish hid his keys to the camouflage Mercedes in a locked security box. On the third morning, Trish woke up to find him in the kitchen. He had neatly laid out all knives and sharp garden tools on the counter. He sat staring at them.

Later that day, Trish closed her door to talk with Vincente.

"Vince, his aberrant behavior is frightening," she said. "I don't know if I want Tommy exposed to this."

"What are you suggesting, Trish?"

"I think he needs to be – "she sought the word, and tears flowed, "sequestered. Institutionalized."

Vincente sat dumbfounded, recognizing how far and fast JW had declined in the few weeks since his encounter in New York.

"What would it take to do that, to institutionalize him?" Vincente asked.

"I don't know all the layers of bureaucracy, whether we need a doctor's referral or a court order. I don't know if you need a family member to formally commit him. I don't think I qualify. We're not married. We've talked about it but the situation is, just fucked up.

But you. You're his father. You could have him committed."

"He'll probably hate me the rest of his life."

"But he'll be alive. And safe. We'll all be safe."

"As much as I'm not ready for it, we need to let JW's mother know and have her come up and stay with JW for awhile or have JW stay with Jayne at her house in Layton," Vincente said. "Trish, I think you need to make the call, and let her know that I'm here. I don't want our reunion to be over the telephone and related to these circumstances."

That afternoon, Trish called Jayne and explained the situation with JW, which she herself knew haunted her son, and told her that Vincente was at the house. Jayne was stunned by the news and could hardly talk but agreed to come see JW.

Trish also made calls to institutions in Utah and neighboring states. They told her there was no chance. They were full, with waiting lists that would take years for an opening. One administrator said, "It's that damn Heaven Ride. And we don't have a clue how to treat those people."

Later, she told David of her frustrations.

"No way!" David said. "You can't send him to a mental hospital or treatment center. The only reason they haven't killed JW, or me, is because of you. You can't send him away!"

Trish knew he was right, but she did not know the answer. David suggested having a psychiatrist come in for house calls. Even that was fraught with risk.

Their talk was disrupted by the sound of breaking glass in the mancave. David looked at Trish and sprinted down the stairs.

"Vincente, come quick. I need you!"

David got to the mancave to find broken glass on the floor with chairs toppled to the floor. JW was gone. Vincente got there half a minute later, and ran into another room to look out the window.

"He's heading to the pond," Vincente said.

He and David caught up to him just after he entered the barn where the Ghost Camo Mercedes was parked. David blocked the elevator while Vincente talked with him in soft tones, trying to calm him down.

"Leave me alone! There's something I have to do!" JW bellowed.

"We can do it tomorrow. Together," Vincente said.

"No! I have to do it alone," JW said.

Vincente stayed the course with firmness.

"It will be better if we do this together. Let's you and me get on it first thing tomorrow."

JW relaxed.

Vincente rubbed his back and told JW about a book he thought would be of interest.

"What was it you needed to do today?" Vincente asked.

"What do you mean?" JW said. He lost all recollection of his important task.

*   *   *

That day, Trish contacted a psychiatric counselor for in-home therapy. Dr. Joseph Ramos agreed to take on the challenge. Dr. Ramos had a long list of professional accolades and published papers. Because of his career success, he was unable to clear space in her schedule for another week.

For the next few days, the family and David were on edge, but JW was well-behaved. They speculated what JW was off to do without any solid answer. They surmised that given JW's state of mind, the results would not have been positive. Several days of quiet served David well.

David finished another arduous early-morning workout, listening to Breaking Benjamin through his Monster iSport Victory earphones. Since his workout in the Ukraine on the weight bench with Aliona, David found it difficult to lift without thinking of her.

As soon as the music stopped, he heard yelling from upstairs. JW was very angry over something. David ran down the hall and up the stairs to the kitchen, where his best friend was blocking the door so that Tommy could not get out.

"Where's Trish?" David asked with urgency.

"Mom went down to the city. She went shopping with Uncle Vince," Tommy said.

JW was still focused on arguing.

"Tommy, sit down and eat your breakfast," JW screamed.

"No!" Tommy answered loudly. "I just want to go to my room!"

"You sit down and eat, or I'm going to make you sorry," JW threatened.

"Hey, hey," David interrupted. "Give the kid --"

"David, you stay out of this," JW said. "I made the kid what he wanted for breakfast, and now he refuses to eat. Sit down, you little shit – "

"Cut it out, JW. Just cool it." David could feel himself getting hot under the collar.

"Back off David. Tommy, you sit down and eat!"

"I'm not going to eat. I ate a half hour ago. Let me go to my room!" Tommy said.

"Wait a minute," David said. "Tommy, you already ate breakfast? Today?"

"Well, yeah, if it was a half hour ago, it was today."

"Don't be a wiseass, Tommy, I'm trying to help," David said.

"Oh, big help you are," JW said. "What are you gonna do, Captain America? You gonna hit me?" JW got in David's face.

"Tommy, go to your room," David ordered the boy. "Go ahead."

"Oh, great!" JW said, throwing his hands in the air. "Let the kid have his way all the time."

"JW, calm down." JW reached for Tommy, who scampered out of the kitchen. David blocked him from succeeding. "Stop it! JW, Tommy already ate. Even so – let it go!"

"But I made breakfast," JW whined.

"What did you make?"

"Cereal."

"Cereal?" David asked, incredulous. "This is about a bowl of cereal?"

"It's about the principle," JW said.

"What principle? The Cap'n Crunch principle? JW, you just threatened a ten-year-old boy over a bowl of cereal."

"It's the principle," JW said, calming.

"JW? You hearing me? You can make him cereal tomorrow. Okay?"

Once again, JW became enraged.

"What have you got against me, David? Come on, let's have it out!"

"No, JW, you need to sit down – "

JW snapped, pulling everything he could off the counter that wasn't weighted or connected with an electrical cord. Cookbooks, flour and sugar canisters, kitchen utensils all flew onto the floor, making a mess. David grabbed JW and wrestled him against the wall, He didn't relinquish his hold on JW, and once he was subdued, David held him in an embrace.

"Take it easy, big guy," David said.

"Fuck off, Davy Boy!" JW said.

"What did you call me?" David said in a concerned voice.

"I said Davy Boy. Steinman was right. You're just a prick with all the right answers. Always telling people what to do. You're a guest in my house so you should do as I say or get the hell out."

He pushed David away and stormed off. JW slammed a door behind him and sat in the garage. David called to the guard house. "Hector, hey, it's David. Don't open the gate for any reason. Only if Trish and Vince come back. Uh-huh. Yeah, we need to keep JW on the premises."

An hour or so later, Trish came back. She and Vincente were laughing as they parked and got out of the SUV in the garage. JW surprised them when he stood up.

"Oh! Hi," Trish said. "Want to help bring in some groceries?"

"No, not really."

"Were you going out?" she asked.

"No. Listen, we need to talk," JW demanded.

Trish did not want to give in to JW's demand. She popped the trunk door open and began unloading groceries with Vicente. "Okay. We have groceries to unpack. Meet me in my office in fifteen minutes."

While they put groceries away, David told Trish about JW's most recent fit. She ran to check on Tommy. The boy was fine, playing a computer game. Trish talked with him, and he expressed concern for JW.

"Is he going to be all right?" Tommy asked.

"We're going to try our best," his mom told him.

When Trish went to her office, JW was pulling books off her shelf and stacking them on the floor.

"You're full of surprises today," Trish said, keeping her voice light and pleasant. "You wanted to talk?"

'Yeah. You wanna sit down?" They both took
that you and Tommy should leave."

Shock registered on Trish's face.

"You want us to leave?" Her jaw dropped, and
what else to say.

"And David, too. For his own safety."

"This makes no sense, JW."

"It's not that I don't love you," he said, emotionless. "It's
because I do. I don't trust myself. Today, I really wanted to hurt
Tommy."

"I heard about that. It was over nothing. Nothing at all."

"It was not nothing! He wouldn't eat his breakfast!"

"It was cereal, JW. I made him a big breakfast before I left."

"I think it best if you leave."

"Did you also think about what would happen to you and
David? If I leave, you both are unprotected. Teutonic will kill you.
There's no doubt. They will kill you both without my protection."

"Maybe I don't care anymore," JW said. "Maybe David and I
deserve what is coming to us."

"No, you can't believe that."

"You know what I believe? I think this "safe zone" and
protection thing are just fake stories you made up."

"They're not. It's very real."

"Prove it."

"I told you. Martin has a deal with me. He won't allow harm to come
to me or Tommy."

"There is no logical reason why he would protect you."

"It goes back to some work I did for him some years back."

"Not buying it. Martin doesn't have a kind bone in his body. It would
have to have been some important job for you to get that kind of
guarantee."

"It was important, JW. I had his son," Trish said bluntly.
"Tommy. He's Marty Martin's son."

Chapter 16: Back to the Beginning

A cable news network reported:

The U.S. economy is clicking, and the national debt decreased to the lowest amount since the Truman era. Senator Bob Thomas called it "growth by diminished decline." He said that government programs that were slashed led to a more productive workplace, and America's good health practices rolled back health care reimbursements to levels not seen in more than three decades. Democratic congresswoman Betsy Tinsdale agreed that the picture is rosy, but for different reasons. "Health care reimbursements are lower for one reason, and one reason only. Suicide. We're paying less because our loved ones are killing themselves in record numbers.

Some are calling this "the Heaven Ride Effect."

In her office, Trish closed her eyes, in deep meditation. Physical consciousness returned, her awareness focused not on her surroundings but on her inner strength. Ideas flowed and she sifted through possible solutions that would help JW. Trish sorted through the contact list on her iPhone. Finding the name she sought, she called.

"Hi, Jayne. It's Trish."

"Oh, Trish, I was just thinking about you and JW. How are – is everything all right?"

Trish had never called Jayne directly before, so JW's mom

became concerned.

"Overall, yeah. Yeah, we're all good," Trish said. "Hey, I wondered if you might want to come up to visit for a few days. I think it would be good for JW, and the two of you haven't had much time to spend in awhile,"

A pause infiltrated the conversation.

Trish added, "Vince is here, too. I know he would love to see you again."

*   *   *

David decided he needed to speak directly to Jonah. He called.

Jonah looked at his phone as it buzzed and pocketed it. He was with Martin and Steinman and had drawn the conclusion he was being sacked.

Martin criticized Johansson in especially cruel terms. Jonah shrugged, "I knew this day was coming. Let's do this with grace and integrity."

"Shove the integrity right up your ass, Jonah. You were supposed to create an impenetrable shield of defense. Today, we learned that some of our assets were stolen," Martin said.

"I know," Jonah said. "I've looked at this every way possible. I don't think we were hacked."

"But some of the energy stores are missing."

"Just a small amount. But we weren't hacked. It was an inside job."

"Bullshit," Steinman said.

"I'm telling you what I know. The three of us here in this room are the only ones authorized to access Helios – the cloud that stores our energy. If it wasn't one of us, somebody with H2H stole our access code. The hit came from an H2H server."

"Jonah, we respect you and your reputation," Steinman said.

"We expected more," Martin said.

"I'll find out who is responsible."

"That would be advisable."

Jonah paused on the street before entering a coffee shop. He logged into a H2H program, using Steinman's username and passcode. He made one last transaction, like the one Steinman made himself earlier that day.

He redialed the call he received earlier.

"David, hello!" His voice was cheerier than it should have been. "What can I do for you?"

"It's JW," David said.

"Oh, no! Did he...?"

"No, Jonah. He's still being a pain in the ass. But Trish is looking into having him institutionalized. It's gotten really bad really fast."

"I'm sorry to hear that," Jonah said. "Hey, listen, I have a lot going on. Is that the reason you called? Well, I can't help. Sorry. I just can't."

Nothing could have made David feel emptier. For all his divine knowledge, he couldn't see a solution for JW, a means to reunite with his family, a way to win back Alison or a way to bring down Heaven Ride. When JW was whole, David could trust in his brilliance and his heart. Now, that trust was compromised.

David sought counsel from Vincente. They talked about the keys they had collected. For all David's efforts, the keys were just a random set of ideas and words that had no connection, so far as they could see.

"Two keys are left. One of the remaining keys is Steinman, Vince," David said. "I think I can tap into that with some effort."

"How do you do that?" Vince asked.

"It's a concentration thing. Just like there is a wavelength for traveling to heaven, there is a separate one for cracking into somebody's mind," David explained. "I'm almost ashamed to say I use it all the time. JW calls it my Jedi mind trick."

"Are you going to crack the code on Steinman?" Vincente asked.

"To be honest, I haven't been successful yet. He has ways of blocking me. I know he was tapping into my head for some time, but I think I've locked him out."

"So you're not even going to try?"

"You're right. What have I got to lose? Other than getting another irritating call from him."

David went downstairs to his room for privacy. He could not find an open door into Steinman's psyche for awhile. Finally, be broke through, but found very little cognitive thought. He risked outing himself by planting some questions in Steinman's head. "What is happening to the energy harvested by Heaven Ride?"

"Go back to the beginning," Steinman said.

"Too vague," David said. "What beginning? To heaven, the beginning of the trip back?"

"You sound different," Steinman said, now confused. "I'm very tired. No, before that. The beginning of Heaven Ride. To the lab at the space center in Rostov-on-Don. There is a top-secret file labeled Gold Star Hero. Go back to the beginning. Were you there?"

David cut off the communication. He realized that he intruded upon Steinman while he was asleep.

David immediately sought Vincente.

"I need to go to Rostov-on-Don, to the Russian Academy of Rocket Sciences. Supposedly something there will lead us on." He was reminded of a quote he loved, by author C.S. Lewis: "You can't go back and change the beginning, but you can start where you are and change the ending."

"Wait a minute," Vincente said. "You can't go there. It's suicide. Rostov-on-Don is the most crime-ridden place in Russia. Small time crooks, extortionists and racketeers. Thieves and murderers. Rostov-on-Don has a reputation for lawlessness that makes our wild west look like the merry old Land of Oz"

"I have to do this," David asserted.

"Fine. Then I'm going with you. I know a guy who knows a guy. He'll get us in where we need to go."

JW entered the room. Vincente turned his attention to his son.

"David was just going to look up some baseball statistics. To settle a bet," Vincente said. "I may be old, but I still remember those old ballplayers," Vincente said. David left them alone, and they had a long talk. JW opened up about Tommy and Trish – and Marty Martin. Vincente pointed out how unfair it was for JW to judge Trish on past events.

"It would be like the world judging you on your 7th-grade science fair project."

"That was the only one I didn't win."

"Right. I know that. You know that. But the world might cast a critical eye, if winning and losing were all that mattered." JW nodded in agreement. Vincente continued.

"I know you forgive me about what happened to Petey all those years ago, and thank God, your mother does, too. Petey does, for God's sake. Your love for me tells me that you don't judge me for what happened in the past. We can't change that. You need to think this way about Trish and Tommy."

"I just can't imagine sitting across the table from Martin at Thanksgiving just because he's Tommy's dad," JW said. "He's an evil man, you know.

"I was just getting over the fact this whole Heaven Ride thing was a set-up, a façade, and could I trust that Trish and Tommy weren't actors on a reality TV show. Now I learn the man I despise and is trying to kill me, and my worst enemy is the father of my girlfriend's son, and I love both so dearly. That fact is real and will never change for as long as I live. This is just crap, and I'm not sure I can handle it."

"Maybe it's not for us to judge. You have people who love you and will help you through this," Vincente said. "Son, you've probably got things in your past that Trish has overlooked."

JW's thoughts turned to the lab experiments, where he accelerated the deaths of many patients under the auspices of scientific research. Trish never knew about them. She could never know. She would probably never forgive him. He snapped his head to one side, trying to shake the images of the dying men and women. He was haunted by the vision of Paul Harrell, the hospital orderly, who witnessed his most daring experiments. If Trish knew, she would have left him long ago. These phantasms of the past played in his head while his father's voice went on.

"Look at it this way. Martin has provided safe haven to you and Trish and Tommy, and David, and now for me. We have this sanctuary, that you earned, but that Martin has helped protect. Look, JW, even if we are bad people or do evil deeds, there are things we do for the love of our sons. And their mothers. I know that you love Tommy a great deal. I see that. Don't stop loving Trish for something that happened in the past. From what I can see, she's an amazing woman who loves you a lot, and I would be proud to have her as a daughter."

"You mean? You think I should marry Trish?" JW let that

thought sink in for a moment. "I just asked her and Tommy to leave."

"I know. And Trish is very hurt by that. It's not just because she felt rejected. She's thinking about what might happen to you if you don't have Martin's sanctuary. Son, you've got to think this through."

JW pulled his knees up to his chest and rocked in silence.

Early the next morning, David received a phone call on his burner phone. It was Steinman.

"Davy boy, I'm ashamed of you," Steinman said.

"Okay, I'll play. For what?"

"You took something from me. You took advantage while I was asleep."

"Asleep?" David processed the information. In the conversation lapse, he heard background noises and voices. It sounded like Steinman was in an airport. "So, you're so old that you're taking afternoon naps?"

Steinman was taken aback by the jibe. David was now in his head, and Steinman was flustered. As always, he responded with cruelty.

"Sometimes I do. Unlike you, I don't have a little friend going off the deep end. But listen up, sweetheart. You crossed a line. You're now a problem. I don't have a reason to keep you around anymore."

David decided to play a hunch that Steinman was unaware of what he told him.

"Tommy baby, you got nothing on me. On the other hand, seems like I've got some real dirt on you."

"There is no dirt you could possibly have that would hurt me." David could feel Steinman trying to enter his subconscious, and he repelled the effort. David let a pillow of silence cushion the suspense. In it, he heard background voices. They were speaking Russian.

"David? You have nothing to say?" David played up the power of silence. Steinman continued, "Okay, just understand that I know your little game, and it's over. Before you finish your little quest, I'm going to squelch your sources. And Davy boy, you should begin saying your final goodbyes."

"Is that all you got, Tommy baby? I think we're done for now."

For good measure, he said *"Proshchay,"* which is Russian for "goodbye."

In the middle of the St. Petersburg, Russia, airport, Steinman just stared at his phone.

* * *

After ending the call, David sought Vincente.

"How would you like to be a bodyguard on foreign soil?"

"I told you that it was a good idea to provide protection for you."

"Not for me. Steinman is in Russia. I think he may try to take out Aliona. She may be critical to our success."

JW poked his head into the room. "I thought I heard you guys. What's going on?"

"We're going to the Ukraine," David said. "We'll just be there a few days, to meet with Aliona." Both JW and Vincente cast looks of curiosity at David.

"Remember?" David queried. "I told you guys about Aliona."

They both shrugged with no recollection.

"What will I need to pack?" JW asked.

"We're tackling this one on our own, kimosabe," David said.

"It's better if you stay behind, JW," Vincente said. "Your condition – you're not in any condition to be involved with this."

JW displayed his disappointment. Deep down, he knew his father was right.

"At least tell me what you're doing there," he said.

David started to share, but Vincente shut down the inquiry. "Need to know basis, JW. We'll tell you if we have anything that concerns you directly."

JW started to anger, but this time, he quelled those emotions.

Vincente recognized JW's internal struggle and offered a solution.

"Why don't you spend some time with your mother? And maybe your grandmother. You can take a day trip. Your mom always loved Steamboat Springs. I was checking the other day – not that I was going to ask Jayne out on a date – but they've got a Western Art Festival that they do every year, and if you get bored, there's a

Warren Miller Film Festival with some of the greatest ski movies ever."

"You were going to ask mom out on a date?" JW asked, ribbing his father, but also expressing gleeful surprise.

"After seeing your mother for the first time in more than 20 years, it reminded me why I loved her in the first place and never stopped. She has a healing heart and mind. I think you should go somewhere, or at least take her up on her offer to stay with her for a while. You'll have plenty of security to protect you. What do you think?" Vincente asked.

"I've been thinking about mom a lot, and seeing you together hugging and talking made me feel happy. Secure," JW said. I think you're right. I haven't been to the house in a while, and I might try my hand a grandma's chili recipe."

The next day, Jayne arrived to surprise JW. It turned out to be a grand reunion with him and Vincente. All three were buoyed by the visit.

Vincente and Jayne spent some time together, but after chatting with Trish, Jayne devoted most of her attention to JW.

Over the next few days, Vincente taught David many ways to be inconspicuous. At David's request, Vincente taught him some self-defense techniques of the Navy SEALs and special forces. David was in great shape and the learning came easy.

To avoid suspicion from casual observers, Vincente arrived at the Salt Lake City airport on the shuttle twenty minutes before David. David wore a knit ski hat with no logo, and a very authentic long beard. David sat midway through the plane, and Vincente took an aisle seat far in the rear. It was sixteen and a half hours in the air, after a brief stopover in Atlanta with another plane change in Istanbul.

David never flew on Turkish Airlines before. The attendant at the desk got into a shouting match with a customer in line ahead of them. David was able to translate the beef as a dispute over meal choices. Vincente, pretending to have met David for the first time, leaned over and told him to speak sparingly, and just nod when possible. Other than the boarding desk altercation, the flight was uneventful. Almost. After more than two-thirds of a day, it was wheels down in Odessa. The pilot warned passengers of the upcoming violent tumult before setting the jet down on the craterous runway.

Once they landed in the Ukraine, David could see a different set of behaviors for a professional spy. Vincente was Special Ops for the Air Force, dating back to the first Iraq war, when JW was an infant. Then, he traded his rifle for a desk job, becoming a special assignment ops commander. With age, he developed into a top-notch covert ops guy. A spy. He retired from the military, but was sometimes brought in as a mercenary, whether for a military mission or for corporate protective services. Just as JW and David felt obliged to put an end to Heaven Ride, Vincente experienced guilt for ever bringing it back to the United States, although at the time he didn't realize that was what he had done. Returning to Russia, or even to the Ukraine, posed some difficulty because he was a wanted man by those around long enough to remember.

Vincente expected to buy a new burner phone that would have a Ukrainian number. No such luck. The tiny airport was devoid of any amenities, save for a small duty-free shop that seemed to specialize in candy and vodka. He and David made do with the phones they registered back in the states.

Vincente made a call while David located the taxi stand. Vincente caught up.

"Never mind that. Duke is coming." David thought he misheard, but they walked a few thousand yards away from the airport to a fenced-in field across the street from the airport runways. Wind whipped across the open parcel of land.

"Are we stranded in a foreign country?" David moaned. "I feel like we are stranded. And who the hell is Duke?"

"Duke is Duke, and no need to know more," Vincente said. Vincente said nothing for the next fifteen minutes until their ride arrived.

Duke arrived and vowed to stay within an arm's length for the duration of the stay. Before letting them get into the car, Duke opened the trunk to reveal a cache of arms and artillery, with just enough room for their two bags.

"The usual?" he asked Vincente.

"Yeah," said the senior mentor. Duke handed Vincente a pistol, and a smaller handgun that Vincente concealed in his sock. Duke spoke to him in Russian, gesturing to David.

"You ever fire a gun?" Vincente asked David.

David swallowed, feeling unmanly. "No."

Vincente pointed to a pistol, like his own. "Duke, give him that one." To David, he warned him, "Don't let the girl get this, okay?" He bristled at Vincente's distrust of a woman he never met but said nothing.

Duke extracted a small jewelry box from his coat pocket and revealed a pin that was just a laurel wreath encircling a platinum disk. He pinned it to the collar of Vincente's jacket.

"GPS," Duke said. "I'll be able to track you. Try to stay together."

David could see that Vincente forged a strong relationship with his Russian ally, who seemed loyal to the core. Duke was a burly man with a chubby face and a fat mustache. He wore a Hawaiian print shirt under a leather coat. His hair was cut short giving the appearance of a very square head perched on a thick neck. His overall thickness was the result of years in the gym that had given way to bad dietary decisions. He opened the doors for his guests to get in. The interior of his car was equipped with two law enforcement-style radios and mount for his iPad.

From memory, David directed Duke to Plensky's Dine, and an evening rendezvous with Aliona. Duke dropped them at the end of the block.

"This is the old world," Vincente commented.

"If you like Eastern European food, this is the place," David replied, opening the heavy wooden door.

Vincente cased the joint like he was a cat-burglar, noting the low ceilings. He was particularly interested in the exits – just the main front door, and from David's story, the one that led out of the kitchen to an alley on the side. As before, a front table was occupied by six men, construction workers it seemed. Vincente nodded to the man at the end of the table who watched them enter. Without losing eye contact, he used his acute peripheral vision to take in every aspect of the man. He was intrigued by his socks, which were not socks at all. *Portiyanki*. Military issue linen that soldiers twirled around their feet, much like wrapping a burrito. They were replaced in 2013 by regular socks. These men were not construction workers at all, but old-guard Russian soldiers.

Aliona greeted them at this door. This time, she wore a tight red sweater that accentuated her curves, a skirt that came down to her mid-calf, and some ankle-high boots that seemed less appropriate for a restaurant job than a night out on the town at fashionable places. Aliona's hair was pulled back and had been woven into cornrows. She shook Vincente's hand firmly, then pulled her body against David's for a hug. Her scent brought back memories of their first meeting. She kissed him several times on the cheeks.

"I knew you'd come back," she whispered in David's ear.

He took note of the clientele. The tables near the front were more occupied than before, with two couples, a few tables with women, and the long table occupied just like before with men, speaking loudly over one another. The men at the table enviously watched her lavish attention on the American. She looked back at them, saying, "Friend of my brother."

Aliona acknowledged Vincente. "You're the papa?"

"JW's father," David corrected.

"Sit," she commanded. "Sit over there in corner. More private for us to talk. I'll be back, one minute. Let me bring you something to eat."

"We're not hungry," Vincente said. "We had something at the airport, although it wasn't very good."

David glared at him because he was very hungry.

"Maybe you change your mind later," she said, her eyes looking squarely into David's. She retreated to the kitchen to prepare the check for the other group.

"I don't trust this situation," Vincente told him. "I don't trust her after you told me about her expertise with poison."

"I trust her, Vince."

They took a seat at the back-corner table, while Aliona delivered the bill and cleared plates from the construction table.

"I don't like this situation, David," Vincente repeated, taking a seat where he could survey the entire room. "This is not what it seems to be."

This mission had no immediate objective. He trusted in David's intuition that the woman, Aliona, would turn up the linkage to the keys David collected and the final resolution. David forewarned him that she was brilliant and beautiful. This had no bearing on Vincente's role, so he took it as a confession from his young, seduced friend. But it gave him ammunition to chide David.

"You mean, I'll be standing watch while you get your rocks off?"

"Nothing's going to happen," David said, watching Aliona interact with other men. "Well, almost nothing. Yeah, okay, I might want a little privacy."

Aliona joined them and sat next to David. He laid out the situation, telling her that they had intelligence leading them back to the Russian Academy of Rocket Sciences. Vincente listened studying Aliona's facial expressions and body language while keeping an eye on the Russian soldiers. They lingered even though they had finished, and their bill was apparently paid. The longer they stayed, the more uneasy he felt. He tried to stop David from revealing his hard-earned Heaven Ride keys, but David sought Aliona's opinions.

Her phone rang, a popular Ukrainian song flowing from a pocket in her skirt.

"*Dobryj den*," she answered. In Ukrainian, she told the caller, "You call at a bad time. I have guests."

She excused herself from the table and took the call back in the kitchen.

The oldest of the soldiers rose from the table, and the others stood up. He walked toward the corner table and addressed Vincente.

"I think I know you," he said. "You are the painter, right?"

Vincente's memory took him back more than 12 years to the day when he and Sanders pulled off their heist of the Heaven Ride technology and the Infinity Reader. His right hand drifted down to the butt of the pistol near his belt.

In perfect Russian, he replied, "Fuck off! I am not a painter and I don't know you."

The soldier squinted, checking Vincente's face for signs of fear.

"Sorry. I thought you were someone else." He turned away.

The soldiers in their construction worker disguises paid their bill and left.

The coincidence of being recognized by a customer at Aliona's restaurant in Odessa worried Vincente further. When they were out the door, the elder special ops commander told his young companion, "Let's go to the hotel."

"Hotel?" David said, puzzled. "We can stay with Aliona."

"No." Vincente said. "Trish booked a hotel. Send her telepathic flowers or something, but we are leaving. And be ready to pull that pistol when we get outside."

Aliona emerged from the kitchen with a paper bag.

"Leaving so soon? We barely finish our talk."

"Yeah," David said. "Something came up."

"I thought you were staying with me," she said, pouting.

"I thought so, too. Vince made different arrangements." "I know you may be hungry later. I made you dog bag. For you to share with Vince."

"No, that's okay," Vincente said. "Very nice of you, but – "

She handed David the bag, and he smiled. "My specialty," she told him.

He pulled her closer and kissed her on the lips. "No, that's your specialty," David said.

Vincente was already at the door.

"Come on, David. Let's go."

Cautiously, he slid out the door, looking in every direction for soldiers. He used his cell phone to call Duke.

"Are you nearby? Pick us up where you dropped us off."

He walked briskly down the street. Evening had fallen quickly. The shops were mostly closed, and homeless men and women began taking residence in the doorways. Vincente quickly grabbed the bag out of David's hand and tossed it toward an old, bearded man huddled in one of the doorways.

"What the hell?" David said. "That was our dinner, Vince."

Vincente said nothing, but continued walking at a fast pace. They walked two blocks to the main avenue and heard a ruckus behind them. A car screeched to a halt near the doorway, and police pulled the old man to the street and beat him with night sticks and bare fists.

Duke's car pulled to a stop, and they got in. David looked back at the glare of the police headlights trying to make sense of what happened.

Chapter 17:   The Diabolical Deception

Steinman arrived at a Moscow restaurant, Cafe Pushkin, where bankers and businessmen, shysters and thieves, cajoled and connived for no honorable cause. Known as "the library restaurant," some of the walls were floor-to-ceiling bookshelves. Gilded staircases whisked one back through two centuries, while Gustav Mahler's Symphony No. 6 emboldened one's senses to commit acts of war, or peace, or deeds that lived in one's soul.

That's where Steinman met Alexei Polzin, who described himself as an investment banker. Polzin was tall, about 6-foot-4, and lanky. He wore an expertly crafted wool suit and a striped silk tie. He spoke impeccable English.

"I must say, Mr. Polzin, that is quite a fine suit," Steinman commented. He would know, as he was a fan of expertly tailored clothing. "Russian-made?"

"No, Italian," Polzin said. "Thank you. In my line of work, people judge 'how nice' by what they see, and 'how wise' is implied. But I'm surprised a man of such fashion integrity didn't comment on my shoes. They're New & Lingwoods I picked up last time I was in London. This style Russian Calf closed the sale for me."

Steinman was slightly impressed, but he was wearing a $2,000 pair of Stefano Bemer shoes, made by the former Gucci footwear designer. After a small amount of small talk, Steinman told Polzin that he had large sums of money to transfer, and wanted a tax haven that would not be trackable in the U.S.

"I do that all the time," Polzin said. "We create a shell account in Cyprus, and the money is dispersed through several accounts here in Russia through Alfa Bank. They are virtually impossible to track without your personal security."

"It sounds easy. How do I know this is true, and the money is there when I need it?"

"Mr. Steinman, I work with billionaires around the world," Polzin said. "My clients are many of the wealthiest men in Moscow, where we have more billionaires per capita than anywhere in the world. If you like, I'll take you on a tour of Ostozhenka, the street of rich men, and you can ask them directly whether I am a man of my word."

Steinman gazed into the eyes of the young man for a few seconds, and determined he was telling the truth. "I believe you," he said. "But I wonder if you might be too honest for the job at hand."

Polzin grew thoughtful before answering. "Honesty is just a thin veneer of a man, Thomas. As for money, money is the great lie. Actual money is worthless pieces of fabric woven together or scraps of metal dug from the ground. But it represents something of value. Whatever it is used for becomes part of that great lie. Lies of grandeur, lies of intellect and the greatest lie, the lie of power. Power that is bought vanishes the instant the wealthy man dies."

"But it's wonderful while it lasts," Steinman said. "Those are wise philosophical thoughts, Mr. Polzin. Worthy of that fine suit. But I will prove you wrong. My wealth will endure, and the power it creates will change the world. And while I sit here with you today, the world will never see me as a man of power. I assure you that when I die, the power will transcend my being and any other force that mankind has known."

Polzin absorbed Steinman's words, and while they were delivered with a sinister tone, the investment banker wanted to create the infrastructure that his client was seeking.

"Now, what we need to do is create a seamless transfer of funds from 23 different sources to our invisible account. Simultaneously, to the last micro-second. Poof! It disappears, like some magician's act."

There in the Cafe Pushkin, amid gilded statues, cloth-bound first editions of classic Russian literature, and museum-grade, authentic

musical instruments that created enduring symphonies and concertos
in this former church, Steinman and his Russian banker plotted the
greatest deception since Satan slithered down the branch of a tree.

* * *

Steinman rode the Sapsan bullet train to St. Petersburg, enduring
more than three hours. Sapsan, Russian for the peregrine falcon, flew
smoothly across the tracks at 155 mph. Business class seats were
four abreast with an aisle in the middle, much like airline seating
with wider, more comfortable chairs. Steinman ordered a Pilsner
Urquell, and some food. The galley was out of his first two choices,
limiting him to either hot or cold fish. He chose the cold, and it came
with a small loaf of bread wrapped in plastic. Aside from the food
service, the efficiency of the train made him envision a Heaven Ride
center in St. Petersburg. In fact, when he closed his eyes, it reminded
him of his Heaven Ride journey so many years ago.

At the St. Petersburg station, he stood beneath a gaudy red and
yellow military crest and was approached by an English-speaking
chauffeur.

He was driven a fair distance from the station to a wealthy
residential area. A circular driveway brought them to the front door
of one of the most impressive mansions on the street, although
Steinman thought it a bit inferior to the house he once inhabited in
San Francisco's Presidio neighborhood.

Steinman was escorted into a parlor, where he was greeted by
his new business associate, Nicholas Ulyanov.

They talked for more than an hour about bringing Heaven Ride
to Russia. Ulyanov laid out his plans to offer Heaven Ride in five
cities, meeting with rabid encouragement from Steinman.

"And my fee for delivering this technology to you?" Steinman
asked. "It is as we discussed?"

"Yes," Nicholas said. "One billion American dollars for you to
share with the other parties involved."

"Oh, there will be no other parties," Steinman said. "Maybe we
can become neighbors. Do you know any good real estate people?"

"My good man," Ulyanov said, "I know everybody in Russia."

"Really?" Steinman responded, his interest piqued. "Perhaps

you can help with one nagging detail."

When they finished the meeting, Steinman promised to have contracts sent the next day. The chauffer dropped him off at the hotel. In his haste, Steinman almost forgot to tip him. He doubled back and gave $100 US to the man. "And if anyone should ever ask, you don't know who I am and have never seen me."

From the hotel, Steinman called the number that Ulyanov gave him. It was printed neatly on card stock below the name "Miss X."

"Hello, Miss X?' Steinman started.

The answer took a moment to come. "You call at a bad time. I have guests."

"I am Thomas Steinman..." There was a pause on the other end, and background noise subsided.

"I know who you are. What is it I can do?"

"I don't necessarily want to do this over the phone. Can we meet someplace?"

"Meeting costs extra. We do business over phone."

"I don't care about the extra cost. This is a highly sensitive matter."

"No meeting. I have integrity to protect."

"But, really, I would prefer to discuss this in person."

"No meeting. What is it I can do?"

"This is weird, saying this," Steinman said. "I mean to a stranger on the phone." He hoped for a reply but got none. "I was told you can help me with a certain problem."

"You need somebody to no longer be a problem?"

"Yes, exactly. Is that what you do?"

"Among other things. Here's how it works. You give me information, you forget your problem, and in short time, problem is gone. Of course, it is service we charge for. "

"Yes, of course."

The feminine voice, Miss X, gave him instructions for providing information and a down payment. Miss X told him she could begin the process right away, which delighted Steinman. The effort was begun. *Amazing what lots of money can do*, Steinman thought. *I don't even have to leave my chair, and I can have this major pain in the ass taken out. If I didn't strike first, it would be my ashes scattered in the sea.*

Steinman's phone rang. It was the police in Westchester County.
"Mr. Steinman, are you all right?"
"Of course. I answered the phone."
"Yes sir. That's a good thing. An explosion just destroyed your
house. Was somebody staying there in your absence? We recovered
a body."
"That was my house boy, Jean-Paul. How terrible." Steinman did not
feel obligated to provide details of how he provided Jean-Paul,
Steinman's flavor-of-the-week, his robe and some clothing, and
assigned chores that might resemble things that Steinman might do
himself. He hoped that his paid killers would be more effective than
those who destroyed his house without him in it. He hoped they
would be quick because once their failure was discovered, the hired
guns that set out to kill him would try again.

                          *   *   *

Ignoring Vincente's advice, David invited Aliona to meet them
for breakfast the next morning.
Vincente also warned David against sharing the keys with
Aliona, but David did so anyway. She provided insight and a distinct
course of action they should take to shut down Heaven Ride.
The following day, Duke arrived to escort Vincente and David
across the border into Russia, to Rostov-on-Don, and the Russian
Academy of Rocket Forces. Aliona lobbied to crash the military
installation with them, but Vincente outright refused. The stalemate
was settled with the boys taking the guns and deceptively fast car,
leaving Aliona behind.
Through Aliona's insight, David decided that the clues led them
to learn more about the Russian professor, Dr. Dmitri Gogol, and the
other Russian riders who suffered and died in the process.
At the immense white stone building, Duke helped them break
in using false badges. They were Americans on a technology
exchange, and Duke assumed the role of a Russian scientist.
"I forgot my key card," he told the security officer. "Can one of
you let us in?"
A young security detail intern brought them up to the 7th floor,
Room 714-B, where the academic labs were located. Aliona was

already inside the room. She had her hair braided tightly, and now brunette, giving her a very different look. She wore glasses and a white lab coat with the nametag of a woman who was now drugged and locked in the trunk of her own car. David recognized Aliona immediately by the diamond aura.

Vincente was focused on his recollection of the RARF, and he silently lamented that this room was next door to the one he broke into 11 years before. It suddenly dawned on him that the brunette was Aliona.

"I wonder, what is in the next room over?" he asked the intern who escorted them.

"That's not on the tour today."

"Oh, come on," Gomez said. "We came all this way. I'm just curious if all the research labs are like this one."

David looked the intern straight in the eye. "You want to show the world how advanced science is here at the RARF, right?"

"Yes. We want the world to see how advanced our science is."

He took them to Room 714-A. In the corridor, Vincente recognized Aliona. "Get the hell out of here," he spouted under his breath. "You're going to mess things up!"

"No," she said resolutely. "I am here to help." Vincente tried to grab her, but she pulled her arm away. "Don't touch. First warning," she said. Vincente took heed of the warning, although he deduced that she somehow realized that he had been trained for deadly combat. He sensed a small dose of fear in her reaction, as though she was sizing up his capabilities in case they needed to use them for fight or flight.

For Vincente, the room brought back a memory of his previous trip, even though equipment had moved out and rows of file cabinets were added. Dmitry Gogol no longer had his office here.

"This is it!" David said. "Right over here." He went to a computer and without hesitation, logged in and using the Russian Cyrillic alphabet, found the files for the X-energy program. Aliona went to another computer, logged in and located files for herself and one of the other less fortunate riders. Then, she accessed the administration identity and pulled Dr. Gogol's files.

David saved files to a flash drive, then flipped it over to Aliona to do the same.

The intern returned with several security personnel. Vincente and Duke were ready for them and subdued them with doses of long-lasting sedatives. The intern ran toward the door, but Aliona got there before him.

"Where are you going so fast?" she asked him. He tried to move around her, but she matched him, while unbuttoning her lab coat. "Take a look at this," she told him in Russian, and he stopped, mesmerized by her toned physique. Vincente came from behind and plunged a small pin-sized needle attached to a minuscule vial into his neck. He struggled against the serum, but then fell helplessly to the floor.

"Got what you need, David?"

"Yes. Aliona, give me the flash drive."

"Oh, right." She pulled it from her lab coat pocket, looked at it, then tossed it to David.

They took the elevator down to the lobby. Two armed security men approached them.

"There is no diplomatic tour today," One said.

"Nope," David agreed. "You're right, it's tomorrow. My bad."

The other guard drew his pistol, but did not shoot as the group of three, plus Aliona, left the building.

David felt for the flash drive in his front pocket, knowing this would be their last chance.

In the parking lot, Aliona removed her lab coat and tossed it to the ground. Beneath, she wore yoga pants and a tight pink satin workout shirt. The three men looked at each other as she climbed in the back seat. Vincente nudged the Duke. "I can't believe the Cold War lasted so long. How did Russian men ever get anything done?"

Vincente got in back with her and watched her apply lip gloss. She acknowledged his distrust. "Remember. No touch."

Smiling beneath his signature sunglasses, Duke drove them to the airport. He and Aliona accompanied them into the ticketing area. While Duke shook hands with Vincente, David said goodbye to Aliona. She kissed him, pulling his hips close to hers.

"I miss you already," she said, her hand lingering near his crotch. "Maybe I come to America for visit."

"Maybe," David said. "I have a lot of work to do, but maybe after that."

She pulled back, gazing into his eyes. "I know you don't mean that. You love Holly. But what we had, it was very nice." Moistness filled the corner of her eyes.

"I do love Holly," he said. "But that situation may be impossible. Our situation, you and me, might be impossible, too. It would be nice to see you again when Heaven Ride is destroyed."

Vincente motioned for David to come along, and he kissed Aliona on the forehead before continuing through the small airport.

Vincente and David boarded the plane, speaking sparingly. David reminisced about the time he first realized he loved Holly, when she greeted him at the airport, then cooked him a meal with all his favorite things. Now, he was even able to accept that her name was Alison, and at least for now, they could not be together. Vincente tried to sleep. Somewhere over the Atlantic, on that Turkish Airline, David pulled out the flash drive, inspecting it closely. It was a replica. Aliona!

He replayed the scenario when they kissed goodbye. She put her hands on his hips. Could she have pickpocketed the original? His memory went back to the lab office. She pulled a flash drive out of her pocket and looked at it before tossing it to David. That was where she made the switch!

The last half of the flight was miserable. David felt ignorant for being seduced and betrayed. It seemed to be a recurring pattern. But I have the gift he thought. The gift is my protection from this type of two-bit swindle. He woke Vincente and told him of the theft. He expected a lecture, but Vincente offered none. What was done, was done.

Once on the ground, Vincente called Duke. He told David that Duke would take care of Aliona and retrieve the flash drive. The phone rang. Four rings... five... six. Aliona answered.

"I'm sorry. Your friend had terrible accident. And he lost all his guns."

"Listen here," Vincente raged.

"Put Davit on," she said. "Now!"

Vincente handed the phone to David, whispering, "She killed Duke."

David's stomach turned when he heard her voice.

"Davit, I am sad to say, you were outbid for final piece of

puzzle. Capitalism is so grand!" He started to respond, but she continued. "Wait! Someone wants a word with you."

David heard a discussion with a male voice.

"Davy boy!"

Thomas Steinman's voice sent chills down his spine. "I want to congratulate you on your excellent legwork for the Heaven Ride grand finale. But that won't be happening anytime soon. You see, the lovely Miss Aliona is clever beyond belief! The good news is that she may be on her way to the U.S. to pay you a visit."

"Steinman, you –" David screamed.

"Oh, I'm sorry, David. We were just in the middle of celebrating our victory. And you know how naughty your Russian girl can be."

David shut down the call and handed the phone back to Vincente.

"I need to be alone."

"You've got to stop pouting and – "

"I'm not pouting. I just need a goddamn room and peace and quiet."

Chapter 18: Hard-Pressed for Answers

In the days that followed, the internet news show "Livestream" ran a segment titled "Heaven Meets Hell." In it, reporter Abby Romand documented case after case of violent crimes where perpetrators suffered from Post Heaven Ride Syndrome.

Romand identified more than 400 horrific murders that were related to Heaven Riders. They included 26 workplace homicides where a worker turned on bosses or colleagues. In New York City, Matt Bradley used a nail gun on an 8th-story scaffold to kill one worker, and a second fell to his death. The most widely publicized one took place at a Modesto, Calif. petroleum company where a woman entered a conference room for a meeting and opened fire on eight executives, then turned the gun on herself.

Romand revealed that a very high-profile tragedy was recently found to be caused by a severely affected man who brought an axe to the Thanksgiving table, and killed 15 relatives with five children among the dead. The Thanksgiving Axe Murder made national news and headlines, but it was only within the past few days that killer Malcolm Patrick Barksdale was being treated by a VA psychiatrist for his Heaven Ride torment. Barksdale was awaiting a hearing to determine whether he was mentally fit to stand trial. ABC showed the crayon drawings he made, which looked similar in style to those in Bridget Moynihan's portfolio.

Romand wrapped up her report questioning whether Heaven Ride introduced some participants to hell, given the nationwide violence.

Not all perpetrators were successful. A cable crime network identified more than a dozen criminals who were foiled in their attempts to enact large-scale violence.

The Wall Street Journal reported a congressional movement to ban Heaven Ride centers, but that was quickly thwarted. A bill introduced in the Senate was killed immediately, with Sen. Bob Sanders of California making headlines with his rebuke.

"Each of those killers also drove a car in the weeks leading up to the event. Does that mean that we need to outlaw automobiles? It's absurd to legislate against a product that is not proven to be directly related to the violent event." The legislation was withdrawn because of a lack of support.

In Massachusetts, a new coven of witches credited Heaven Ride with supplying them with ideas for desecration of churches and synagogues near Boston.

But for every act of violence and destruction, supporters dialed up stories of invention and goodwill that appeared to have been heaven-inspired.

From the lower level of a frat house in New Haven, Connecticut, a white paper was disseminated to major opinion leaders, editors, media executives, and politicians on the local, state and national levels. In it, proof was offered that Heaven Ride was the catalyst for more income generation and charitable deeds than any single product, business or event in history. The statistics in the white paper were widely quoted in nearly every discussion of Heaven Ride merit or atrocity.

Chapter 19: Flashing Back

The phone rang in an office at the San Francisco Veterans Administration Medical Center.

"This is Dr. Sneed. Oh, yes, hi Jonah."

"I was just calling to check on our patients. Phelps, Herman, English, Root and Warneke."

"I have some bad news for you, Jonah. Woody English passed away. I think it was on Tuesday. The other four are still the same. You know, they have their ups and downs."

"Tell me, Emily," Jonah requested, "what happened to Corporal English?"

"He became very agitated. His blood pressure elevated. I should say, it rose higher than usual. All of them have very high BP. We restrained him with some difficulty. He struggled, then just succumbed."

"What was the cause of death?" Jonah asked.

"Ruptured brain aneurysm," Dr. Sneed told him. "Just like Malone a few years back."

"Is Warneke doing any better?" Jonah asked.

"No, he's consistently unstable." Dr. Sneed paused. "We have him in restraints around the clock. He has severe hallucinations. He stopped eating dinner. He only takes one meal a day now."

"Have any of them had visitors? I'm curious about Root. His

condition seemed to brighten when his daughter visited."

"No, no visitors for any of them."

"I'll send flowers to English's family," Jonah said. "We're down to four out of the original six."

"I'm so sorry, Jonah. I admire you for checking on them every few weeks."

"Yeah, well, thanks, Emily. Even though they all volunteered and signed waivers, I still feel responsible."

"Don't feel too bad, Jonah. It was ten years ago, or more. You've done as much as you can."

Jonah terminated the call, feeling a knot in his stomach.

A voice in his head told him, "You have NOT done everything you can. There is more."

The six servicemen volunteered for Operation Special K. They were the first ones Jonah tested with the energy-stripping code during Heaven Ride. Two others took Heaven Ride before them and survived with the surplus energy. The intensity of energy stripping diminished with each test as Jonah witnessed mental health defects in the subjects. The Heaven Ride tests were halted so that Johansson could test what became known as the robber virus.

Before Jonah's tests were completed, Steinman already presented several scenarios to the Department of Defense, the Department of Homeland Security and the Central Intelligence Agency, receiving their endorsements and support to implement a plan to store and use the energy. Jonah witnessed the traumatic effects of the Heaven Ride procedure, but found himself in a situation that compromised his integrity, His boss, and now his country, pushed him to move forward with this procedure to denude victims of their soul and a cosmic energy that, to his understanding, was essential to life.

Chapter 20: Change of Heart

Upon arrival at the new Salt Lake City terminal, David called Trish.

"Hey, we survived the Odessa airport and two transfers, and we're back. Can you come to pick us up?"

"David, I'm so glad you made it home. Did you hear that Steinman was killed yesterday?"

"He wasn't killed. That scumbag has nine lives. How soon can you get here?"

"I don't think I should," Trish said. "It's JW."

"Oh, no," David said. "What's wrong with JW?" Vincente perked up and put his head as close to David's to hear.

"He's – angry. I had to ask Hector to board up the barn. JW tried to escape. Well, he did get out, on foot, and we caught up to him on the road. He stayed outside all night in the yard, pacing. Pacing manically along the wall. I called the company for added security to watch him through the night."

"It's cold out. March is still pretty cold."

"Yes, and he's just out there in a long-sleeve T-shirt and shorts. I'm waiting for the second security agent to arrive. I've been up all night, worried sick that he might drown in the pond. I tried to talk him into coming in, but he wouldn't."

"Okay, we'll get our own way back."

Trish cried into the phone. "David, I think he's lost it for good. It's like his brain is in another world."

"Vince is here, now. He'll bring JW back to earth," David said.
Before David could hang up, Vincente said, "Let's go!"

He rented a car, and they drove quickly to the gated mountain
road that led up to Five Rings.

It was unsettling. David stood next to Trish. Vincente put his
arm around her to comfort her, while his own mind tossed and
turned like the ocean. David said a prayer. He did not know what
else he could do.

JW stomped along the length of the north wall as if on a
mission, past where the wall ended and a boulder-strewn cliff
receded down the mountain. While snow had receded in other parts
of the yard, about six inches of icy snow crunched under his feet. His
long strides made him look sub-human. In his current plight, he was.
The majority of the perimeter was a steep grade down the mountain,
and on the other side, a steep grade up.

"I'm afraid that this is the way it's going to be," Trish said. "I'm
afraid that I won't be able to trust him, never enough to be my
husband. And Tommy – I'm afraid that Tommy has lost his best
friend."

"You know, it's remarkable," David said softly, "that nearly
anyone who got to know JW thought of him as their best friend. I
mean, there's me, there's Tommy, there's Kelly, there was Karl, and
there was half of America who got to know him through TV and
magazine interviews."

Trish's voice changed, a deeper octave tinged with wickedness.

"Don't you talk about JW as if he were dead," she scowled at
David. "You, of all people!"

David felt ashamed but did not know how to address her. He
looked at Vincente, who shared her hurt.

His throat clenched, and he could muster only a whisper. "I'm
sorry."

Trish's phone rang. She walked away, fumbling to find it.

David told Vincente, "Keep an eye on her. I wouldn't put it past
Steinman to call right now."

When Trish turned, she was on the phone and her countenance
had been uplifted.

"How soon? Really? Oh, my word. No, it's not a moment too
soon. We're having a rough day today. We'll keep an eye out. I may

not be in such good condition to get there, but David or Vince will. Oh, thank you. Thank you, Jonah."

David lightened when he heard Jonah's name. "That was Jonah? Jonah Johansson?"

"Yes." Trish came over and hugged David. "He's on his way here. He said he had a change of heart."

"Alison. I bet Alison was behind it," David said.

*   *   *

Two days later, David found himself navigating his way to the airport in the Smart Camo Mercedes. He parked and entered the airport, lingering at a kiosk that was their designated meeting spot. The plane was late. David's senses were on high alert, but he was hardly the focus of any of the airport passengers and personnel. He wore a black Salt Lake City Bees T-shirt, and some eyeglasses that altered his appearance just enough to make him invisible. Or so he thought. Finally, Jonah strode through the concourse toward him.

"David? Wow! You look so athletic!" Jonah said.

David shook his hand. "And you look like a miracle worker. You look great, Jonah. Come on, and I'll get you out of here. Let me carry your bag."

"We have to wait. I brought someone with me." An involuntary smile creased David's face. His heart beat a little faster, anticipating that this might be his reunion with Alison. He carried on a conversation with Jonah that he would never remember, and Jonah pointed him toward the baggage claim check. There, luggage began to cascade onto the carousel like little children pouring out of school after the final bell. Jonah pulled a pink suitcase off the belt. That wasn't Alison's style, David thought, and it wasn't Jonah's, but it certainly was easy to pick out of the scores of bags.

After the two men stepped back from the carousel, David felt a presence. Not Alison. It was Kelly Bryant. David's jaw dropped. He concealed his disappointment the best he could, and astonishment took over. He looked inquisitively at Jonah, who seemed pleased to facilitate this reunion. JW and Trish occasionally discussed Kelly, and how they felt betrayed by her alliance with Martin and Steinman. Kelly had been part of the team, and one of the first

Heaven Riders in the new era. They laughed together, celebrated together and mourned the loss of friends together. When Alison reeled off the names of those who betrayed David and JW, he was perhaps most surprised by Kelly.

David socked those images away and greeted her with a hug.

"David Brownington! Look at you! You look like a UFC fighter. And you even have a few scars, tough guy."

"Thanks to some of your friends, perhaps," he said. He looked into her eyes, and his comment put a damper on the moment. He picked up her pink bag. "Come on. We'll talk in the car."

He decided it would be best to not let them know about the camouflage. Sadly, he couldn't trust his friend, Kelly.

In the car, Jonah perceived the tension. "Kelly has to be here," he said. "She worked with me tirelessly on the research and the algorithms for bringing JW back. All-nighters. Kelly calculated the dose and the formula for the transfer. She convinced me to help, and she did it all because she cares."

"Trish and JW aren't going to put their trust in you again."

Kelly started to argue with David, as her wrath escalated. Jonah intervened.

"You know, David, I'm insulted!" Jonah said. "I wouldn't have come if there was even a remote chance that this operation was sabotaged."

"Yeah, we didn't think she would sabotage us, either!"

"Whoa!" Kelly said.

"Then turn the car around and we'll go back," Jonah ordered.

David weighed his options. He kept driving toward Five Rings. After half a minute, he apologized. Looking at Kelly in his rear-view mirror, he warned her, "Don't expect hugs and kisses. It might be rough."

David brought Jonah inside and told Kelly to wait outside while in the garage. Joyous celebration met his arrival. He was distracted by the fact his assistant wasn't with him. Finally, David told them that Jonah brought some help along and wanted to give them a head's up. Before he could explain, Kelly entered and stood near the door. She captured JW's attention first. His face went blank, like a witness at the scene of an accident. Vincente did not know Kelly and had no reaction. Trish immediately became enraged.

"Get out of my house!" Trish said. "You don't belong here!" Trish lunged toward Kelly, but David intercepted her.

"Hold on, Trish! Kelly is here because she helped Jonah design the energy transfer."

Jonah piped up. "Trish, please calm down. Kelly wanted to regain your trust. She worked for days and nights on end, weeks – with me – to help me find the solution. Kelly? Say something."

"I want her out of my house!" Trish said.

"Wait a minute, Trish!" Kelly said, defending herself. "In case you forgot, you were in on the whole thing, too."

Trish stormed off to her bedroom.

"JW, is it okay if Kelly stays?" David asked. He looked at Kelly, and she felt him probe into her mind. After a brief pause, he continued, "She is sincerely trying to help."

JW approached Kelly, standing inches away from her face. Her jaw tensed, bracing for some unexpected reaction from a man whose cognitive controls were short-circuited. She didn't back away, not for fear, but for guilt. For trust. For love. Vincente was about to intercede, but Jonah stopped him.

He looked into her dark eyes, and the dark skin on her face. Small beads of sweat caused her cheekbones to reflect the ambient light in the room. She did not turn her gaze away from his.

"Why did you do it?" he asked, like one lover to another. "Why did you betray David, and me?" He said it like two separate questions.

"I had to," Kelly said. "I was in too far. I didn't have a choice." She turned to David briefly. "Neither did Alison." Her hands fidgeted. "They would have killed us."

"They?" JW asked.

"Martin. And Steinman. When he killed Karl, he sent a message. We were terrified to go against him. And dude, I was totally in love with your creepy ass. When Jonah came to me asking secretly if I wanted to do something to help JW, I jumped at it like a grasshopper on a hot August day in Texas. I jumped at this. For you. Steinman doesn't know I'm here. Martin doesn't know I'm here. I'm here because I need to be your friend again."

"Steinman knows you're here," David said. They did not understand, so nobody asked for an explanation.

JW showed little emotion. He checked David's response and saw him nod. JW hugged Kelly and drew her close. "Thanks for coming to help. And welcome back to our team."

Kelly hugged him tightly. "I'll try to never let you down again."

JW broke the embrace and called Trish. "Trish, come on out. We're giving our guests a tour of Five Rings."

Trish did rejoin them, JW kissed her and held her tightly. Trish's eyes were ringed with red, and residual tears glistened on her cheeks.

"They're going to make me better, babe. They're going to make me better." For comedic effect, he added, "I know you didn't think it was possible for me to be any better, but Kelly and Jonah are going to do it." He began kissing her neck until she pushed him away.

"On with the tour," JW said. "We'll skip my office, because it's a little messy."

David disagreed. "Naw, I think it's important they see it. JW has mad interior decorating skills, except he uses a baseball bat."

After the tour of the house and grounds, they ordered in dinner from Siciliano's Italian Restaurant. Vincente drove down the hill to meet the delivery man. After dinner, they discussed the Transference.

The Transference was the product of Jonah and Kelly working deep into nights for the past two weeks.

"We're delving into the unknown," Jonah said. "The process is an offshoot of Deep Brain Stimulation. We'll use electrical current to depolarize neutrons in specific parts of the brain, the amygdala, then add significant amounts of our stored energy to create a more efficient array. We don't know for sure the correct amount to transfer."

"Based on my analysis, "Kelly said, "we need 500 joules of energy added slowly to replace what JW lost, and the average loss for the Riders in the system."

"Double it," David said. "You've got to counteract the momentum of the rapidly declining loss. There is more ground that needs to be made up."

"Joules?" Trish asked. "What is the equivalent of 500 joules?"

"Five hundred joules could be compared to the energy used by a .357 Magnum to fire a single bullet," Kelly said. "Except we'll be adding it slowly in a measured trickle."

"Double it," David insisted.

"Are you crazy?" Trish shouted.

"No, David," Kelly said. "Too much will kill him. Or cause complete memory loss. As it is, we are going to have to numb parts of JW's brain over a long, slow period. Four hours. Maybe more. With every minute after that, his risk factor triples."

"Double it," JW said.

Chapter 21: Supercharged, or Super Dead

Jonah laid out the game plan. He had not yet contacted the Heaven Ride Center in Salt Lake City. They didn't know he was about to be fired, and he wasn't officially gone, yet. But he told JW and David that he needed a pod for at least seven hours and complete privacy.

"I have a pod," JW said, while David chuckled. Jonah and Kelly stared at him incredulously. "And it's at the most secluded place you could imagine."

"Complete with monks who bake bread for the big guy," David said.

Trish cast a quizzical gaze at JW. "You never told me you had a pod. I never knew where you two were going off to. The monastery. It all makes sense now, because I saw JW's donations show up on bank statements."

"They're going to shut down the monastery," JW said. "I've talked with Abbot Brennan about buying the land and turning it into a home for retired monks. That way, we can keep our office and provide a service for those guys."

"How much?" Trish asked.

"Still negotiating. We'll talk later. It's still a year off."

"I'm going to require some specialized lab supplies," Jonah said.

"Like what?" JW asked.

Jonah outlined the supplies he would need and JW directed him to Dr. Cheryl Redmond at the University.

"Don't mention me, though. She was a turncoat, but she'll work with you, Jonah," JW said. They talked further into the evening, developing and scrutinizing their plan. Kelly would oversee procurements, and they would go to the monastery the next day. Before Jonah and Kelly left to check into the hotel, Jonah spoke earnestly.

"I don't know about all this," he said. His voice trailed. "I don't know. I can't give you any guarantees."

Jonah pulled Vincente aside for a private conversation.

"You know you're one of the reasons I changed my mind about helping JW. You risked your life securing the technology from the Russians all those years back. You did it without questions. When I learned JW was your son, something I just recently found out, by the way, I could not let him be destroyed by something you helped save. For the greater good, no less," Jonah said.

"I really appreciate it and thank you for being here. I'm still perplexed how the government entangled my son in this Heaven Ride technology. Was coincidence or was it by plan?" Vincente pondered.

"Because Steinman's involved... it was by design," Jonah said. "He's..." Jonah refrained from using harsh invectives. "He's Steinman. He had some intricate selection process, and I don't think it involved the collateral damage to family and loved ones. Steinman is focused only on results, and his own best interests."

The two talked for a few minutes more then Jonah addressed the group again. Vincente's respect for Johansson was restored, and he was confident that the genius in his midst would not purposely try to harm his son.

"Listen up," Johansson told the group. "With Kelly's help, I have designed a procedure to restore energy from a secure bunker in the computing cloud. As with all science and experimentation, it should work – on paper. Given my precarious employment position, this is probably the only chance we'll have to do this. It hasn't been attempted *in vitro* and I can't forecast the outcome. Trish, JW, I have to be totally honest – this could kill you. Or, as I predict, it could work and restore you to your previous self. Kelly volunteered to assist me because she admires you so much, JW. And I'm here for the same reason. In the past year, I've been at the helm of this ship that you and David launched. You took it far beyond what we created a decade earlier. I hope that this procedure will do two things: prove that it can be done and set some parameters for other restorations in the future."

"And to give you and Trish the quality of life that you have earned," Kelly added. "I can't change what happened before, but I do have a say in what happens going forward. Jonah trusted me enough to work on this surreptitiously. I really want your trust, too. Trish, I would never do anything to hurt JW."

Trish nodded. She was still troubled.

Later that night, while JW slept, Trish and David talked about the return of Kelly.

"Why did you react so strongly?" David asked Trish.

"Because you trusted Kelly before, and she turned on both of you. Kelly was responsible for inserting this... this plague... into the code. She did this! David, she knew that Heaven Ride would pose a danger to everyone who took it. She knew this would be bad for JW and everyone else."

David tried to be a voice of reason.

"I don't know, Trish. She took Heaven Ride, too. There is more to that story. And yours. I think we will find out that Kelly has a dark secret that Steinman and Martin would have exposed if she hadn't worked with them. She is very sincere in her desire to help now."

"Well, you've been wrong in your character assessments before, David."

"You are absolutely right, Trish. And I may be wrong again. But not this time."

"I have doubts. But I'm also a realist. We're out of options."

"Yeah, I'll give you that. If Jonah is close to being booted from H2H, our time is now. I think your main concern, if I can speak freely, is that you consider Kelly a rival."

"What? How dare you!"

"Trish, be honest. There was something between JW and Kelly. It never got physical because they were both in denial. Kelly fabricated a story about a boyfriend back in Texas. JW buried himself in his work, of which Kelly was a big part. But here's the truth."

Trish grew red in the face, about to explode. "No, listen and hear me out," David continued. "JW loves you. He wants to marry you. Not Kelly. When the story is finally written, Kelly is going to be one of the two people who give JW his sanity back. You are going to be grateful for what she has done."

"Or regret that I listened to you. David, I'm afraid that Kelly is here to destroy JW once and for all. She cannot be trusted."

"Look at JW now," David said. "Two days ago, he was destroying this house, himself, and you. This is the reality. Remember that Kelly is under the supervision of Jonah. She is the hope." He let those words sink in. "Do we really have a choice?"

"That's my problem with this whole scenario. We don't know if we can trust Kelly. We don't even know if we can trust Jonah. We don't have a choice."

* * *

JW woke before Trish turned in and was up most of the night. He fell asleep just about 15 minutes before the alarm clock sounded.

"Man, I was out for most of the day, wasn't I?" he asked Trish. "I feel great!"

Trish put on her happiest of faces and the most optimistic attitude she had in her possession.

David drove the Ghost Cloaked Mercedes to the hotel and picked up Jonah and Kelly. They brought a Styrofoam cooler and a backpack with items they needed for the transference. Jonah also carried a hard-sided toolbox with a device he designed that would measure the energy transfer. The SUV was crowded. David suspected that they were being followed from the hotel parking lot. He exited I-15 and took a right turn, pulling into the back of a convenience store lot, where he activated the smart camouflage. The following vehicle slowed and drove past. In full camouflage, David drove back to the highway heading toward the monastery.

"Who knows you are here?" David asked Jonah.

"My secretary. And Alison. Why?"

"Because one of them told the feds that something is going on, and they followed us from your hotel. They can't see us. They are gone, for now."

David drove about 40 minutes to the monastery. They arrived at 9:15 a.m. Kelly set up the pod while Jonah made adjustments on the computer and connected the Transference Protocol Apparatus. JW sat on the sofa with his dad, the elder Gomez milking the moment just in case they were among JW's last. Trish walked outside in the garden. David watched over Jonah and Kelly, making sure their preparations were above board and seemingly legitimate. The prep lasted about an hour.

Trish returned and got an update from David. She asked JW if he would go for a walk with her. Trish hid her doubts from JW, and outwardly shared his optimism. She made note of the sunshine on the mountains and the flowers in the garden and told JW that the beautiful things in her life were because of him. She called Tommy who was with JW's mom and let him talk to JW for some time. Trish had only told the boy that JW was going in for an operation, but Tommy seemed to know it was more serious than that. JW talked with his mom, who wanted to be there but was a nervous wreck, and instead offered to take care of Tommy. The call ended with JW in tears. JW hugged Trish.

"I have to get through this," he told her. "Your kid challenged me to a game of Scrabble."

They went back to the room. Before climbing into the pod, JW addressed Jonah.

"You forgot to connect an important piece of equipment. Jonah disagreed.

"Oh, yes, my friends. As before, we have to have a send-off song." He used Bluetooth settings to connect his iPhone to the computer. "Before we play the song, I need to say a few things. Jonah, at one time, we were rivals, of sorts. But you are a man of honor and an elite scientist. Respect, my man. Thank you. Kelly Bryant, you surprise me. You made a lot of this happen. You were one of my closest friends, and here you are again. To Karl – Karl Mann, who is not with us today. We did good things together. Fuck you, Thomas Steinman. To my Dad, Vincente Gomez. You weren't with me for a lot of years – but you were. I had no idea about your secret life, but here you are, with me now, and from here on out. David Brownington. Best friend a guy could ever want. Sometimes

we fight like brothers, but when everything is on the line, you are
there for me. I love you, my brother. And Trish. I know these last
few months have been especially hard on you. When we finally shut
Heaven Ride down, it will be because of you and your work behind
the scenes. I love hearing you laugh. I love hearing your stories. I
love you. So, when I come back – after this procedure today..." He
took a knee. "I don't have a ring, but will you marry me?" She bent
down to kiss JW, and he rolled her on the floor.

They kissed and laughed.
"Yes! I'll marry you, you big doofus!"

They got up off the floor. The frivolity ended momentarily until
JW introduced his music selection.

"You all know I love '80s new wave. But on this day, I couldn't
resist something more recent, because – I'll let the song say the rest.
Tommy loves this song. One of the reasons why I picked it."

He hit the play button, and the first notes of a familiar song
played. "Best Day of My Life" played loud on the speakers.

"The American Authors!" JW shouted over the music. JW
started dancing, and clapping his hands over his head, and smiling,
the others followed suit. JW turned Kelly square dance style by her
arm, then did the same to David. He grabbed Trisha in a big hug and
lifted her in the air. Vincente stood clapping and laughing. David
pulled Jonah to his feet to get into the mix.

When the music ended, JW bellowed, "It's all about friends and
family! I have the best friends. Together, we can do anything!"

The high note came unexpected to David, and especially to
Trish. This was the JW of old whom they expected craziness and
zaniness to follow. David watched JW climb into the pod, and he
realized that JW made his departure so positive because he feared
the procedure would fail. His joy pervaded because his anxiety was
real. The equipment Jonah brought included an updated skullcap.
When placed on the head, 23 of 26 sensors automatically found their
marks with precision, and only three had to be put in place by hand.
As JW's skullcap was placed, Jonah explained a few things.

"As I told you, we have never done this before. We're pulling
pure energy from a remote source and inserting it into your brain. If
we go too fast, we might fry your neural receptors. Even then, we
don't know if your brain will accept the energy. More things can go

wrong than can go right. But that was true of the original Heaven Ride, and you did that, too."

"I have faith," JW said.

Jonah squeezed JW's shoulder. "You're a good man. You ready, JW? Okay, Kelly. Let's do this."

"Wait a minute," David said. "The long-term comatose state. Won't that cause brain damage after four minutes?"

"Not as long as we provide minimal electrical stimulation to parts of the cortex and cerebellum," Jonah answered. "just enough, so that we don't wake him."

"He's right, David," JW said. "Just make sure I have an oxygen source. Don't put a plastic bag over my head."

"The program I wrote has sequential electrical impulses going to essential neural sensors throughout the brain," Kelly said. "An unconscious state isn't completely necessary, but we feared that if you were conscious, the energy will stay concentrated with active neural centers, and not be evenly dispersed."

"Shall we get on with the transfer?" Jonah said. "How are you feeling right now, JW?"

"Great. Happy. Hopeful. Ready to become myself again."

"All right, Kelly. Are you getting signals from all sensors?"

"Affirmative. Ready to initiate sequencing."

"Just like the initial Heaven Ride, JW, we're replicating the start with a protein injection." He readied the needle and swabbed JW's arm with alcohol. Once the shot was administered, he pointed to Kelly. She began a countdown.

"Trish, David get over here!" JW said. They came to the pod, one on each side. He held onto their hands. "If this doesn't work, you know what to do."

David had long suspected that those who entered the comatose state without fear performed better, so he asserted a positive influence. "JW you are in the best hands possible here with Jonah and Kelly. We are all here for you. And that send-off – best day of your life!"

"Okay. You're right, man!"

JW closed his eyes, and Jonah put a finger to his lips.

Jonah had Kelly move out of the chair at the computer. His fingers typed furiously on the keys, accessing secret panel upon secret panel, delving further into a digital realm that only he had crossed before. Before, it was to give, and now it was to take back. One final password, and the process stalled. For an instant, he worried that he might be locked out of the cloud.

"David, how reliable is the internet signal here?"

"We had problems with the DSL lines," David said. "JW paid to have fiber optics installed. And we're less than a mile from the hub."

"If we lose connectivity, it will fuck up the whole thing," Jonah said. "Excuse my language." Jonah's fear was alleviated when the cloud accepted his password and brought him to the gateway page.

"You are now accessing a security zone of the United States of America, which requires a Level 6 security clearance. Trespass beyond this point may be punished to the fullest extent of the law. Do you wish to continue?"

Jonah clicked on "Yes."

Dots followed each other in a circle... working... working...

A graph appeared, showing how many teragigs of joules of energy were stored and those that were in transit from various centers in real time. Jonah ventured into a territory he had never been before. He clicked the DOWNLOAD link. It opened a panel where Jonah was able to direct the energy to the circuitry for the pod.

"Select the rate of transmission." Jonah selected the lowest rate possible.

"Select Total Amount."

JW's mind slowed, and he felt a series of electrical pulses radiate through his brain. They were not in a predictable sequence, and the more he concentrated on the zapping, the further from the room he felt. There was a tingling below his scalp. He wanted to scratch it, but his arms felt like lead. He couldn't lift them. The same with his legs. He heard a voice that might have been Kelly.

"Entering Phase Three."

Ahh, that's a warm sensation.

I am relaxed. I haven't felt this good in a long time.

This is like lying on a beach. Every sense, magnified. Apple pie, I smell apple pie. I can even taste it.

Gone. Now it's gone. Like a cool breeze blowing. Chill.

Now I feel warm. I need a hat. Shield me from the heat. Oh, no!

The apple pie. It's burning!

In the room, Kelly announced that five minutes had passed. "We are 3 percent complete."

"Is that for the initial install, or the double?"

"The initial," she said. "I thought the 200 percent transfer was just an option."

"No," David said. It's what he wanted."

"Okay, then we're approaching 2 percent."

JW reclined in the pod, watched over closely by Trish and Vincente. His eyes were closed, but his eyelids moved ever so slightly. An hour passed with little change.

"Sixty minutes in. The transfer is 25 percent complete." The fluttering in JW's eyelids increased, and the left side of his face twitched slightly. Inside the pod, his fingers moved marginally, involuntarily.

It's the hottest day of the year. I wish I could sweat. I don't think I can even sweat. Grandma's chili is boiling on the stove. The smell is so thick in the air, I can taste it. I need ice. Isn't there anyone here who can give me ice? Why am I alone in this hot place?

"One hour twenty minutes in. The transfer is at 33 percent. Body temperature is elevated. It's 100.2 degrees. What do you think, Jonah?"

"A temperature of 100 is acceptable," Jonah said. "Increase the lapse time between energy transfers."

"How are his other body functions?" David asked.

"Blood pressure is elevated just barely," Kelly reported. "Everything else looks good."

At the two-hour mark, Kelly gave another report. "The transfer is 44 percent complete. His temperature is 100.4 and his BP is elevated just a bit more."

JW's skin was reddish, and blotchy. The facial movements increased.

David stayed with JW the entire time. The others went out for a late lunch and brought him a sandwich. JW approached the 100 percent mark. His skin started bubbling, and he experienced a sudden increase in body temperature. "It's 104 degrees. His blood pressure has spiked into a dangerous zone. His pulse rate is up to 135 BPM. Trish and David stood over him. His forehead rippled like soft cheese under a broiler. They whispered to each other.

"Should we cut this short?" David asked.

"JW said not to," Trish said. "I promised him."

"Me, too. Let's go a little further. We've got monitors on almost any bodily function. We'll know if his condition becomes critical. We have to cool him down, though."

David started to the door. "Vince, Jonah, come with me. There's a kitchen in the other building. There's got to be an ice machine. Let's pack the pod with ice to bring his temperature down."

The kitchen was open. The ice machine was very old. The ice machine was only a third filled, and the ice was watery.

They found buckets and filled three of them as full as possible. They hurried across the grass, sinking into the moist March soil. When they got to the room, David found some pillows, and they used the pillow cases loaded with ice to wrap around JW's neck, and they crossed his arms and put one over his wrists. For their effort, JW's temperature dropped one degree. He was at about 112 percent when Kelly pleaded with Trish and David to let her stop the flow of energy to JW's brain. They said no.

David sensed all the prayers in the room. He said another one. Then, he took a moment to make contact with Alison. He let her know that he was there with her grandfather. He conveyed to her the reason for him coming to conduct the first brain energy transference on a civilian. He told her that JW was beginning to struggle with the transfer, and that she might say a prayer for him. Alison was very concerned.

"Promise me you will listen to my grandfather if he tells you JW has had enough. He's a good man and wouldn't hurt anyone."

By all appearances to anyone else in the room, David sat in a prayerful trance, consumed with concern. He feared the outcome for his friend. In the same instant, he sought comfort and thought of the love he shared with Alison.

Kelly gave the word: 140 percent, 20 percent above his pre-HR levels. Body temperature stable at 103. Blood pressure high, but stable and his rapid eye movement had increased to an extraordinary level. "Not sure what that means," she said.

In the next hour, she saw sporadic spikes in almost all his body functions. At once, all the sensor readings redlined. He was still breathing, and his heart rate jumped to 152 BPM, but his brain waves slowed or stopped. Warnings beeped and blinked, and the observers in the room went into a state of panic.

"We've got to shut this thing down!" Kelly said.

"How far along are we?" David asked.

"At 156 percent," Kelly answered.

Jonah leapt behind the board. Trish looked at David, fear in her eyes.

"I'm shutting this down," Jonah said. "We're cooking his brain," Jonah finished shutting down the program and securing the energy cloud. Kelly came over and tenderly removed the skull cap and sensors. They stuck to his head, and when she pulled it away, bits of his skin and hair were baked onto the diodes. It left burn marks surrounded by dark red blistering on his head.

David pushed past the others to view his friend, frozen in a pose like figures in a wax museum. JW did not move at all.

"Is he – dead?" David asked.

Chapter 22: Alison

Trish's eyes burned. Red from crying, the dry air made them feel like they were on fire.

"Do you think Kelly had this planned?" she asked.

"No," David said. "Not a chance. She was as horrified as any of us."

"We need to get him to the hospital," Trish said.

"No. The security risk is too great. How do we explain what happened? We'll all go to jail for it."

"We can work those things out. I just want JW to live," Trish cried. "The University Hospital..."

"A teaching hospital?" David questioned. "I don't know, Trish."

"What about the university, itself? Perhaps one of the profs or experienced doctors from there."

"Then Cheryl Redmond will know. She's one of the traitors who set us up."

"We can't just leave him up there in that room We don't know if this is a life sentence, a few months or a few weeks. But we can't leave him up there in this room."

David knew Trish well enough that she wasn't going to back down. She was right, from a practical standpoint.

"Let me do a little research. I'll be quick. Within the hour."

David searched websites and he made two calls to identify the top neurosurgeon in the area. He and Trish met with her that afternoon while Vince watched over JW at the monastery lab.

Dr. Renee Bellows was about 40 with a pretty face sabotaged by a very stern disposition. Dr. Bellows agreed to a consultation with JW, and under HIPPA and other confidentiality clauses, his case and identity would remain a secret. He would be admitted under the name James Raines and Dr. Bellows would attend to him personally. JW was transferred to the University Health Center later that afternoon. Jonah and Kelly met David, Trish and Vincente for dinner at a restaurant not far from the Heaven Ride Center. They ordered cocktails and discussed the events of the day. "He was so upbeat, and fun," Trish said. "That's a JW we haven't seen in months, but he was himself."

"We have to be pragmatic about this," Vincente said. "JW is in a coma. I can't blame anyone. He wanted to do this. But it doesn't look good."

"I'm not a doctor," Jonah said. "I don't know. I think we overloaded the synapses in his brain. We should have stopped at a more modest pinnacle."

"You did exactly what JW wanted," Vincente said.

Trish's phone rang, and she excused herself to take the call.

"David, you know what this reminds me of?" Kelly said.

"Yeah, I know. But it's not the same." He explained to the rest of the group. "Kelly is saying that this is similar to when she and I and JW and Karl got together after our initial pitch to Steinman's group, and we found out about Bridget's suicide. But, hey, we've got to think positive thoughts for JW. We did the best we could for him. He was miserable and becoming a threat to himself and others."

Trish came back. "David, you've got to come with me. Jonah, if we're not back in an hour, will you take Vince back to your hotel?"

"All right. Is this good or bad news?"

"I don't know yet."

"I'll call you guys once we find out," David said.

At the hospital, Dr. Bellows shared some test results and wanted some answers.

"I know you've seen exhibits before showing thermal dynamics of brain waves, basically the action in the cortexes of the brain during certain activities. I'm going to show you on my computer the average brain scan for a 32-year-old male. You see certain hot spots of brain activity. This is very normal. Now, I want to show you the scan we performed on JW just over an hour ago."

She clicked to an MRI image of another brain. This one was completely glowing.

"We conducted advanced tomography. Nearly every synapse in the frontal lobe of his brain is in use, even though his body is almost completely shut down. The frontal lobe is responsible for reasoning, advanced thinking, problem solving, emotions and a variety of other functions. While most ordinary people use 10 to 15 percent of their brain, He's way up there, 70 percent or better."

"So why isn't he cognitive?' Trish asked while David gushed in amazement.

"James suffered severe cranial burns. I'd liken it to burning the roof of your mouth with hot pizza. I'm theorizing that he is focusing his mental capacity on healing energy. I want to caution you. His brain may literally be fried. All this activity could come to a screeching halt. Right now, I have to say I am encouraged."

"So, he's going to be okay? He'll come out of the coma?" Trish asked.

"He should, but we don't know for sure. When he does, he'll probably have a lot to say."

"Oh, great," David mumbled. "I mean, I'll be grateful when he's back, but the world may not be able to handle a supercharged JW," David said.

They went back to the restaurant and shared the news with the whole bunch. The somber mood lifted, and Vincente ordered shots of tequila for everyone. The waitress brought a round of margaritas and talk turned to a party celebrating JW's return home. Just when the celebration seemed to be ending, a woman entered the restaurant and glided towards them. David sat with his back to the door.

"Ally Angel!" Jonah exclaimed.

"Grandpa!" came the reply, as Alison hugged Jonah tightly. David watched, startled. He stood, waiting for her to come around the table. Her face brightened with excitement to see David. "I wasn't sure you would come," David said.

"I know. I blocked you out the whole way. I wanted to surprise you." David started to introduce Alison to Vincente, but she stopped him.

"How is JW?" They shared the events of the day and their

cautious optimism that he could regain his faculties. David was thrilled to have Alison in her physical presence. He hugged her tightly and rubbed his fingers through her hair. They talked and embraced forgetting that the others were there.

Jonah walked over to the two love birds.

"Thanks for coming, Angel. We're celebrating 'cause we had some good news about JW. He's not out of the woods yet, and he's still in a coma. But his brain is active. Hyperactive. How long are you staying?"

"For good? Naw. I took a week off. They didn't like the short notice, but too bad."

"Maybe they'll fire you and you can stay," David suggested.

She slapped his arm playfully. "I don't want to be fired. It has been almost a year. I thought this might be a test."

"A test of what?"

"A test to see if we're still right for each other. I wasn't sure if you had moved on. I started seeing a guy in D.C."

"The guy from the coffee shop?"

She seemed annoyed. "Yeah. God, do you have to know everything about me?"

"Believe me, it might help in our relationship. I had no clue what you were thinking before I developed The Gift."

"It's a little troubling. Like stalking, only on a much higher level."

"Honestly, I was with somebody, too. We ended up being geographically incompatible."

"Oh."

"Let's say we move this party back to Five Rings."

"Five Rings?" Alison asked.

"JW's ski house. That's the name of it. I'll tell you the story on the way. And when we get there, you'll meet Tommy, Trish's son."

"I booked a hotel here in the city."

"Unbook it."

"No, I don't want to impose. It's easier if I stay in the hotel."

"Believe me, it's not easy at all. Hey Trish, we got room for one more back at the ranch?"

"Of course!"

"See? She said of course. Her tone of voice said, 'Why would anybody in their right mind stay anywhere else?'"

"I never said I was in my right mind," Alison said. "I went steady with you, didn't I?"

"Ooh, that hurts!" David said, grimacing. "All the more reason for you to stay secluded from society. You are obviously mad. Where are your things?

"My bag is up at the front desk. I was going to Uber it to the hotel room that I reserved."

"Go get your bag and we'll put it in the Smart Mercedes."

"Don't tell me what to do," Alison protested, laughing all the while. "And what the hell is a Smart Mercedes."

"I'm not telling you what to do," David said calmly. "Now go get your luggage because the last train up the mountain is leaving soon."

"That's fine. I have a hotel room waiting right down the street."

"If you're not going to come willingly, I'll be forced to kidnap you and hold you for ransom, until your grandfather pays me one million – no, one billion dollars."

"I'm right here, David," Jonah said.

"I know. Expect a note from me in three or four days."

Vincente commented, "You two are hysterical."

"See? David said. "'You two' implies that we are a couple and should be together. And JW would want this. And you're going to help us plan his Coming Home party."

Trish stepped in. "David, shut up. Alison, let me help you with your bags. You're staying at the house."

David laughed, as Alison just got a dose of "You don't mess around with Trish." Of course, her protests were all for fun, as she didn't travel all this way to stay at a hotel miles away from her love. David beamed, finally reunited with the love of his life.

David took great delight in demonstrating the Smart Camo on the Mercedes.

"This was JW's big thing. He had this designed, so we could occasionally travel off the reservation."

On the drive to the mountain home, they reminisced about JW's idiosyncrasies and some of the sweet things he had done. It brought Alison back to the time JW opened up the house to let her cook all of David's favorites. These memories solidified the fact that JW was a kind and selfless human being.

David carried Alison's bags to his room while Trish showed her around the massive house.

"In D.C., I have about 600 square feet that costs $2400 a month," Alison lamented. "This is just amazing."

Tommy woke up and stumbled out of his room\, followed by Jayne who fell asleep in his room.

"How is JW? Is he okay?"

Trish went over to him and hugged Tommy tightly.

"Darling, I should have called you. JW is still asleep, and he might be for awhile. But the doctors think there's a good chance he'll be okay."

"Why did he have to do this?"

"Well, part of JW's brain stopped working right. The doctors put electricity into his head to bring those parts back to life."

"Like Frankenstein?" They all laughed, except Trish.

"No, not like Frankenstein. There are no body parts from other people. It's all JW. But while he heals, his brain decided it would be faster if it went to sleep. But this is why I always nag you to wear your bicycle helmet. Brain injuries can happen easily, and sometimes, they can't be cured."

"Okay, Mom. But JW's, it can be cured, right?"

"Honey, we don't – "She stopped herself. She didn't want to instill any doubts for the boy. "The doctor told us JW would be better than ever. Before you go back to bed, say another prayer for him. Come on, I'll tuck you in and we can say a prayer together."

Trish gave Jayne a hug and thanked her for watching Tommy. She assured JW's mother that her son would come out of this okay and gave her a kiss on the cheek.

"Who is the pretty lady?" Tommy asked. Alison blushed.

"That's Alison," Trish said. "She's a good friend of David's."

"Oh, yeah he talks about you all the time. Except he calls you Holly-slash-Alison." They laughed, and he went to Alison and offered a handshake. "I'm Tommy Raines. It's a pleasure to meet you."

"Tommy, I'm so glad to meet you, too. David, your mom and JW have told me a lot about you. But you're even better in person."

"Well, I try," he said. "I should be going to bed now. I have school tomorrow."

He scampered off. Alison looked like she would melt.

"Oh, my God, he's such a doll."

"Yeah, he's a good kid," David said. "He and JW are thick as thieves. Tommy's been a really good influence on JW."

Trish returned. "It's been a long day," she said. "I think I'll turn in. But first, I'll call the nurses station to see if there's any change with JW."

She called on speaker phone, and the nurse said he was still "critical, but stable."

Even though the news wasn't any worse than what they already knew, it cast a sorrowful pall over Trish. She excused herself to be alone. David was caught in between two emotions. Heartache, for his best friend, and elation to be with the woman he truly loved.

Alison seized on those emotions. When David showed her the lower half of the house, she protested when they reached his room.

"What are my bags doing in your room?" she said. "Are you sleeping on the couch, or in the man cave?"

"No, I-I-" David stammered.

"Did you think we were going to sleep together?"

"Well, yeah, I assumed we would."

"You've got this all wrong, David. We've got some talking to do before we get back to the way things were."

David put his hand on Alison's waist to pull her close.

"We can talk in the morning," he said softly.

She wriggled away.

"No," she ordered, and a certain fired raged in her eyes that David had never seen. "Don't touch me. After everything that happened, we aren't just picking up where we left off."

David tried to show understanding, although he was confused by Alison's emotional change. He moved closer and reached to caress Alison's cheek. She recoiled and slapped him hard across the face.

"You don't get it, do you?" she asked. "You have no idea of the pain and suffering you have caused me."

David was stunned. He could not think of a word to say.

"I told you, don't touch me," Alison said. "Do you remember what happened the last time I saw you? When you came to my apartment? You grilled me over Heaven Ride, and you grabbed me and pushed me in a threatening way. And I told you what I knew. What you needed to know. You gave me an engagement ring, expecting that I was going to just swoon and fall into your arms. Then, you left, just before the FBI got there."

"I remember that like it was yesterday," David said.

"Do you know what happened after you skipped off to the airport?"

David was beginning to feel guilt and rage and a variety of other emotions.

"Yeah. There was a guy on the plane that was going to try to kill me. Did you have anything to do with him being on the same plane?"

David heard multiple voices in his head. He tried to concentrate on Alison's, but she was being drowned out. He read her lips to discern what she was saying.

"I don't know anything about that," Alison offered. "Within minutes, the FBI came knocking at the door. They weren't coming for you. They came for me! They had a search warrant to take my laptop, my phone, my letters, everything. They were looking for information about you, and us. I told them that you and I were through. Then... that fucking ring! They saw the little box with that ring, and it refuted everything I told them. Hell, my story didn't even sound true to me anymore."

Alison stifled tears as she spoke, her voice raising a half-octave higher as the words caught in her throat. The other voice in David's head turned to derisive laughter. The combination of laughter and tears flummoxed him.

"At that point, I told them I wanted to talk to my lawyer, I watched them search my apartment and carry my stuff out the door, anything they thought might do them good in a case against you. They took me with them to the FBI office for further questioning."

Now, the tears started flowing. The other voice competing for David's attention took charge. It was clean, female and free from any accent or distinguishing quality. Now, it overwhelmed him.

"They took me to the Department of Justice Building to interrogate me. It was surreal. I just sat there. They bombarded me with questions and I just sat there. Finally, my grandfather came. He asked Marty to make some calls, and when Jonah Johansson shows up, well, it improves your stature a lot.

"The FBI let me go," she said. "But," she said, her voice squeaking, "I lost my job. I lost my security clearance. I lost everything I worked so hard to get, David, because of you. And because of that fucking ring."

David couldn't take anymore.

"Stop it, Aliona!"

Alison's anger vanquished the tears.

"What did you call me?"

David reacted with a sympathetic look. He realized his blunder, but didn't dare try to explain. He wanted to hug her but refrained. In his head, Aliona gleefully chastised David for his foolishness.

"She doesn't love you anymore, naïve boy," Aliona told him. "Things will never be the same." Her taunting was compounded by echoing laughter. David tried to block her, with only moderate success.

"You don't even know my name," Alison said, combatively.

"Something strange just happened. I'm sorry. I didn't know all you went through."

"Yeah, so I come here out of respect for JW, and you treat me like I'm your personal plaything. And now, my name is Aliona. I-I just don't know what to say."

"To be honest," David said, "You are still Holly to me."

From the ether, Aliona took great delight in David's current struggle. She chimed in sarcastically, "I thought I was your Holly."

Simultaneously, Alison's barrage continued. "I don't mean to offend the giant ego of the almighty David Brownington, but I'm not going to sleep with you tonight. In some ways, I wish I never met you."

She paused to let the words sink in.

"You never said anything when we talked," David pointed out.

"Oh, you mean the periodic mental jibber-jabber where you invaded my head at inopportune times. I guess that was convenient to you. No, I never said anything. I wanted the least interference in my life from you as possible, and if I told you, it would have opened the door for you to try to shed that whole lifetime of pent-up Catholic guilt, to try and *help*." She used air quotes for emphasis. "I didn't want your sympathy."

David pouted. The truth was hurting.

"So why did you come?' he asked, wounded.

"I told you," she said. "I came out of respect for JW. It was a chance to see my step-grandfather, because his neck might be in a noose very soon. And," she looked upwards before looking David in the eyes. "I wanted to let you know the living hell I've had to endure, because – to be fair to you – you had no idea. And I know that my anger at you, well, some of it is displaced. And I also knew that in the worst case, if JW doesn't come out of this thing okay, that it will be devastating to you. While I'm mad as hell at you, I don't want you to experience that kind of grief by yourself."

David looked down and paced before responding.

"Thank you," he said, a disturbed quietness to his voice. "But JW is going to be fine. We may not agree on everything anymore, but we have to believe that."

Alison forced a smile. She took a deep breath, beginning to calm.

"Okay, you're right. Faith. It's one of your best qualities."

Alison picked up her bag and took it upstairs to get another room designation from Trish. She did not feel invigorated by her outburst. More than anything, she felt ashamed that she waited so long to tell David the many aspects of their parting that bothered her.

David felt humbled, and alone. He focused on the last part of Alison's discourse. *What if JW doesn't survive? How will I be able to handle it?*

*   *   *

In the morning, David showered and went upstairs to the kitchen to make breakfast. Trish and Jayne were already making scrambled eggs and bacon, and Vincente sat at the table reading the news on an iPad and sipping his second cup of coffee. David solicited a hug from Jayne and wished her a good morning. Alison entered, her hair still wet from her shower.

"Damn, you two were noisy last night!" Vincente said. David was horrified to think that Vincente heard their argument.

He winked at Alison and told him, "I thought you were wearing your noise-canceling headgear!"

"You haven't changed a bit, Vin. I don't think that kind of questioning is appropriate," Jayne said.

"Ah, I'm just kidding," he said. "These two like to joke around."

Although Alison always liked a good laugh, this time she wanted to set the record straight.

"I slept in the room way down the hall from this one," she said. "Nothing improper going on last night."

"That's true," David concurred.

"Sit down, everybody," Trish said. "I'll bring breakfast in."

Vincente quizzed Alison about her work at the White House. She answered with great candor about her days there, then informed him she no longer worked there.

David asked, "So does Martin know you are here?"

"Oh, no-o-o-o," Alison said. "If he knew, I'd be in big trouble. No, this was a spontaneous decision. I need to start looking out for my future."

"So should Martin," David said. "If all goes according to plan, Martin will be unemployed."

"Alison should move here and be my wedding planner," Trish said.

"Oh, my God! JW asked you --"

"Yes. Right before he went in the pod for the transfer."

"That would be an honor. No decisions yet. I would have a target on my back just like the rest of you."

"Not a problem. You would have a personal bodyguard." David said, taking a bite from a slice of bacon.

"Oh, David. That's so chivalrous for you to be my bodyguard."

"I was talking about Vince." Waving the remainder of his bacon, David said, "I've seen him kill a man with a single slice of bacon."

"It's true," Vincente said, pushing scrambled eggs onto his fork with his knife. "It's my weapon of choice."

"Okay, visiting hours start at 11. The party bus leaves at 9:45," Trish said.

"How are you holding up?" Alison asked her.

"I'll be okay. I had a nightmare last night that JW – "Trish began crying.

"Trish, JW is going to make it fine," David said.

"You're not a doctor, David. We don't know if he's going to make it or not. If you're done, I'll take your dishes."

"Let's give his nurse a call," Jayne suggested. She led Trish into an adjacent room.

David leaned over toward Vincente and quietly said, "I'm not going to say a single word all day long. I can't win."

* * *

Jayne returned a few moments later. Only Tommy and Vincente remained at the table.

"No way!" Tommy said. "Hockey is way better than baseball."

"Baseball has been around – professional baseball – for more than 150 years. It possesses that contest between one man and the pitcher, yet it's wrapped up in a battle between teams, where each man contributes to the success or failure of the team."

"Hockey is like that, too," Tommy said. "The first pro league started in 1904, but the National Hockey League, as we know it today, began in 1917. It has the contest between the skater and the defense, and the skater and the goalie. And the defense against any of the offensive players rushing. That's all one part of the battle between two teams. And there's action all the time. Baseball is boring."

"Baseball is not boring!" Vincente said, his voice raising in tone and volume.

"Dear, come on. Let's you and I go talk," Jayne said, trying to de-escalate the argument.

"No, wait," Vincente said. "I have one more point to make for Tommy to think about. Now, I love hockey, too. But you said baseball is boring. It's only boring if you're not looking. By that, I mean that there is always something going on. A catcher giving signs to the pitcher, a manager signaling to his third base coach, or infielders telling each other who covers the base. Then, it comes down to the batter versus the pitcher. Those moments of silence in baseball are filled with meaning. Tell you what, Tommy. I'm going to take you to a Salt Lake City Bees game, and I'll show you all the amazing things that go on during the game. Then you can take me to a hockey game and we'll scream our lungs out for the home team. Deal?"

"Deal!" Tommy said. They shook hands on it, and the truce took place.

"Can I have a word with you, Commander?"

"Sure thing."

"Let's go outside. The sun is shining," she said.

The went out by the driveway.

"You always were good with boys," Jayne told him.

"Boys are all young men," he said. "We all share something. It's just a matter of finding what that is."

Along the walk was a bench made from a tree trunk that was halved, polished and polycoated for a smooth, shiny finish. Jayne sat, and tapped the bench, urging Vincente to sit with her. He did, his knees cracking loudly.

"That didn't sound good," she said.

"No. I'm not young anymore, Jayne," he said. "Working on that Alaskan fishing boat didn't do me any favors. I lost almost all the cartilage in my knee."

"So you really did work on a fishing trawler?"

"I did," he said. "Big operation. Family run. Really nice people. And hard working."

"And you faked your death?"

He paused for a moment. "Yeah. I did that, too. But not for reasons you might expect." Jayne said nothing so he offered more. "The government found me. They asked me to get involved in a highly classified project. We had to make Vincente Gomez go away. For awhile, at least."

"It broke my heart," Jayne said. "It broke JW's heart, too. I'm not sure if I hurt more for myself or for him."

"I'm so sorry, Jayne," Vincente said. "I didn't mean to hurt you, or anybody. I can't make excuses. I was lost. I was hurt. I lost Petey. On that day, I lost you, too."

Jayne looked down at the sidewalk.

"I know. We never had a chance to grieve together. I was wrong. I heaped all that guilt on you. You left and then I felt guilty for chasing you away. I didn't know how to handle the loss of our son."

She looked at Vincente, tears rolling from the corner of her eyes.

"And now, I might lose JW." She cried loudly. The tears gushed down her cheeks. She sought refuge from this outburst of grief by burying her face in Vincente's shoulder. He put his arm around her shoulder and pulled her close. His tears fell on the back of her head.

"I can't lose another boy," she said.

"He's going to be okay," Vincente said, trying to convince himself as much as Jayne. "You know how stubborn that boy always was."

Between sobs, she let out a chuckle, and she raised her head.

"Do you remember the bike rally, when he was eight?" she said.

"I think he was nine."

"No, but when he was eight, he lost. He thought he had the best decorated bicycle, but he finished second. Ooh, he was mad!"

Vincente laughed. "He spent the next twelve months figuring out a way to beat Donald Smith. And he did."

Jayne full out laughed. "He made his bike look like a rodeo bull." She could barely get the words out. "And he made me take him out to buy a checkered shirt and a cowboy hat. My God, that was funny."

"The kicker was when he asked for rope to make a lariat," Vincente said. "He took out books from the library on how to spin a lariat, and by golly, eventually he taught himself."

Their laughter subsided. Jayne slipped her hand in Vincente's.

"You're right," she told him. "JW's too stubborn to let this keep him down. He'll bounce back."

He squeezed her hand slightly and adjusted his arm over her shoulder."

"It's quite a view from here," Vincente said. "Remember what's over that ski run over that way?"

"Refresh my memory," she said. "I'm not a skier."

"Hill Air Force Base has a ski lodge over there," he said. "And that was where I first met a shy, beautiful seventeen-year-old girl, Jayne Prentice."

"That's over thay-er? I guess it would be. Remember my friend, Marilyn? She had a date with an enlisted man and invited me along in case it didn't work out."

"I remember him. His name was Gus. Gus the womanizer," Vincente said.

"That's right, it was Gus."

"How did that work out?"

"For Marilyn? Not very well," Jayne said. "For me? Well, I met the most handsome and charming man that night."

"Did you go home with him?" Vincente asked, stifling a chuckle.

"No. Not that first night. Marilyn needed me to rescue her from Gus the octopus. My gentleman politely asked for my phone number and then escorted Gus away."

"And let me guess. He called you the next week."

"He di-id. And then I had two bay-bies with him." Jayne laughed, wiping away her tears. She turned serious. "I can't lose JW, too."

Vincente was at a loss for what to say. The mirthful exchange seemed to be over.

"Oh, look!" Jayne said. "Those are some purple four o'clocks. Remember how they used to grow wild near the house."

Vincente smiled, admiring Jayne for compartmentalizing her sadness and anxiety.

"So, you took the Heaven Ride?" Vincente asked.

"I di-id," she said. A long pause followed as the details brewed inside her." Petey was thay-er. It wasn't Petey, the boy we knew. It was him, for sure. But he was – I guess you would say he was in spirit form, still a boy, but all grown up in a spiritual sense. He knew everything that was going on with us. He was watching over JW then, and I'm sure he's watching over him now, as we speak. I asked him why you weren't there to see me. He said, "Why would he be here? His time hasn't come yet." I had heard about your fishing boat accident. My aunt Emma, she's into genealogy, and she dug up a newspaper article that said you died at sea. Even though you had been gone for a long, long time, my heart ached when I read that. It was then that I realized I never apologized to you for how I made you feel. All those years, I made you the center of everything wrong in my life." Jayne choked up, sniffling. "I never once thought I was the one inflicting pain. On you. On JW. Too many years have gone by, Vince. I can't expect you to forgive me. But it was Petey, in heaven, who told me that forgiveness was the only way we could be a family again. I know it wasn't your fault, Vince. I'm so sorry."

"We all grieve differently, Jayne. I bore the brunt of the tragedy. I wore that badge the community gave me, 'Bad Father.' I left, and I had no one. Then, those son of a bitch monsters set me up to kill my other son. I have trained all my adult years to keep my emotions under wraps. No one could have trained me for this. I'm still struggling with grief and guilt. And anger. Inside me, the pot is boiling over. All I can think of is getting revenge on the people trying to harm JW."

Jayne looked aghast.

"Vince, you can't. I mean, we are all together now. You've got to let that dog lie."

"Let's wait and see, Jayne. Right now, JW is in crisis. I'm taking things one step at a time."

"I don't want you hurt, too," Jayne said. After a brief pause, she addressed an issue that burned inside her.

"While you were away, were you with anybody else? Was there another woman?"

"It has been a lot of years, Jayne," he answered. "Yes. I saw some women. But my focus was healing myself. I couldn't have been a good partner for anyone. Were you with anyone else?"

Jayne turned away. It was difficult for her to speak.

"I dated men. Some of my friends would introduce me to guys they knew. After I heard that you were dead, I got in a serious relationship with a very influential man, a state senator. I was engaged. But when Petey let me know that you were still alive, I broke things off with Rand."

Vincente tried to process the information, a variety of emotions swarming him like bees.

"Well, we were apart for a long time. It's only natural," he mumbled.

"I dreamed – for all those years, I dreamed that we could be together again. When I broke thinks off with Randolph, I told him you were still alive. He promised to try to find you. He came back and said it was futile. In every database he checked, you no longer existed."

Vincente absorbed the information. He chuckled and said, "That may be quite an advantage on April 15.”

Jayne did not laugh, and fidgeted with her hands.

“Is there hope for us to be together again?” she asked.

“We absolutely need to be together for JW. We have to give him our all. After that, let’s see if we can pick up the pieces.”

“Would you be willing to go through marriage counseling with me?”

“Let’s fight one battle at a time,” Vincente said. “C’mon, dear, let’s get over to the hospital.”

He rose, and extended his hand to help Jayne to her feet. She looked drained from the emotional interchange. Vincente pulled her close, hugging her at length. Jayne’s worry evaporated, and they walked hand-in-hand back to the front door.

* * *

David and Alison stepped outside to pass time while the others got ready for the day-long marathon at the hospital. They walked the grounds outside, and they stopped at the pond. It still had a small oval cake of ice in the center, but the outdoor hockey season melted away with every March day filled with sunshine. David told her about his skating sessions on the ice and how he began to teach Tommy some of the finer points of the game, and that the kid was getting quite good.

“I'd be scared about security,” she said. “I know Marty would come after me. He really wants nothing that will make you happy. And now, he's afraid of you, and what you might do to Heaven Ride.”

David's phone rang.

“There's only three people, or four including Jonah, who have this number,” he explained. “Hello.”

“Hey, slacker!” It was JW. “Get your ass to the hospital and break me out of here. These nurses don't want to let me get out of this dress. I think they're enjoying the view. Do you need my room number?”

“JW! No, I don't need that. I was with you all day yesterday!”

“I thought that was you.”

“How do you feel?”

“It's a little like those old Looney Toon cartoons where the anvil falls on Wile E. Coyote's head. But as soon as I woke, my perceptive abilities seemed to be back. Like, I could hear the nurses way down the hall, and the smell of the antiseptic spray is overpowering. It's not Lysol, but some industrial strength chemical. Very offensive."

"So, did you talk to Trish yet?"

"No. Get down here and sign me out of this place. I want to surprise her."

"No way. You can't do that. She's worried sick about you."

"I know. I can visualize the surprise on her face when you bring me in."

"Listen, JW. You can't do that. In fact, you should not let her know that you called me first. Hang up and call her. I'll drive Trish, and your mom and dad, and – well, I have a surprise for you."

"Huh. A surprise. Okay. You really think I need to tell Trish?"

"Yes. And talk to your dad. He's spooked by the whole procedure."

"Okay, I'll trust you, Big D. One last thing..."

"What's that?"

"Kelly did great work. We can trust her."

"I knew that."

"Well I didn't."

"But you went anyway?"

"Yeah. Because I trusted you. You wouldn't have put me in a death trap."

"For the record, JW, I think you were officially dead at one point. But you sound incredible now. One last thing. You remember that you proposed to Trish right before you went unconscious?" David asked.

"Holy shit. That's right. She said yes, and hasn't changed her mind, has she?" JW said nervously.

"Of course not, you nut! Now make your calls and we'll get the car ready."

"We?"

"Um, yeah. The royal we. Stop talking and make your calls." David ended the call.

Alison laughed. "Stop talking and make your calls. Isn't that an oxymoron?"

"Only you, Alison!" He ran up the hill toward the house. "Come on!"

When he got to the house, Trish was talking with JW on the phone. Hearing Trish overjoyed with the news, he didn't interrupt, but rather hugged her and showed his own happiness with two thumbs up. He shouted a couple of "Whoo-hoo's" for realism and went downstairs to get ready for the day. He couldn't wait to see JW, if not to verify that his friend was back from the dead and dying.

David and the entourage drove to the hospital in two separate cars. David phoned Jonah to tell him the good news. Jonah was still in town, so David invited him and Kelly to come to Five Rings later for a celebration.

As soon as he saw JW, he could tell his buddy had changed. A heavenly glow over JW's head was bright, but only David could see it. Excitement beamed from his eyes. And JW grew even more animated when he saw Alison.

The hospital had not officially discharged JW. David made a few calls and reached Dr. Bellows, who issued the release order by phone.

JW rode with David, Alison and Trish in the Smart Mercedes, but directed them to stop at a natural food market near the university before heading toward the mountains. He talked non-stop, filling Alison in on the purchase of the ski house and several of his adventures with Tommy. All the while, he filled the cart with spinach, jicama, beets, a box of avocados, several pounds of blueberries, bananas, walnuts, pistachios, fresh garlic and powdered turmeric. From the cooler, he depleted the store's stock of wild Alaskan salmon and then bought six cans of mackerel.

"I've never seen you eat any organic foods, except maybe the garlic. What's up?" Trish asked.

"I'm just craving this stuff."

David arrived from the bulk food aisle, where he poured a half-pound of raw honey from a self-serve tap. "What on earth are you doing?"

Alison grabbed David's arm. "He has cravings."

"He's never eaten any of this in his life, except maybe the garlic." They all laughed, and Alison explained that Trish just said the same thing.

"JW, these are vegetables, you know that? You can't make

burritos out of any of this."

"Mind, body and soul, David. Mind, body and soul." Before David could remind him that he didn't have a soul, JW added, "I know, I don't have one. But this is what my body is telling my mind that I need."

David whispered to Alison that JW's behavior seemed odd for someone just coming out of a coma and on the edge of death. "Don't take this wrong but JW is scary cured. I sort of expected him to act like someone with a bad hangover. You know barely able to walk or put two words together in a sentence. I'm wondering what this energy transfer did to his brain. Maybe be was faking it all along"

"Really? Faking it? I can't believe you just said that. I think you're nervous you might be out gifted by JW and he'll run circles around your intelligence," Alison responded, while punching David in the arm.

Amid David's skepticism and his energy and sudden interest in healthy food, as soon as they got back to the house, JW made and avocado and swiss cheese sandwich with coarse mustard, and a salad of fruit and nuts.

JW told David he was eager to get back to work on "the beast." He suggested that David give Jonah a call.

"Oh, yeah, he and Kelly are coming up in a bit. We're throwing a little celebration party in your honor."

"Nice. I need to talk with Jonah. Oh, man – we're going to need food!"

Trish, Jayne and Alison had already begun to make some hors oeuvres, but JW jumped into the fray.

"Let me get that batch of chili leftover from the Super Bowl. We can reheat that."

"So, is your health kick over?" Trish asked.

"Oh, no. But this is good chili. My grandma finally parted with her recipe. Alison, you should have been here for the Super Bowl. We had so much food. And not many guests."

Trish took over the story. "My mom came out to visit, and JW's mom and grandma, and their neighbors. Oh, and JW's old football coach. It was the geriatric ward, and almost everyone was on a restrictive diet. So, we've got a boatload of JW's chili left in the freezer."

"Honey, I don't think it will thaw in time," Trish surmised.

"Nonsense. I'll be using laws of thermodynamics that Bobby Flay never dreamed of."

"I love Bobby Flay," Trish said.

"I know you do, my love. But he can't hold a candle to JW when it comes to scientific principles in the defrosting of a block of chili."

"Should we invite Bobby over?"

"You could. Tell him to come over at about, let's say, one-thirty-three, and he can have a piping hot bowl of chili."

"I could make some of my mom's chili from scratch. No need to eat the freezer burned stuff," Jayne told JW and Trish.

"Mom, you know it taste even better having been in the deep freeze," JW said.

Jonah and Kelly arrived slightly before the chili reached its peak temperature, but they had plenty to talk about with David and Vincente. JW ushered them downstairs to the man-cave while Trish, Jayne and Alison brought the food down. As much as Trish wanted to poke fun at JW, his chili reached 165 degrees at 1:33 p.m.

Tequila was the flavor of the day at the bar. It was the perfect venue for this type of gathering and JW was proud to give his party hall a workout. After the Barmaster X conveniently prepared a pitcher of margaritas and a second with sangria, JW quieted everyone down to make a speech.

"Barmaster, make seven shots of Tres-Quatro Cinco," JW ordered his machine, which dutifully followed his order. David distributed the shots while JW moved to the center of the bar. Alison helped David, then clung to his arm as JW spoke.

"I'm not going to lie," he said. "The last few months have been shitty. But three things happened. My dad came back. He shot me with a high-powered rifle, but he's back. And we hide his ammo when alcohol is served. I love you, dad. My mom and dad have reunited. I'm not suggesting anything but it's just nice to see you together, whether it's just friends or something more."

Jayne and Vincente smiled but gave JW the stare down.

"Next ... I can only imagine how hard it was, but Kelly and Jonah – you did it! You made scientific history. You were able to transfer the Heaven Wave energy back into a human. Jonah, I challenge you – and Kelly – to find a healing purpose for the procedure for the thousands, maybe millions out there like me. It's possible it could cure diseases and be put to a peaceful use.

"It's been two days, and I feel great! It's hard to describe, but my whole life, I've had this deep, analytical thought process. Then over the last year, it was gone. I was frustrated, I lost control, and There's Tommy. Little man, you stuck with me even when you didn't understand what was wrong with me. All of you stuck with me when I was at my ugliest and most selfish state.

"Well, now, I'm back!"

"Hear, hear!" David interjected. Kelly and the others applauded.

"Kelly. Jonah. In science, and in life, you are brave warriors. Thank you for coming back to be by my side, and now, forever in my heart."

Kelly came to him for a hug, and she wiped a tear from her eyes.

"Lastly, I have this vague memory from before the procedure. I believe that Trish accepted my proposal of matrimony. Tommy, your mom and I are going to be married."

Tommy jumped up and down and yelled "Hurray, hurray!"

"I can't wait. I'm going to be the official ring bearer," Tommy said.

"That's right son, I mean nearly son. And, today, David accepted my invitation to be best man. In between adventures to save the world from Heaven Ride, we will set a date. Stay tuned, cuz everyone who's here must be there.

"So, let's drink. To being alive, to friends old and new, and most of all...

TO THE WARRIORS WHO WILL NEVER BE DEFEATED!"

Everyone in the room knew the war to which he alluded. Jonah raised his glass, then set it on the bar without drinking. He was, after all, still employed by the enemy they sought to vanquish. JW watched him and could tell Jonah was preparing to leave.

JW hugged Trish, informing her that he wanted to thank Jonah, and gave her a kiss. He moved to Jonah at the bar.

"That's quite a Rube Goldberg bartending rig you've got there."

"Rube Goldberg?" JW said, puzzled. "No way, that's a David Brownington original."

"David invented that?" Johansson said in astonishment.

"Impressive. Of course, these days, everything is voice activated."

"He did that nine years ago, maybe ten. Way ahead of his time. So, what's the deal, Jonah? That's Tres-Quatro-Cinco you left in the glass. It's $360 a bottle."

"I'm sure it's very good. You know I can't drink to your so-called war. I'm still employed by your enemy."

"Today, yes. Tomorrow? Not so sure."

"You're right. None of us knows what tomorrow might bring. You, of all people, understand this. After all you've been through. Tomorrow, you could have a setback and that beautiful genius could be compromised."

"I have faith."

"We need to stay in touch. I want to know that you are doing okay."

"Sure, Trish has your number. "So tell me, Dr. Johansson, does the newest iteration of Heaven Ride have a kill switch?"

Jonah frowned. "No." He stroked his beard. "And there are 368 reasons why I couldn't tell you if it did. I can't be part of your plot, JW. But I must say, you're the first person to call me doctor in a long time."

"I have the utmost respect for you, Jonah. Even when I think you're making a huge mistake. You're playing with fire when you deal with Stein-mare. Come on, Jonah, at least give me the password so I can go and poke around."

Across the room, Alison came into view. "There's my Ally-Angel!" Jonah motioned for her to come over and she responded to his gesture. Turning back to JW, he told him, "You should have paid attention before when I said no. Oh, and that babble earlier about the transfer technology someday saving lives and curing diseases all goes away with the end of Heaven Ride. Just remember that my friend."

Alison bounded over, carrying a spoon and the remains of a bowl of chili.

"Grand-dad, you've been here for two days, and I've hardly had a minute to talk with you." She set her bowl on the bar. "Give me a hug." He pulled her tight and swung her in a tight circle. Alison pointed at him when she informed JW, "Best hugger, ever! Oh, and O-M-G! JW's chili! Wow! Good job!"

"Ally-Angel, it's good to see you again." To JW, he confided, "This young lady means everything to me. So what's the secret ingredient in your chili?"

JW smiled. "Enlightenment. Go ahead. Try some."

Jonah was bewildered, "I might just do that. Enlightenment, eh?"

"Yes. It's the precise combination of capsaicin and caramelized sugars and the molecular bonds that take place in the heating, cooling and re-heating process. Then, there's the quality of the meat. I used Buffalo tenderloin from Colorado. Tenderized in pineapple juice. No ground beef in my chili."

"I should have known better than to ask a science nerd. 'Cause I'm one of you," Jonah said. "Ally, show me where I can get a spoon and a bowl of Enlightenment."

Before they dashed away, JW stopped him by grabbing his forearm.

"Dr. J – thank you, from the bottom of my heart."

"JW, I'm no hero. You would've done the same for me."

"But I didn't. And you did, when you didn't have to."

"I didn't want to be governed by some regret in the future that couldn't be resolved," Jonah said. "Well, you're welcome. And congratulations on your decision to marry Trish. She's an amazing woman."

Jonah acquiesced to Alison's tugging on his arm and went off. JW spotted David across the room talking with Kelly. He joined them, putting his arm around Kelly's shoulder.

"Has David gotten around to asking when you're coming back to work for us? I'll put you on the payroll today if you say yes."

David seemed a little shocked at JW's blunt approach, but Kelly wasn't rattled.

"No, he didn't. And no, I won't. This is a beautiful place, but I'm more of a city mouse."

"Work via distance."

"No, thanks. I don't want a target on my back, like you two in your war on the government."

"At least give me a nugget I can use."

She squinted, wondering what information JW wanted.

"Tell me about Jonah's Third Cloud.

"How do you know? Did Jonah tell you?"

"He told me a lot of things. So, are you encrypting with TKIP-1 or TKIP-2."

"I didn't know there was a TKIP-2," Kelly said. "We use AES."

"Oh, yeah, that makes sense," JW said. He peppered her with questions and purported theories that seemed innocuous, and Kelly took it as a test from her former mentor. The questions he asked were part of a puzzle that JW was solving, forming a map in his head while making lightning-fast calculations. Before reaching a point arousing suspicion with Kelly, he changed the subject. How was living in New York? Done any traveling? Been back to Texas? Do you cross paths often with Martin and Steinman?

David asserted himself into the conversation, injecting some levity that made Kelly feel like she had never left. Before too long, it was time for Kelly and Jonah. JW had promised Trish he would play Fortnite with Tommy, but before he left, David grabbed him by the arm.

"What were you doing? What were all those questions?"

"David, this new brain of mine is somethin'! I'm functioning at a higher rate than ever. My senses are heightened. And get this, I was able to read Jonah and Kelly's minds, just like you. The questions were just distractions while I mined my way in. My explicit memory is more explicit, my semantic memory, declarative memory and procedural memory are vivid and fast as lightning." David was riveted. "This tequila, for instance. I can taste every nuance, and I envision myself standing in an agave field in Mexico. The pleasure side of my brain is wide open. Between you and me, I can't wait to have sex with Trish. I'm operating on a level I never experienced before. Is this what you've been experiencing?"

"Yeah. Maybe not to that degree. Do you know what you are, JW?"

"Yeah! I am SUPERCHARGED!"

* * *

Alison stayed one more full day before leaving. Jonah and Kelly left the following morning. Jayne became a more frequent guest in the days ahead. Trish began asking JW all kinds of questions to plan their wedding. Life became very different at JW's house, and he liked it.

Chapter 23: The Woman with a Shovel

JW slept for twelve hours each of the next two days. In the hours of alertness, he was manic. He worked out with David with the same intensity, although not at the same level of weight or repetitions. When David complimented him on his work ethic, JW just said, "Mind, body and soul."

JW played street hockey with Tommy in the driveway, since the ice was melted. His reactions were quick as a cat, frustrating the boy because he couldn't score with JW in the net. His appetite was voracious, sticking to the healthy foods but in great quantity.

Before turning in early, Trish asked if he was okay.

"I feel great," he said. "But this is going to take some getting used to. I can solve three or four problems simultaneously while still holding a conversation. My powers of concentration are exaggerated."

On the second day, while JW slept, David drove Alison to the airport. He failed in his efforts to convince her to stay. He did, however, reap a promise for her to come back to visit as soon as she could arrange more time off. David felt heartbroken seeing her wave goodbye from the security gate at the airport. He knew he needed to focus on his task. Although he expected the energy transfer to make JW a viable asset in the mission, so far, his host slept a lot, carried on fast-paced conversations, played games and burned through a box of avocados in two days.

David paid the airport parking fee, and his phone rang. He

transferred it to the car speakers. It was Steinman.

Before Steinman could speak, David expressed his annoyance. "Whaddya want, old man?"

"Oh, Davey Boy. I know how annoyed you must be. Your girlfriend is on her way back to Washington. Back to her boyfriend there. She did tell you about him, didn't she?" David didn't respond, other than to grit his teeth. "Oh, Little David. She didn't tell you, did she? Another heartbreaking betrayal."

"What were you doing in Russia?" David asked.

"Simply put, David, I was conducting a business meeting. You will know the details in due time. Once again, I will be victorious."

"So, Heaven Ride will have a center in Russia?"

"You never were one to grasp the big picture, Davy boy. Why must you assume that I was here meeting about Heaven Ride?"

"If it had nothing to do with Heaven Ride, you wouldn't be calling me. Just answer my question."

"I don't need to answer your questions. But, I'll be polite since you asked. You need to add an 's' to center. Russia is a very lucrative market for us. There, you have your answer. Hey, I heard your boy, JW, was in a coma."

"He's not my boy. He's my best friend. And you know, he wouldn't be seeking your condolences."

"I wasn't offering any. Without him, you're kind of in a pickle, aren't you?"

"No. I've witnessed lesser people do fine with fewer intelligent resources. Going back to my original question, whaddya want, Steinman."

"I want you to back off, David. I know what you are trying to do. End Heaven Ride. You may succeed, but your lovely girlfriend, Alison, may meet with horrible consequences."
"Alison knows what she's up against."

"Then, there's your parents. Tsk. Tsk. You know, your father is retired now. His life ahead of him. It would be a shame if say, on their way to morning Mass, some horrible life-ending accident occurred."

"You've crossed a line, Steinman."

"I have no problem doing that. I don't have any lines in my life. And you have so many you try to defend. Such a shame. So."

Steinman let the word hang like a noose. "Back off, David."

Click.

David took solace in the fact Steinman was wrong about JW. Or was he? Perhaps JW slipped back into the darkness of his comatose state.

He called JW. No answer. He called Trish.

"Is JW okay? I called but he didn't pick up."

"He's asleep. I'll wake him if you need me to."

He thought for a split second and decided against it, just in case something was indeed wrong. "Naw. I'll see him when I get back."

David drove on the bounds of recklessness to get home. He entered through the main gate and screeched to a halt across the driveway. He ran up the stairs, fumbled with the house keys, then entered.   He asked Trish if JW had woken yet. She answered to the negative.

"I'm going to wake him."

David went into the room. JW lay motionless on his back, his head propped with a single pillow. David could not tell if he was breathing. He moved closer, knelt beside the bed and put his head on JW's chest. Through a blanket and comforter that wrapped his friend, he heard nothing. He shook JW with urgency. JW punched at the air with his right fist and connected with a glancing blow with his left. David leaned back, allowing JW to become alert, then he leaned over and held him down.

"Get off of me!" JW said, pushing him away.

"Just showing appreciation that you are alive," David said. "You were completely motionless in your twelfth hour of catnapping. I thought maybe you fell back into a coma."

"I was asleep. My brain was still working. By the way, you have a spot of blood above your eye."

"Yeah, somebody just punched me. But it's okay."

David then told him about Thomas Steinman's call, explaining his nervousness. He told JW that with most people, he could connect telepathically, but not with him.

"Yeah, I can tell when you or Stein-worm are probing into my brain. It's creepy. I learned to block it."

"I can teach you how to block Steinman, but let me through. It's easy."

"It's still creepy. No, thank you. I don't want either of you snooping into my thoughts."

David resented his comment a tad, but let it go.

"I'm hungry," JW announced. "I'm going to have some breakfast, and then you and I can go to the office. The monastery. Jonah gave me all sorts of information."

"I was there," David said. "He really didn't tell you anything."

"*Au contrere, mon frere*," JW said. "Maybe to the untrained mind, but --" JW paused. "He told me without telling me. I told you I could read Jonah's mind."

David shook his head. "You amaze me. I don't understand why, but you amaze me. Get cleaned up and meet me outside when you're ready."

At the monastery, Abbott Brennan presented the boys with a warm loaf of bread and fresh creamery butter. He sported a cut over his left eye.

"Did JW clock you, too?" David asked, evoking a hearty laugh from the monk.

"No. We had a burglar attempt to break in. This building, in fact. I wrestled with him a little. Got in his way more than anything. Then Tildy, our housekeeper, hit him over the head with a shovel and pulled his gun away. He ran off. Got into a dark-colored SUV and sped off into the darkness."

"But you're okay? And how about Tildy?" David asked.

"Oh, she's fine," Fr. Brennan said. "Tildy is from sturdy, Irish stock. And me, I'm fine. The old monastery, though..." He didn't finish his thought.

"What about it?" JW asked.

"Well, you see, the lock is busted. I reported the incident to my superiors. It just provides more fuel for them to sell the property. The youngest one of us here is 67. They have concerns about our security."

"Don't you worry, Father," JW said. "David here was looking for some investment property, too. We just might invest in this together. In the meantime, would it be a problem if we installed an additional lock on the door?"

"I don't see any harm."

He turned to David. "Do you know how to install a lock?"

"Haven't a clue," David answered.

"Neither do I." JW said. "I'll call my father,"

David said, at the same time, "Call your father."

After the priest left, they discussed the attempted break-in and the security there.

"We were an old woman with a shovel away from losing the pod and your computer," David said.

"Tildy's definitely going to be on our Christmas card list. What are you thinking?"

"That we should move this operation back to Five Rings."

"Oh, I don't think we can," JW said. "We need to stay an arm's length away from Trish and Tommy. You know that Martin might bomb us out just because of his guilt over being an absentee dad. If we were trying to destroy Heaven Ride from the sanctity of the compound, I think his agreement would go out the window." David searched his imagination for alternatives.

"Besides," JW continued, "I think I can have this thing wrapped up in days."

"What thing?" David asked.

"This whole dismantling of Heaven Ride thing."

Without any attention to David's dumbfounded look, JW booted up the computer.

"You mean, this whole matter, the one that has confounded us for months? We're – You're within a few days of taking down H2H?"

"I think so," JW said. "Jonah confirmed that there was a third cloud, a super-secure level of security. If my assumption is correct, I know where to find the key, or the weakest point of attack. Kelly inadvertently gave me some of the encryption key data I'll need. Then I read her mind to verify her blunder."

"Why you sneaky bastard!" David said. "What did Johansson tell you?"

"He said, and I quote, 'there are 368 reasons why I can't tell you' if there's a kill switch in the program. He obviously can't be in collusion with us because he's still tied in with Martin and Steinman. Why did he randomly choose the number 368? I think he told the truth that there's no kill switch. But I suspect that if I go to line 368 in the code of that sector, that I'll find directions to an old lady with a snow shovel. The defense mechanism. He also gave me his personal password."

"What is that?"

"Not gonna tell you yet cuz; I don't want to jinx it. But we'll find out."

"Sounds like you have this all figured out," David said, excitement overflowing from his voice. "Why can't we take it out today?"

"Because I haven't written the program that will destroy Heaven Ride forever. I may have only one chance to break into the third cloud. They monitor that stuff closely. It's got to be ready to go, and it's got to be flawless. And for the sake of my conscience and yours, I need to do this in a way that won't jeopardize any innocent people who may be taking Heaven Ride when we bring it down."

"Sounds like you've got a lot of things figured out?"

"Maybe. A big maybe."

"Have you thought about what's going to happen to us as a result of shutting down this government institution?" David asked.

"What could happen?"

"I'm thinking we might be up for some prison time. We might take the Teutonic thugs out of the equation, but we could get embroiled in a long legal battle with the government."

JW thought about it for a few seconds. "We can't worry about that until it's time for us to worry about it. We have to take this sucker down."

"What do you want me to do?"

"I dunno. Enjoy some fresh-baked monk's bread while it's still warm. And cut me a few slices. I'm about to break into Fort Knox."

Chapter 24: Seeing Red

David and JW sat outside the monastery looking up at the sky. The stars loomed large. Without speaking, they shared the same thought, that the stars really did look like heaven, before the points of light converged upon them. They found peace in the moment, a respite from the business of saving souls. David thought of his own soul, which flew wingless into heaven. He thought of Daedalus, and his son, Icarus, who flew with wax wings too close to the sun, only to crash into the ocean.

JW broke the silence.

"David," he petitioned. "I think I know the reason why God created the stars in the sky. It's for the people who can't get into heaven. So they can see what it's like and imagine the enormity of it."

The thought sank in with David. For the moment he could only enjoy the vision.

It sounded like some of the wisdom imparted to him by his Grandma Hilly. He recalled one of the things she told them when he was visiting on his Heaven Ride. She told him that he should find a good woman to marry and have children. She told him that the angels' singing often sounded like a child's laughter.

"Despite all of the hardships, of being exiled and at risk, we really have been blessed," JW said. "And cursed, at the same time. With a duty. We must put an end to this thing. I feel like we are so close."

"We need to find out who this Sandra Singer is, and what she can tell us," David said. "She's the holder of the last key. While you try to find her, I'm going to find out what Steinman and Martin are doing."

Oblivious to time, they both pursued their missions. David was curious about the H2H corporate leaders, because both of them had recently suffered attacks on their homes, presumably with the intention of killing them. Martin's had come first, and his home was demolished by a firebomb that was intended to look like a furnace malfunction. Three weeks later, an explosion rocked Steinman's house, but Thomas had taken a surprise trip to Russia and escaped without harm. The blast had all the earmarks of the destruction wrought on the Servare Caeli cult as Heaven Ride was expanding under David and JW.

David thought about the people he worked with through Global Reach. He didn't want to sacrifice his privacy by contacting them directly. He knew that Gia McCarren left the company and was now an executive assistant at Levi Strauss in San Francisco. When he performed an online search for Marva Bratton, Martin's executive secretary, he found a very telling blog by her husband, Chet Bratton, a top Wall Street analyst with Unger Financial.

In it, Chet recommended a sell order for Heaven Ride (HEVN) stock due to significant discord in the C-Suite. "Martin Martin and Thomas Steinman will no longer sit in the same boardroom, so how could you expect them to direct a growing company. Jonah Johansson is the glue keeping the H2H company together."

"Hey, David," JW said. "Our Heaven Ride stock may have taken a big hit." He told him about the two-week-old blog. "My pal Jonah is doing his best to hold it all together, but apparently Steinman and Martin are duking it out like street thugs.

"Your pal?"

"Well, since he gave me my life back. Yeah, he's my pal."

"What's the source?"

"Marva Bratton's hubbie, Chet. He's a Wall Street analyst geek."

"Wow. That has some veracity to it."

"Stocks have dipped, but not that much," JW said, rapidly typing on his keyboard. "You know what I think? I think Martin and Dick-Stein tried to knock each other off. If things are that bad, it's not unrealistic."

"If Martin goes, it could be a bad thing," David said. "What will happen to Trish's security arrangement? The house? Everything?"

"So, we better hope that asshole stays safe. Damn!" JW's thought process was taken off track. "Meanwhile, on the west coast, I found just one recent reference to Sandy Singer. From, let's see – about one year ago. She was hired as an assistant director at the Community Housing Partnership in San Fran. In the Tenderloin District."

"So she dropped off the map for about 12 years? Amazing in this day of Google tracking and social media," David opined. "Did you check marriage licenses? To see if her name changed."

"I did. No record. I checked obituaries to see if she was listed as next of kin. Given the nature of her job, I looked at real estate licensing – nothing. Should we try calling her?" JW asked.

"It works better in person. The telepathic vibes work best when both parties are willing."

"What's your schedule like this week? Do you think you can move some meetings around and cancel your business lunches so that we can fly to San Fran? Thursday?" David said jokingly.

"Right. Business meetings. I'll check with my secretary. And lunches? I think I was supposed to have a PB&J sandwich with Tommy. I don't think I can blow him off."

"I think you can. His grandpa can take your place."

"It might be a good idea for Vince to come with us. San Fran is our old home turf. Now, it feels dangerous."

"Dad's got a pretty crazy schedule, too. I'll see if he can make it," JW said with a laugh. "I haven't told you this, but my dad thinks the world of you. He called you a 'tough sonuva bitch' and said he never met anyone who thinks as strategically as you. He says you would have made a great general."

"Nah. Judging from this Heaven Ride experience, I would have been killed by friendly fire," David said.

"At least your own father didn't nearly blow your shoulder off with a rifle."

"True. But my dad won't even speak to me. That's the other thing I need to resolve. Mom and dad."

"Let's get out of here," JW suggested. "I think we earned some take-out from Tuscany. I'll call Trish and get some order preferences from back at the ranch."

Trish opened a bottle of Coppola pinot noir to accompany an Italian food feast. JW bought an extra serving of manicotti, reasoning that "it will keep until tomorrow." Travel plans were made. Vincente decided he would leave Wednesday and drive so that he could pack a gun. "He told the guys, "You may not see me, but you can be sure I'll be close by for your protection."

JW and David saw Vincente off, as he took the Mercedes SUV out the gates at Five Rings. He took what JW called "the dumb Mercedes" because it was not the one with the Smart Camo. Despite JW's urging to live a little, Vincente would stay the night at a modest motel near the Community Housing Partnership offices and "be present" when they arrived. JW and David left the next day wearing modest disguises. This time, instead of the red Utes' hoodie, David wore a light jacket with the stylized grey wolf of St. Bonaventure. Per usual, they sat in different parts of the plane, keeping an eye on each other.

They arrived in just under two hours, gaining one back with the time zone change. They rented an economy car and drove straight to the building housing the Community Housing Partnership, parking in a $9-an-hour parking lot across Jones Street. The CHP was a small, two-story storefront office, and inside the blue door was a pleasant receptionist in African garb. They asked to see Sandra Singer.

"Is Sandy expecting you?" the receptionist asked.

"No. We don't have an appointment," David said.

"Hang on," she told them, and called an extension with the phone. After a brief conversation, she turned back toward the visitors and said, "She'll be right down."

As they waited, David asked JW, "Did you see your father anywhere?"

"No. And I didn't see the SUV following us from the airport. He's here, somewhere. I know that."

They heard footsteps treading lightly down the stairs, and a woman came into full view. She was slender, and attractive, with shoulder-length hair that bounced with each step. She was familiar but dressed casually in sweater and slacks. It was Sandy Steinman.

"Sandy?!" JW exclaimed in a half-question.

A troubled expression darkened her face, like a moon in eclipse. David saw only the bright diamond-shaped glow, brilliantly identifying her as one of The Gifted. She stopped, appearing for a moment to want to run back up the stairs.

David voiced a friendly appeal. "Oh, my God! Sandy! We need your help. It will only take a minute."

"Not here," Sandy said. "There's a coffee shop around the corner. Let me get my coat."

Sandy's reaction earned them the evil eye from the receptionist. When Sandy returned, she asked her, "Sandy, is everything okay?"

"Everything's fine, Tonya. I should be back very soon." She turned to JW. "Fifteen minutes, tops."

She fastened her coat. JW noticed her lapel button, white with a blue polar bear and the letters S-O-S.

She led them down the block, heavy with construction, and turned left, saying nothing. JW attempted to engage her in conversation, but she ignored him for the moment. She took them to the Mint Plaza, named for its proximity to the San Francisco Mint. On the opposite side of an open-air plaza was a coffee shop with blue-tinted plate-glass windows, The Blue Bottle Coffee Shop. Inside, it was unique, with siphons for tea and an Oji water-drip apparatus that looked like a Rube Goldberg invention. The cafe featured dozens of different types of hot lattes, espresso drinks and the Oji-brewed iced coffees.

JW expressed shock. "Holy cow!" They watched the coffee drip procedure, enchanted by it.

David nudged him. "I bet the Barmaster X technology could be used for coffee drinks."

They each ordered cappuccinos. Sandy stepped to the counter and ordered a vanilla iced coffee. David offered to pay but Sandy demanded that the barista accept her cash. "I can buy my own coffee. Thank you. Please make mine to go."

The cold reception surprised JW. They found a table away from other patrons, affording them privacy.

"Why are you here? We have nothing to talk about?" she said.

"Why are you being such a —" JW asked, but he was interrupted by David.

"You have some information that we need."

"Why am I being such a bitch?" Sandy asked, repeating JW's unfinished question? "You two show up out of the blue, obviously having expended some effort to track me down. From what I understand, you two are on some endangered species list. While I care about some endangered species, I don't like putting myself in danger."

Her comment reminded JW of their apparent danger. JW scanned the coffee shop but saw no sign of Vincente. Outside, a man stood with his back to the shop who might have been his father, but he couldn't tell with certainty.

"We did search for Sandra Singer. We had no idea it was you. How come there was no trace of you, wedding announcement?"

"Easy. Because there was no wedding. I was just a plot piece. After the first year, anyway. One thing about Thomas is that he knows how to wine and dine a potential lover. Over time we figured out that we weren't right for each other. I was monogamous, and Thomas was anything but. But we had this great ruse, and I had freedom to do whatever I wanted. And yes, JW, at one point I wanted you. But you were too afraid of Thomas to pursue me all the way."

David got to the point. "Listen, we just need to know one thing."

He nodded to JW, passing the baton.

"When you took Heaven Ride, was there one thing, one thought, one idea that was planted in your brain? The most memorable image or thought?"

Sandy laughed loudly.

"So you figured out that I was one of *them*! The chosen ones. Ha-ha!" She reached across the table and stroked JW's cheek. "My dear JW, what can I possibly gain by telling you my deepest, darkest secret." Her eyes smoldered, and David could understand the lust that JW harbored for her the past four years.

"You would be helping millions of people who weren't quite as lucky as you," JW said.

"That's it? Look at me, JW. You think I'm where I am because of luck? You just told me what I'd gain. It's pretty lame. It doesn't compare with what I'd lose. I live in a mansion. I drive the car of my dreams. I vacation wherever I want to go in the world. When I want to be a good girl, I save entire species. If I help you, I lose all that. Don't play me for a fool, JW."

"I'm not. What we are doing is not foolish. It really has a lot to do with saving humanity. All of humanity."

Sandy stood up and pushed her ice coffee to the middle of the table.

"Good luck, JW. You too, David. Give me five minutes for a head start. It's that danger thing."

She made her index fingers into an X, then blew JW a kiss. They watched her leave, and when she got across the plaza, she stopped to use her phone. Then, she was gone.

David rubbed his face with his hands. He was visibly frustrated.

"We need that last key," he said.

"She gave it to us," JW said.

"No, she refused. What did I miss?" David asked.

"The button on her jacket. She's really into saving the polar bears in Alaska and the arctic. When I had that dinner, where Steinman was trying to buy me out, she made a comment about saving the polar bears on Cooper Island. She organizes fund raisers for polar bears."

"So the key is – polar bear?"

"Yep."

"I don't know how that pertains to – "

"Yeah, I don't know, either. But between us, we'll figure it out."

Before they left, David asked the barista staff to pose in front of the Oji coffee maker. He snapped a few pictures on his burner phone.

One blonde college-age girl was eager to tell him all she knew about it.

David said, "Oji. Like, I pour water in and oh, gee, now I have coffee?"

"Yeah, like that," she said, giggling. "Hey, are you a celebrity or something?"

David paused a moment. "No. But maybe someday. Thanks. Gotta go."

He did that mainly to make sure the five minutes had passed to honor Sandy's request. He explained to JW, "If we ever become penniless, I might want to reinvent that oji coffee maker."

As they crossed the plaza, David told him, "You do know that when we shut this thing down, our shares of stock will be worthless."

"That affects you more than it does me," JW said. They rounded the corner onto Jones Street, and another familiar figure approached them sixty feet away. Simon Sanders. He carried a pistol, which he raised, pointing it at David's head. Bystanders screamed, and a taxi honked. A single gunshot. David saw the bullet rotating, as if in slow motion, moving closer. Then, he didn't.

A loud thud and an anguished groan followed. One of the bystanders dove in front of David to block the bullet. The taxi driver and another witness chased after Sanders, who ran before he could fire another shot.

David was breathless, amazed to be alive. JW knelt down to check on the good Samaritan. He rolled the man over. It was his father.

"Call 911! Call 911!" JW shouted to a woman on the street.

Vincente was bleeding with a chest wound. He grimaced in pain. His breathing was shallow, and words could not be enunciated. JW used his hands to try to stop the bleeding, then pulled the sleeve of his hoodie down to absorb more blood. David knelt and used Vincente's scarf to prop his head off the sidewalk, vigilantly keeping watch in case Simon returned.

The 911 lady approached.

"I'm a nurse. Let me help."

She took over, using Vincente's hand to apply pressure on the bullet hole.

"Chest wounds are tricky," she said. "Depending on the entry angle, it might have hit his lung or his heart. Honey, the ambulance is on its way."

JW spun in a circle, and with his bloody hands tugging at his hair. He screamed, "My God! Oh, my God! This can't be happening!"

David tried to calm JW and whispered, "Be positive. Let your dad hear positive thoughts."

JW cried. Anger crept into his being. "I want to go after Simon. I want him dead."

"Calm down, JW. We've got to get your dad fixed up. Don't

worry, we'll get Simon."

The ambulance siren screamed, although the traffic and construction slowed its arrival. The taxi still blocked one lane of Jones St. The EMTs tended to Vincente. JW had trouble articulating what happened, overwrought with emotion. David squeezed the back of JW's neck and took over the narration.

The female EMT unzipped Vincente's jacket and ripped his shirt open to apply a large, rectangular bandage.

"You're his son?" she asked JW. "Do you want to ride with him?"

"Uh, yeah. Of course."

Softly, she warned JW. "He may not have long."

The words hit him like a brick. He stood on the sidewalk, with all the activity, and flashing lights, and a burgeoning crowd of concerned citizens, his father being lifted onto a gurney and the male EMT attaching sensors and a wrist bracelet. He felt far removed from it. It was as if a thick force field separated him from everything. The distance made him feel alone. His intuition told him this would end badly. Perhaps it was the adrenaline ratcheting upward by the moment, or perhaps it was his inner anger, but he felt like he was burning up. He was no longer thinking lucidly but reacting. His scientific brain conjured all the outcomes, and he calculated the best reactions to them.

David called to the female EMT. "Which hospital?"

"San Francisco Medical Center."

"JW, give me the keys to the rental," David demanded. "You're riding in the ambulance, right?"

"Right." JW tossed him the key. "Wait, David," he called. He approached the gurney that the EMTs placed Vincente on, and pulled his keys from a front pocket, Dangling them to show the citizen nurse. "Here's dad's keys. One of them fits his van."

"I'm going to talk to one of the witnesses. I'll meet you over there.".

"Find his vehicle and drive it to the hospital. Leave the rental here."

"How am I supposed to find it?" David complained. "Is it in the parking garage down the street?"

"He doesn't like garages. Check the alleys nearby. See you at

SFMC."

David rolled his eyes. The taxi driver drove away before David could call to him. Among the onlookers was the witness who chased after Simon, watching the EMTs after catching his breath. David approached him.

"Dude, what's your name?"

"Tyler. Why?" He was a young man, and his tone implied that he expected trouble.

"Tyler, you did a good thing, man. You saved my life. You may have saved a few lives." David extended his hand, and Tyler shook it. "Are you busy now?"

"I was on my way to work."

"Can you call in? I'd like to talk with you, just to hear what you saw and what happened when you chased the guy."

"I really can't" Tyler said, hesitant.

"I'll pay you. Five hundred bucks."

Without delay, he said, "Okay."

* * *

The hospital was familiar to JW. He rushed to keep up with the gurney as it was wheeled to a cubicle. He had been familiar with the ER, having retrieved many DNR patients to study their last moments. Having witnessed the end stages so often, he could not fathom his own father in that dire situation.

The EMTs incubated Vincente in the ambulance and took measures to slow the blood loss. Vincente stared straight up, and JW could only imagine the thoughts running through his head. Over the past five months, Vincente had shared some of his experiences with his son, stories of hits on war criminals and enemies of state, his time in Alaska and other aspects of his double life. Several subjects were cast to the shadows, leaving JW to surmise they brought too much pain for his father to re-live.

JW was not allowed in the treatment room. After supplying information for forms in triplicate, he was banished to the waiting room. After five minutes, the depressing atmosphere became toxic to him. He called Trish. Her worry added to his anxiety. He decided he would wait to call his mother. He walked. Purposeful, he followed the hallways to an unmarked doorway that led down several flights of stairs to the basement. There, he followed the hallway to the basement lab where Heaven Ride was first conceived.

Predictably, the door was locked. Pleasant memories flooded his head. He performed his best work behind that door. An adoring public hailed him as a genius. At the end of the hall, the door to the hospital morgue was propped open. JW ventured down and peeked around the corner. At a desk, playing Mobile Strike on his cell phone, was Billy Hernandez.

"JW!" Billy exclaimed. "Man, it's so good to see you."

"You, too, Billy. You're still here. Everything going good?"

"Oh, man ... It is, it really is. My lady, Naomi, we're getting married in May. That's all because of you, brother." He gave JW a fist bump. "And we have a baby on the way. If it's a boy, you know what we're going to call him?"

"JW?" he said immodestly.

"No." He said it like it was the most ridiculous idea he'd ever heard. "Billy, junior. William, actually."

JW laughed. Billy continued.

"And I'm going to junior college. Gonna get a degree and open my own crematorium. Well, funeral director actually. Eventually, they're gonna shut this one down."

"I'm glad things are going well for you," JW said.

"I owe you, big time!" Billy said.

"Nah. You are just finding yourself. You did it on your own, man."

"You inspired me. It's really good to see you."

"You, too. Take care of that baby," JW said.

As he left, a hospital orderly was opening the door to his former lab. The orderly added a box to a stack of file boxes. The lab was now a storage room, a sort of dead letter office. The sterile hallways, shoes with sanitized booties, the latex gloves, the scrubbed-down faceless personnel behind the masks, it all reeked of death to JW.

JW returned to the waiting room, and momentarily, a scrubbed-down, faceless doctor told him they were going to perform an emergency surgery. The bullet entered Vincente's chest on the right side and cut across his thorax, resting against the right ventricular wall of Vincente's heart. A small amount of internal bleeding would do him in, the doctor said, unless it was repaired in minutes rather than hours.

Minutes later, the doctor reappeared, and told JW that his
father's blood pressure had dropped so severely that surgery was no
longer an option.

"What other options do we have," JW asked.

The doctor looked down at his sanitized booties, and merely
said, "I'm sorry." He patted JW on the shoulder and walked back to
the restricted area.

JW stood motionless. Tears would not fall. Others in the waiting
room stopped their own grieving and coping, empathizing with the
huge grief that JW was feeling. A course of action occurred to JW.
He walked outside the waiting room and called David, who could
not find Vincente's van and was driving the rental car to the hospital.
JW gave him instructions on where to park and told him to stay with
the car.

JW strode back to the waiting room, and through the doors to
the restricted area of the ER. His disregard for the signage earned
protests from the nurses at the desk, but they did not follow. One
receptionist got on the phone.

JW walked briskly through the ward, stopping at a few curtained
treatment areas to check the name on the chart. At the end of the
corridor, he found his father resting. JW turned off the monitors and
disconnected his father from any vital equipment.

He spoke to his dad in low whispers, and as he began wheeling
the bed from the treatment area, he held his father's hand and told
him not to worry, and to trust him.

With several hospital personnel clutching at him, JW pushed the
gurney down familiar hallways and to the far side of the hospital. He
sloughed off attempts to stop him, telling the nurses and doctors
"We've had a change of plans."

He took his father to the loading dock, followed by four scrub-
wearing professionals.

"You can't take him out of the hospital," one of them said. "This
is insane!"

"It's a last wish," JW said, continuing to the edge of the dock. A
steel freight elevator lowered them to street level, and to the rental
car, where David stood, his mouth agape.

"Don't just stand there. Help me get him in the car!"

David opened the rear hatch and they slid the body into the flat cargo area.

"Give me the keys. I'm driving,"

"I'll drive," David said. "Where are we going?"

"Give me the fucking keys!" JW demanded. David gave in and tossed the keys to him.

In the car, JW sped away just as hospital security arrived on the scene. He careened through traffic toward the Transbay Tower.

"Hang in there, Dad. You're going to see Petey one more time."

"This is crazy!" David argued. "You're going to get us killed."

"I know what I am doing!" JW screamed. "Dad hang in there!"

David was silent the entire way, enduring JW's speeding and erratic driving. JW pulled into the underground parking garage, taking the vacant executive spot that used to be his.

He had not thought how to transport Vincente up the stairs. Inside the door, David found a wheelchair. Weakened by his injuries, Vincente appeared the calmest of the three as JW wheeled him inside to the atrium.

"Cover your face," David warned. "They have cameras everywhere with facial recognition software. If we are seen they'll flag us for sure."

"How am I supposed to cover my face and push a wheelchair, David? Sometimes, for a brilliant guy, you say stupid things."

"Here," David said, pulling JW's hoodie up to shade his face. "Keep your eyes looking down." At the elevator, they pushed the button for the 17th floor.

"Dad, we're almost there. We're going to take you to Petey."

The elevator opened, and they entered the plush, spa setting they carefully designed. JW rushed to the reception desk. His harried instructions to the receptionist left her confused.

"Who's the manager?" JW asked.

"I am," Melany said. When JW turned, she gasped. "JW! David! What a surprise!"

"I need to get my dad on Heaven Ride. ASAP. He doesn't have much time left. Can you do it, Mel?"

"Let me see," she took over the computer for the greeter. "Pod 6 is open. Will that be on a charge card?"

"Here, I'll leave you my card. Run it, do whatever, but I'll take care of everything afterward."

David had already started moving Vincente to Pod 6. JW caught up. Once they were in the room, JW began explaining. David assisted him in applying the electrodes and the special helmet.

"I want my dad to see Petey. We had to do this now. Dad, just a few more minutes."

The technician, Kristen, came through the door, and was alarmed to see then tinkering with the equipment.

"What are you doing?" she asked.

"We're in a hurry," JW said. "David, you want to calibrate the computer, so we can initialize the sequence?"

"This is highly irregular," Kristen said. "Who do you think you are?"

"I invented the goddamn thing!" JW shouted at her.

Melany came through the door to check on them.

"Kristen," she said, her voice dropping to a whisper, "he invented all this. It's okay."

"Thanks, Mel. And thank you, Kristen, for being diligent," JW said.

"All the electrodes are signaling," David reported.

Melany asked, "Everything okay? Just wanted to check in."

"Yeah, it's all good," JW said. "Can we have privacy for this one?"

"Sure," Melany said. "Come on, Kristen. Just see me at the desk when you're ready to leave."

"You got it." JW toggled a few buttons on the computer, in final preparation. "David, you want to administer the protein shot?"

"Not sure I know how," he said.

"On that tray over there," JW instructed. "Now, they have these thingees like on Star Trek, all you do is press it on his arm and it will inject the serum. Roll up his sleeve and go for it."

JW stepped from behind the computer to be next to his father.

"Dad, your heart rate is a little slow, and this may be pretty strenuous. These last five months with you have meant the world to me. I love you, Dad. I know Petey loved you more than anybody. When you experience him in heaven, he'll tell you. He was happy – in heaven – and knows the accident was never your fault. I'll be here for you the whole time. Come on back and we'll get you fixed up."

Vincente had tears in his eyes. He gagged a bit on the tube and tried to point to it. JW shrugged to David and removed it.

In a hoarse, slow whisper, Vincente said, "I'm proud of you. Of both my boys. But what if – " He choked up. "What if ...they don't let me in?"

"You'll get in. Everybody gets in. On Judgment day, some souls will be relegated to another place," David answered. "You will get in."

The elder Gomez motioned for the younger men to come closer. "Say a prayer, In case."

They held hands, and David led them in the Lord's Prayer. When they were finished, JW leaned close to his father and whispered some words of gratitude. David checked the computer monitors.

"David, hit the start button. Dad, in a few seconds, you will feel drowsy. Don't fight it. Think beautiful thoughts, of people and places and things you love." Vincente felt the systematic electrical jolts and smiled before closing his eyes.

"He's already at the second stage," David said. "He's in a hurry to see Petey!"

"Can I confess something, David?" JW said, while watching the monitors. "My father has told me many things about his life. He has killed a lot of men, in the name of government-sponsored nation building. He's probably not going to heaven on his own merit. I wanted him to be with Petey. We talked about it and he agreed."

"Bon Voyage, Vincente!" David said. Each of them hoped the journey would finally bring peace to him. They tracked the flow of energy for a moment, and David broke the silence.

"It's not polar bears," he informed JW. "It's charity."

"What the hell are you talking about?" JW asked.

"Sandy Steinman. The key is charity. It fits. I couldn't figure out how polar bears fit the puzzle. Charity."

"Hey, David, check this out. The 27th wave – the media called it the God Wave. Take a look." JW expanded a window on the computer which showed an abundance of colored squiggled lines moving along a similar path in both directions. "It's way busier than we ever saw it before. Even after the expansion."

"It will all come to an end when we shut this puppy down," David said.

Vincente completed his trip but remained unconscious coming out of the pod. JW chartered a medical helicopter to fly his dad to the University of Utah Medical Center. He arranged for Dr. Barrett to have the best surgeons save his father and nurse him back to health.

A surgeon called JW to provide an update on Vincente.

"He's still comatose," the doctor said. "Very slight brainwaves. He's hanging in there, but barely." There was a hesitation in his voice. "His brain scan showed a few small pockets of intense activity. Very small pockets. The rest of his brain, including the part that would regulate involuntary actions, like breathing, those are totally dead. We have him on life support. Frankly, I've never seen this before."

JW told the doctor to keep him going, and to call if his condition changed. "Thanks for the encouraging news."

"I didn't mean it to be encouraging," the doctor said. "It's just... different."

JW hung up the phone, unsure how to feel. He did something rather unusual for him. He prayed.

Chapter 26: Capital Punishment

The next day back at Five Rings, JW woke up early, but heard laughter coming from the kitchen. David performed a mock cooking class for Trish and Tommy. The menu had changed several times in the past 24 hours. David finally settled on Pigs in a Blanket served with a praline whipped cream and fresh fruit salad. JW joined in the frivolity, mocking David in a gentle way.

They ate, and JW grew anxious to finish the deed.

"We need to sit down and go over those keys. The poison pill still needs work."

"I've got this all figured out," JW explained. Jonah gave me the clue to where the system vulnerabilities lie. "Line 368 of the program he added for the third cloud. There's a hidden meta tag. It's inactive right now. As soon as I activate it, the whole program will go down. It will rewrite the functional code in gibberish to eliminate an easy fix. The pods will no longer be operational. I created an error message telling the Heaven Ride technicians to direct customers to a phone number for a full refund. I put in Stein-bum's personal number."

David laughed. "That's cringe-worthy."

"Yeah, pretty harsh, but he deserves it."

"So how does that work? Everything goes down instantaneously?"

"Not quite. I have to enact the changes on three separate servers.

By the time the technicians in San Fran call Rochester to see if their system is down, it will be. "

"That's AWESOME!" David exclaimed. "When can we do this?"

"The day after tomorrow is March 21. You know my sense of the dramatic. It will be 3-2-1- ZERO!"

"Okay. We may want to prepare with some extra security. They're going to suspect we are behind this."

"The safe room will be fully stocked. I'll tell Tommy we're camping out for a night. I'll have Hector bolster security around the perimeter. We'll be fine."

"What time? Can we drop the doomsday bomb during the morning rush hour?"

"Sure. How about 8:08?"

"Works for me. I'll make breakfast at 7. Yep. Arma-gettin' breakfast."

"I get it. An end of the world joke."

"The end of *a* world. We'll be saving a lot of people."

"How do you feel about this?" JW asked. "We're tearing down something, a big thing, that we built. Well, kinda built."

"I'm okay," David said, a little hesitancy in his voice. "I guess I've envisioned the day to take it out for some time. How about you?"

"Honestly? I'm a little sad." David nodded in agreement with his best friend's assessment. "This was the gateway for me to be with Petey. And for my mom. And hopefully it was good for my dad. But, I'm trying to think about what it's like. Maybe like getting rid of a car that you love. You know you'll have a different way to get around, but you'll always have fondness for that old car."

"Everything... everybody... has their time," JW concluded.

"I'm glad you think that way."

"You know what I've also been thinking about? What makes this a whole lot easier?" JW asked.

"What?"

"This may bring you and your parents closer together. That's my hope. We're tearing something down to make room for something else. Something even more glorious."

"Thanks, bud," David said. He cleared his throat, choked with emotion. "I thought of that myself."

"Do you want to know what Jonah's password is?" JW asked.

"I should probably say yes."

"AllyAngel."

"Nice. You figured that out?"

"The most important thing in his life," JW said. "And yours."

"Right on." He fist-bumped with JW. "Right on."

Trish got a phone call, and summoned JW and David to join in. Jonah was on the speaker phone.

"They finally did it, guys. I'm out," Jonah announced. "Martin gave me the news about five minutes ago."

JW looked for David's reaction, and David urgently sought the same with JW.

"Sorry to hear that, Jonah. We're in the middle of something." As he dashed from the room, he called back, "We'll call you later."

Trish was puzzled by their erratic exit but remained on the phone with Jonah.

JW logged onto his computer and rushed to enter the access codes for the Heaven Ride back office.

"We can't wait," JW told David. "Gotta do this now, even if it's not 8:08."

"I know. They might lock Jonah out of the system any minute. Or, maybe they already have!"

"I know!"

"What are you doing, JW?" Tommy asked. He followed the guys into JW's office.

"You have to get out of here, Tommy!" JW said, revealing some of the pressure he felt.

"C'mon, JW. What are you doing? Can I watch?" Tommy requested.

"He can watch, can't he?" David asked. JW gave no reply, completely attentive to the computer screen.

"Tommy, you can watch, but don't talk to JW because he needs to stay riveted to his work. In a minute, I'll tell you what he's doing. What *we're* doing. JW, how's it going?"

"So far, so good. On the first cloud. I got in."

David took time to explain to Tommy the important work JW was doing.

"Why would you tear it down?"

"It has hurt a lot of people. Some people have been hurt really bad. Some people have died. Some bad guys took it away from us before we could change it. So instead of letting them have it, we're going to blow it up. Not really blow it up but disable it. Nobody will ever use it or get hurt again."

"So what dad – I mean, JW, is doing, that's a good thing?" David smiled at Tommy's gaffe.

"It's really good. He's going to be a hero for this."

"He's already a hero."

"Yes, he is."

"Second cloud, I'm in!" JW announced. "Now, this one, I need to go through a lot of gyrations just to get to where I need to go."

Nearly 10 minutes passed. Tommy watched over JW's shoulder. Screens changed, but mostly, it was just a lot of typing. Finally, the boy whispered to David.

"David, this is boring."

"You don't have to stay and watch," David whispered back. "You can go, if you want. But, if you stay, you might see history being made."

A slight smile came upon Tommy. "I'm gonna stay, then. This is important, huh?"

"Yes, it is," David whispered back.

"It's not letting me in!" JW complained. "I'm at the firewall for the Third Cloud. It didn't let me in. I've only got three chances, and then it will kick me out."

"Do you think you made a typo?" David asked.

"I don't know." His answer was angry. "I'll try again."

He typed Jonah's access identity, and then the passcode.

"Denied! It came back denied! Fuck!" JW said.

"Did they delete Jonah's access to the system?" David asked.

"They may have. I can't believe I got this far, and can't get in," JW groused. "If I screw this up, I can't even try again until after midnight."

David looked at JW and did not say what they both were thinking.

Or ever.

"And, I only have about 40 seconds to try again or I'll be logged out of the system. Fuck! Sorry, Tommy."

"Don't worry, JW. I know that word. At school, my friend Josh wrote it in big letters on the dry erase board, and he got in a lot of trouble with Mrs. Davis."

A look of wonder came over JW's face. "Big letters! That's it."

JW began typing again.

"David, I accidentally hit the caps lock key. I was typing in all caps!" He added the password Ally Angel, and before hitting the enter key, said, "Okay, guys, here goes!"

He hit the key and waited. And waited.

"We're in!" JW shouted. "Oh, my God, we're in! Tommy, you're a genius!" JW high-fived him. A huge grin filled the boy's face.

JW pushed the other two out of his mind for a few minutes, navigating through the code, and making sure that his "poison pill" was correct before trying to activate it. He then erased a part of the code that Jonah inserted so that the poison virus he devised would override all attempts to resurrect Heaven Ride on the server.

He uploaded the revision to the H2H server and logged out.

"It's done! The San Francisco server is completely infected with garbage."

He stood up and hugged David, and then Tommy.

"Now I just must repeat that in Rochester, and on the London server. Once it's done, it will be gone for good! I'll be quick!"

"No all caps, JW," Tommy reminded him.

"That's right, Tommy."

The entire process took less than a half hour, and JW was successful in shutting down Heaven Ride in all the cities where Martin and Steinman had set up operations.

Trish heard their excitement and came down to JW's office.

They marveled at the success for a moment, then she told them, "We should get to the safe room."

"Do you think we need to stay in the safe room?" David asked.

"I feel like celebrating!" JW said. "That's why we pay Hector and our security team. Let's put them on high alert, and party!"

"Hey, JW! Look at the clock!" David said.

It showed 8:08 a.m.

"I'm going to bust open that bottle of Macallan!" he said.

"Scotch? At this hour?" Trish asked.

"There is no better time! Damn it all, we're going to drink a toast with the best."

"Macallan?" David asked.

"40-year Scotch," JW explained. "To wash away the taste of a three-year ride to heaven, and hell."

*   *   *

After the Scotch an uneasiness permeated throughout the large house. No one spoke outright but everyone expected some type of reaction to what JW and David had accomplished. There were no telephone calls. No knocks on the door or helicopters flying overhead. The networks and cable channels ran programming as usual. No breaking news stories. David certainly thought his phone would buzz with a Steinman threat, or even an irate call from Marty Martin. Trish checked her phone as she, too, expected Marty to call her.

"How can be sure the poison pill worked?" David spoke aloud and directed his question to JW and all in the room.

"I'm 100% positive it worked. Maybe everyone is so stunned they don't know how to react. I mean this is a major defeat. A complete takedown. Something Steiner and Martin Martin have probably dealt with," JW said.

"I'm gonna call the Salt Lake Center and San Fran to see if anyone's there," David said.

"I'll check out the website. They usually have a chat angel ready to attend to all queries. I'll see what they're saying," Trish said.

David's call went directly to both centers' answering service, and Trish said the website was business as usual. She declined the pop-up chat but said there was nothing unusual. Trish dialed Jonah, but it went directly to voice mail. She texted him and received no reply. Trish thought about calling Marty but didn't want to seem guilty of something. She rarely called Marty unless to return his call or if there was something important to share about Tommy.

"I think I'll call that bastard Steinman just to gloat," David offered.

In unison JW and Trish said, 'No."

"We should be celebrating but it's like we're sequestered. We restored order to heaven. The world should know," David suggested.

"I'm afraid it may be the calm before the storm," Trish observed. "I'm not sure what to expect. But, I can tell you that Marty and Thomas aren't going to roll over and die. We all need to prepare for battle. I'm not even sure Marty will continue to honor my agreement. Tommy may be the only one protected from this day out," Trish said and turned to look outside the giant glass doors opening to the backyard.

JW walked up behind Trish and wrapped his arms around her and gave her a kiss.

"Take Tommy with you to the safe room. I need to go with David to the lab at the monastery and secure a few things there. We'll be back for dinner and by then I'm sure what's ahead for us will be in motion. I'll ask Hector to call in more security to cover the entire grounds and let no one through the front gate," JW told Trish in private. He then called the hospital to check on his father.

"Be safe, hun, and don't do anything foolish. You and David need to be extra careful. I hate to say it but I don't think you and David planned for the aftermath of shutting down Heaven Ride. Maybe it would have been better to left things alone." Trish hugged JW and kissed on the lips and let it linger. She told JW she would call the University Hospital to check on his dad. She then called out for Tommy and walked upstairs to prepare them both for the safe room.

In silence, JW picked up his keys and headed for the garage housing his smart Mercedes.

JW unlocked the front door at the monastery and called for Abbott Brennan but received no reply. They checked the kitchen and the library, both were vacant. David and JW made their way to the secluded lab where the pod and computer equipment were still in the place from JW's transfer procedure. JW began examining the equipment and looking in drawers and under papers for something.

"What are you trying to find," David asked.

JW continued his search and replied, "I just want to make sure I have everything in order in case we have to fire this up again. You know turn over the pod to save our lives."

"I'm afraid there's no firing up anything anymore, my good friend. You've destroyed all the threads and frequencies to make this work," David said as he put arm around JW's broad shoulders.

"What if," he started to say, the words tumbling slowly off his tongue, "what if it isn't shut down. I mean, we don't know if we really succeeded. Jonah – or Martin, or Stein-crook – may have had some other protection in place. It appears that little has changed."

The two sat in the near-dark of the lab and talked for two hours about their lives, what's ahead, whether David's parents would forgive him and welcome him back in their graces. Steinman and Martin weighed heavily on their minds.

"I'm going to New York to confront them. I'll see if Trish can book me a red-eye tonight. I want to make the first move. I want to be the hunter and not the hunted," David said hoping JW would support his move.

"Dude, I don't think that's a smart move. We'd be walking right into a death trap. My dad isn't here to help with security and I promised Trish to hunker done with her and Tommy so we would be on our own. I've seen those guys both pissed and, man, what we just did, pissed is not even a big enough word. I wouldn't be surprised if Martin already pulled out his big dog whistle and has Teutonic on the run."

"I want to go alone. I'm the one that led this charge. It was my idea to shut it down. You reluctantly went along to help me but it's me that needs to face the consequences. I want to stick it there faces, and I want to negotiate a truce, at least for you, Trish and Tommy. I will be the fall guy on this one."

"That's suicidal. What are you going to say when you see them?" JW asked.

David paused for a few seconds.

"I haven't figured that out."

JW interrupted David's answer and sprung up from his chair. "I think Fr. Brennan coming down. God, I hope he's bringing down some bread. My stomach is growling."

JW called out loud, "Hey, Father, we're in here. Just David and me. I hope you're bringing some bread. I think I can smell it."

The footsteps grew louder but there was no reply. The door swung open. A man's frame filled the darkened doorway in the lab. It was much taller than that of Father Brennan's. The figure stepped further into the dimly lit room. The light caught the man's face.

Standing in front of them was Marty Martin.

David and JW were stunned. Stone faced and eyes wide and mouths open. Martin Martin was dressed in an impeccable suit and tie, wing tip shoes and unbuttoned bespoke trench coat. JW tried to reach back into a drawer where his dad had placed a Glock pistol for times like this.

"Don't reach for it, JW. I don't want to blow off your other shoulder," Martin said.

"Who told you we were here? And, what do you want," David said realizing he was the hunted and not the hunter as he planned.

Marty didn't answer David's questions, which he considered irrelevant. He looked David squarely in the eyes and then turned to JW to let him know what he had to say is meant for both. Still standing while JW and David stayed seated, Marty bent down to lock eyes with David.

"You stupid little man," Martin scowled. "You and your buddy here haven't ended anything. Steinman has stolen Heaven Ride and placed it squarely in the hands of the Russians. You have taken away any chance of us being able to stop him."

"He was in Russia for a …" It dawned on David that he had been duped. "... real estate deal. I don't understand," David stammered.

"That's right. You don't understand," Martin scolded. "For all your supposed brilliance, David, Thomas played you like a Stradivarius violin. Your righteous little prank played right into his hands. The Russians intend to weaponize Heaven Ride. The energy that it generates will be used to cultivate an elite force of spies, astrophysicists, global entrepreneurs and military generals. You have the gift, and you, Mr. Wizard Genius, are a recipient of the transfer so you know what's possible. What you both have is only a fraction of what the Russians intend to do. Congratulations, gentlemen. You have just plunged the Western world into the Dark Ages. Heaven help us now."

Martin walked toward the exit, but stopped.

"Oh, by the way," Martin said, pausing for effect. "I've taken Tommy and Trish with me."

THE END

Made in the USA
Middletown, DE
21 May 2022

66056477R00156